PRAISE FOR *POSS*

"Tender, funny, and perfectly observed, *Possible Happiness* explores the mind and heart of the singular Jacob Wasserman. I loved him, and his journey out of loneliness and into an increasingly complicated world is utterly captivating."

—Jennifer Gilmore, author of *If Only* and *The Mothers*

"In *Possible Happiness*, David Ebenbach introduces us to Jacob Wasserman, a shy and witty sixteen-year-old trying to negotiate the treacherous terrain of high school cliques, romance, and his own demons and insecurities. Beautifully crafted, Ebenbach's novel is a coming-of-age love letter to Philadelphia in the late 1980s and to one young man's journey of self-discovery and self-acceptance. Deeply satisfying, frank, and moving."

—Gary Eldon Peter, Minnesota Book Award winner and author of *The Complicated Calculus (and Cows) of Carl Paulsen*

"*Possible Happiness* by David Ebenbach is a luminous coming-of-age novel about Jacob Wasserman, a boy who is, by turns, shy, bewildered, hopeful, and hilarious. Jacob thinks too much, feels too much, worries too much, and is deeply loveable. The book opens with the line, 'Jacob was discovered in eleventh grade,' and he feels like a discovery. I happily follow him through Philadelphia as he navigates the overwhelming world of his single mother's sorrows, his own hope that people might actually like him, and the choppy seas of high school. He ventures into a troubled world with only his uncertain soul to guide him, and we are rooting for him every step of the way. I picked this book up and couldn't put it down. *Possible Happiness* is a definite delight."

—N. West Moss, author of *Birdy* and *Flesh & Blood*

"In *Possible Happiness*, David Ebenbach gives us the tenderly subtle story of a young loner's socialization. Only a writer of Ebenbach's exceptional gifts could have produced this novel that, while devoid of sensationalism and melodrama, is also deeply engaging. One cares about Jacob, his friends, and his family as one rarely cares for characters in fiction—not as protagonists or antagonists, but as vulnerable, thoughtful people. One leaves them behind with a sense of loss and regret accompanied by the wish for them to live long and happily on."

—Peter Selgin, author of *Duplicity* and *Life Goes to the Movies*

"A tender story about learning to forgive yourself, David Ebenbach's new novel, *Possible Happiness*, is an intimate, moving portrait of a boy coming of age in Philadelphia. Jacob Wasserman's teen angst is real and relatable, as is his heartbreaking struggle to come to terms with his parents' divorce, his place in his school's complex ecosystem, and the ever-treacherous dating landscape. Ebenbach has given us a poignant, wrenching tale that will make adult readers grateful that high school is behind us and younger readers hopeful that there is light at the end of the tunnel."

—Clifford Garstang, author of *Oliver's Travels* and *The Shaman of Turtle Valley*

POSSIBLE HAPPINESS

David Ebenbach

Fitzroy Books

Published by Fitzroy Books
An imprint of
Regal House Publishing, LLC
Raleigh, NC 27605
All rights reserved

https://fitzroybooks.com
Printed in the United States of America

ISBN -13 (paperback): 9781646035021
ISBN -13 (epub): 9781646035038
Library of Congress Control Number: 2023949028

Cover images and design by © C. B. Royal

Regal House Publishing, LLC
https://regalhousepublishing.com

The following is a work of fiction created by the author. All names, individuals, characters, places, items, brands, events, etc. were either the product of the author or were used fictitiously. Any name, place, event, person, brand, or item, current or past, is entirely coincidental.

Printed in the United States of America

This book is dedicated to Carole Nehez,
who took a mixed-up kid seriously

1

Jacob was discovered in eleventh grade. Not in a Hollywood way, where he was catapulted to stardom by a movie studio or something, and also not in a murder mystery kind of way, like *The remains of Jacob Wasserman were found floating in the Schuylkill River*, but more just that he was discovered to exist. It surprised him as much as it did anyone else.

The way it worked was that previously, pre-1989, he had been basically background, walking the halls of Central High School ruminating, mixed in among the crowd, a small, interchangeable piece of the setting of everyone else's lives. Nobody harassed him, but nobody shouted out his name when he turned a corner like he was Norm from *Cheers*, either. He just slumped on by, more or less two-dimensionally. Then, in the fall of 1989, he told one joke in class—not even an especially good one—and that started a cascade of events. It was as if suddenly someone turned around and said, *Hey—you're Jacob, right?* And then everyone else turned, too, and saw him, and said, *Jacob, huh?* The extended results of which were that he was discovered to exist in 3-D, already there in front of the world.

In a way, it had started the summer before that.

Jacob had been working summers and weekends at the Philadelphia Zoo since he was old enough to legally be allowed to work, giving kids rides at the pony track in the children's zoo. That was where he'd met Leron, and Ty, too, who now he rode the subway to school with, almost like friends. Anyway, maybe it was his uniform—red polo shirt and tan shorts—or his hair, which wasn't as curly since he had gotten a short and preppy cut in June in the summer before his junior year, or the fact that he kind of liked working at the zoo and so was a little happy, or some other thing, but actually he was first discovered at the zoo. It didn't count as *the* discovery, because most of the kids working there didn't go to his high school, so his newfound status didn't transfer back to Central. But still there was this surprising thing where people were noticing him. Specifically, *girl* people. More than one. When he discovered that a few of the girls working there thought he was *cute*, Jacob felt like his life was being pushed into motion all of a sudden. Zero to sixty. Or twenty, at least.

He'd even had a girlfriend that summer. Only four weeks, and they spent about half of that time trying to figure out how making out worked—what exactly were you supposed to be doing with all the different parts of your face?—but nonetheless it was a very big first for Jacob. He felt that he'd crossed a line on the journey to manhood there. A no-turning-back kind of line.

Dating, Jacob learned, apparently showed you sides of yourself you hadn't ever thought much about. For example, his summer girlfriend—her name was Barbara—had thought he was funny; she told him so. His mother had always told him that too; it was his jokes that would cheer her up when she was down. But this was the first person outside the family to notice. Barbara said it a lot, in fact, including at times when he wasn't intending to be funny. Like one time when they were eating their bag lunches on a bench in front of the tiger enclosure—she worked at the zoo too—and he said, "I wonder what it'd be like to be one of those tigers. I think I'd get tired of pacing around." He'd really meant that seriously—there was something a little painful and unsettling about the pacing—but Barbara said, "You're funny." That was a pretty good example of how their dynamic went.

But he had brought this slight increase in his confidence and this perception of himself into eleventh grade, and sometimes he would notice a moment in class that had the potential for humor, and then in his head he'd tell a joke about it. Like one time Ms. Terrell, the Elementary Functions teacher, was pointing at the letter x she'd chalked on the blackboard, and she asked, "What is this?" looking for the word *variable*, and Jacob, in his mind, called out, "A blackboard!" That kind of thing. His grades were high enough that teachers would have probably just rolled their eyes and kept going if he did say some of this stuff out loud, but what would the other kids do? Would they laugh? How would Jacob feel if they did?

Anyway, so one day—it was late September—he was in Advanced History, listening to Mr. Nowacki talk about pre-revolutionary America. Jacob couldn't decide whether Mr. Nowacki was a cool guy or not. He owned a sports car, which you could sometimes get him to talk about in class, and he was informal with the students, in the sense that he would call on kids with lines like, "Okay, smart guy, whaddaya got?" and would respond to wrong answers with "No, but thanks for playing," and he dressed like he was actually living in the late 1980s, whereas a lot of the other teachers were practically still in the 70s. Jacob liked him, but he did sometimes wonder if Mr. Nowacki was cool or just *trying* to be cool. Regardless, he was friendly toward Jacob, and on this particular day when he asked, "Who can tell me who was living in the colonies at this time?" Jacob actually, without pausing to think about it, called out what had popped into his head. "The colonists!" he said. Immediately afterward Jacob felt his face burning—he was as shocked as a house cat thrust suddenly outdoors—but Mr. Nowacki just twitched his dark mustache and said, "Thank you, Shecky. Shecky Greene, everybody."

Jacob, still burning, did then give Mr. Nowacki the answer he was looking for, which was people who had fled Europe to escape religious persecution, and Mr. Nowacki said, "Okay—I guess his brain still works," and things got back on track.

But after class, in the swarming hallway, while Jacob went over that moment again and again—he had a habit of second-guessing himself, except that he usually couldn't stop once he'd started and so it was more like frenetic fifteenth-guessing or hundredth-guessing or nine-hundredth guessing—someone called Jacob's name. Jacob turned and saw Eric Strudwick's head of feathered red hair bobbing up like a balloon over everyone

else; Eric was already more than six feet tall at age sixteen. He
knew Eric, a little. The two of them were in the same history
class, which was not the first class they'd been in together, and
they both lived in West Philadelphia, too, as relatively rare white
people, and in fact Eric was also similar in that he hadn't been
discovered in the high school universe yet either, though Jacob
suspected that more people noticed Eric, at least because of the
tallness and the red hair. In any case, despite all the similarities,
for some reason they had never really hung out, aside from
a couple of times in middle school. Eric and his family had
been away—Canada, maybe?—for a couple of years in there,
so maybe that was part of it.

Eric closed the distance through the crowd now and said,
"Jake" again, extending his hand to be shaken. "You are hilarious."

It felt a little strange and formal, and Jacob had to wonder if he was being teased—he felt really, really stupid about
his joke—but it didn't seem like it from Eric's face, and Jacob
shook his hand. "Thanks," he said, almost like a question. The
crowd swirled past them, everyone on their way to their next
classes.

"How are you doing, man?" Eric said. "Which way are you
going?"

Jacob, who didn't know what was going on, pointed in the
direction he was headed, and the two of them started walking
together. Everywhere around them were other people, going
various places loudly.

"That class is pretty cool," Eric said, thumbing back in the
direction of Mr. Nowacki's room.

"Yeah," Jacob said. So that was a vote for Mr. Nowacki being cool, which Jacob noted. "I like it."

"Listen," Eric said, with some intensity. Jacob remembered
that even back in middle school, the energy level always seemed
to go up around Eric. "I'm having a party in two weeks," he said.
Still in motion, he flipped his book bag forward so he could
open it and pull out a manila folder, from which he extracted a

crisp flier. "Music, dancing. You should come," he said, handing the sheet to Jacob.

Jacob didn't really see the flier at first—he was taking his time processing the idea that he was being invited to a party, and not like a birthday party but like a *party* party. "Wow, great," he found himself saying. "Totally." And then he checked the date, as though there was any chance he was going to be busy then. The flier gave the date, and times, too—*8pm to midnight*—over the words *Fresh Dance Party!* The whole thing had been handwritten and Xeroxed. "Thanks. I can totally do this."

"Great," Eric said, settling his backpack on his back and shaking Jacob's hand again. "And feel free to invite anybody else you want, too, if they're cool."

"Okay, sure," Jacob said. He was looking at Eric's extreme, almost translucent whiteness and his preppy button-down shirt and his jeans rolled up, and thinking that probably Leron and the guys wouldn't be interested in this party.

"Especially girls," Eric said.

"Definitely," Jacob said.

"If they're cool."

Jacob nodded as if to say, *I know exactly what you're talking about.*

Then they walked on a little further, down the big hallway now, which was just swarming with people. The rumor was that Central's administration was overenrolling the school so that they could make an argument for a new science wing. Jacob wasn't sure that kids would actually have access to that kind of inside information, but it was a plausible explanation.

"Hey—have you ever seen the movie *Evil Dead?*" Eric said now.

Jacob had not. He didn't usually go to see things.

"That movie is crazy. I've gotta tell you all about it," he said. "I'm turning here."

And before Jacob knew it, Eric had turned down another hallway—the school was shaped like a capital E and this was the middle line of the E. Jacob stutter-stepped, which made someone crash into him from behind. "Come on, man," the person said. And Jacob's face went hot and he apologized a few times and got himself moving again, off to English class, his thoughts all over the place, holding the flier uncertainly in his hand.

2

Jacob didn't invite anybody else to the party that week. On the subway home with Leron and the guys, for example, he didn't mention it at all.

He and Leron and a few other guys all took the Broad Street Line together down to Center City, and then the 34 subway-surface car out to West Philadelphia. But riding together happened more because they all lived in West Philly than because of any deep bonds between them. Mostly Jacob would spend those trips half-listening to Leron talk about whatever new game he'd gotten for his Commodore 64, while Derrick and Ty asked follow-up questions and Omar agreed with everything Leron said, even if he had no way of knowing what Leron was talking about. Every once in a while, Leron would say, "What you think, Jacob?" and Jacob, who had usually been sitting there silently distracted by his persistent thoughts about how awkward everything was and how sad it was that things were awkward, would just shrug, and everybody would laugh, including Jacob, because he wanted to go along to get along. He was sort of their pet white person. Some afternoons they would actually go to Leron's house on Fiftieth Street and play one of the games, like *Mike Tyson's Punch-Out* or something—"See what I was talking about?" Leron would say, knocking Bald Bull or Kid Flamenco down, and Omar would say, "Aw, yeah"—and Jacob would feel this sharp, familiar aloneness in the midst of everyone, and then after a while they'd all go to their different homes to do homework and have dinner.

And now there was this party, which he didn't mention to those guys.

What he did do was ask his mother if he could go, the next night that she wasn't working, which was Sunday. It was actually the end of Rosh Hashanah, too, which he didn't realize until his mother mentioned it, and she only mentioned it because someone at her hospital had mentioned it. "I guess we didn't do Rosh Hashanah this year," she said. They were at the dinner table together, just the two of them. Jacob's sister, Deanna, was off at college—Cornell—and his father had lived in Chicago since Jacob was twelve. So it was always the two of them at dinner, unless Jacob's mother had an extra shift—she was a nurse, and took extra shifts whenever she could get them, because they for sure needed the money—in which case he would heat up a frozen mac 'n' cheese dinner in the oven and eat that in front of the television. But on this night they were together.

"I guess not," Jacob said. They usually didn't go to services even on the High Holy Days. They were not a big family for doing stuff.

"We could still go to Yom Kippur. What's that, ten days from now?"

Jacob shrugged. He was distracted, thinking about whether to ask his mother about the party. Between when Eric invited him and when he broached the topic with his mother he had started the second-guessing process—had the invitation maybe even been a prank?—and was no longer sure how it would make sense for him to be at a party. How could it possibly lead to anything good? And so the way he asked was this, abruptly, instead of answering her Yom Kippur question: "There's this thing coming up that I wanted to tell you about. I don't have to go or anything. It's not important." He handed her the flier.

"Oh, wow," she said, her hand on her mouth, looking at the flier. "It has an end time. I love this." And then, "Eric Strudwick?" she said. "I think I remember that kid. He was a nice one."

"He still is, I think," Jacob said.

"Well, this looks great," she said. "You can certainly go."

"You think I should go?" Jacob said. Because of course he could just stay home.

His mother took a drink from the glass of gin she was having with dinner. Then she smiled and gathered her dark curly hair up behind her head into a momentary ponytail and said, "Lovey, you can't always stay home. It's not healthy." Since her hair wasn't long enough to be in a ponytail, it just sprang back. She had the same hair as him, but a bit more of it. And, he could see now, there was a little gray sneaking into hers too.

"Okay," Jacob said, jangly inside, picking up his turkey burger just to have something in his hands.

"It'll do you a lot of good," she added. "You spend way too much time locked up in this house. It's important to do fun things."

"I think something's backward," he said, his mouth part full. "Aren't you supposed to be *stopping* me from going out all the time?"

She said, "If you did your part, I would do mine."

He almost choked on his food a little at that. "That's a pretty good one, Mom," he said.

His mother smiled, but Jacob now saw that she hadn't been joking.

It wasn't that Jacob was *anti*social. He did hang out with Leron and the guys sometimes, even on the weekends—well, he worked on the weekends, alongside Leron—and he had a few friends from work or elsewhere who he saw sometimes. Or at least every once in a while. But it was more like *Well, you're here, and I'm here, so I guess we're here together* instead of something more significant. And there wasn't a rhythm to it. If anything, there was a rhythm to *not* doing it. The fact that he was home most weekend nights, the fact that he usually didn't call people to make something happen—that was more inertia than anything else. Plus it was easier to keep himself distracted at home.

Jacob had found that he needed distraction because when he was out in the world, on his own or with people who were not especially close friends, he'd often find himself overwhelmed by bad feelings. He called that the howl. He would be walking down the street and see a dent in a car, for example, or he'd be on the bus and he'd hear two people arguing bitterly, or he'd look out a window and see a person walking slowly by themselves, or he'd be with sort-of friends and see how nobody was really connected to anyone else, or maybe there would be no reason at all, but suddenly it would rise up inside him: an awful moaning feeling, a keen wind. Maybe it was because he lived in a poor, rundown neighborhood, or because his parents were divorced, or just because life automatically produced a lot of problems everywhere in the world, but somehow his life was full of these kinds of moments. Each time it was like he was witnessing something essential and tragic about the universe, and his insides would just start howling like a lone coyote. And he'd want to fall onto his hands and knees into the deep sadness of it.

And sometimes things got a lot worse than that.

So he usually spent his weekends working at the zoo during the day and then, at night, playing video games on his Commodore 64, or he'd watch television. He especially liked anything that was funny, or at least trying to be funny, but he would watch anything—Jacob even watched shows he didn't particularly like, just because they were on, one after the other. He liked *Perfect Strangers*, but nobody on earth could possibly like *Full House*. Still, he watched it because it was on after *Perfect Strangers*. And then there were other shows after *Full House* and other shows after those first other shows and then more other shows and you could watch them or play video games pretty much forever. And so he did these things on and on, and time passed and suddenly it would be very late or even into the morning and he wouldn't know where all the time had gone or even what had happened, exactly, and he would feel wonderfully blank.

His mother called these "lump nights." If she wasn't working, she would peek into his room and say, "You're not having another lump night, are you?" And he would shake his head because everything was fine—he was making sure of it—and she would say something like, "Don't you want to call a friend? Or go to the movies? Or something?" and he would shrug and she would look concerned. "I want you to be happy," she would say. And he would say, "I'm fine," really just wanting her to leave him to his TV and video games before the distraction crumbled away. But it was a routine they had. Sometimes they even did it in reverse, when it was her turn to get stuck in place. He would suggest card games and stuff like that. So they went back and forth.

Not all nights were like that for him, but they were usually his best option.

And it was going to take force to break that inertia and pull him away from his distractions.

The party seemed to exert that kind of force on Jacob. The morning after his mother told him he could go, he woke up with some energy. Nervous and otherwise. The party was still almost two weeks away, but still. He ate his cereal that morning with vigorous chomps. And at school later that day, in history, he sat down at the desk next to Eric's and said, "I'm all set to come to the party."

"Awesome," Eric said. Another handshake. So it really didn't seem like it was a prank. "Definitely invite people if you want to."

"I will," Jacob said. Class hadn't started yet, so there was time to talk. "Hey."

"Yeah?"

"How come I never see you on the subway before or after school?"

"I get in a little early," Eric said, "and I stay a little late." He ran his fingers through his hair, feathering the redness.

"After-school clubs?" Jacob said.

Eric shook his head. "I need time to settle in. And time to settle out, I guess."

That made sense to Jacob. "Where do you...?" He didn't know how to end the sentence.

"Settle in? I just sit in the hallway by my locker," Eric said, pointing in what might have been the right direction.

"Huh." Now that Jacob thought about it, he remembered

seeing Eric sitting there a couple of times. Their lockers were on the same hall.

"You should hang out sometime," Eric said.

"I will," Jacob said before he could think about it. And spent the rest of class too nervous to pay the best attention.

In any case, that afternoon he chickened out and went home at the regular time, riding with Leron and the guys. They talked about video games. Which was better: Winter Games, Summer Games, or World Games? Winter Games was the consensus. Jacob tried to picture Eric shaking all of their hands. "What you thinking about?" Leron said, and Jacob shrugged, and everybody laughed, including Jacob.

But a couple of mornings later he got out of the house a little earlier than usual—"What's the hurry?" his mother asked him, and Jacob said, "No hurry," as he hurried out the door—and got to his subway-surface stop on Baltimore Avenue fifteen or twenty minutes before he usually did. He didn't know anybody on the subway-surface car when he got on. There were kids around his age, quite possibly going to Central, but he didn't recognize them. They all went down into the tunnels together, not knowing each other.

He did recognize a few people on the Broad Street line, but they weren't people he really ever talked to. So he just sat back and his mind bounced around while the thing rocketed north toward school, stop after stop. Jacob could feel, among other things, that he was going somewhere. It was an interesting feeling.

His stop was the second to last. Olney. It was a big one, where just about everybody would get off, right in the heart of rough-and-tumble North Philadelphia, with its blocks of concrete and empty street corners and old cars and houses falling apart all around. There weren't even any trees. West Philly at least had some trees. The dust at the curb made this neighborhood feel something like a desert.

There was one stop beyond it, though: Fern Rock. Jacob had never seen Fern Rock, but just from the name he had a picture in his mind of this beautiful meadow covered in grass and ferns and the occasional tree making shade, all alongside a little stream lined with rocks. Sunny. He pictured sun and shade and green, spreading out in every direction. It sort of made him want to cry.

He had never told anyone about that picture in his mind. For sure not Leron and the guys, who would have just called him a *pussy*, guaranteed.

Jacob got to school with a little time to spare before the bell. And he was already fiftieth-guessing himself and feeling pretty sure that this was a stupid idea and wondering what was wrong with him, but then there was Eric, sitting and leaning back against his locker, his hands behind his head, his long legs way out into the hallway. He looked like he was contemplating the nature of the universe.

Jacob walked up and Eric said, "Jaaaaaaaaaaaaake." It was so drawn out that Jacob actually had time to think about how long and drawn out it was. *Wow*, he thought. They shook hands and Jacob sat down. His own locker was just twenty feet away.

"What were you just thinking about?" he said. "When I came up?"

"Oh," Eric said, pushing up the sleeves of his blue-and-yellow rugby shirt. "I was thinking about Hamilton, Ontario."

"Hamilton, Ontario?"

"Yeah—remember? That's where I went for two years for my father's job."

"Right," Jacob said, though he wasn't sure he'd ever known the exact place Eric had gone.

"Yeah."

"What was that like?"

Eric shrugged. "Boring. Cold and boring. That's what I was just thinking: man, that place was cold and boring."

Jacob nodded. Was Philadelphia boring or not boring?

"Philly's cool, though," Eric said.

So there was that vote. "Yeah," Jacob said.

"Hey—what kind of music do you think I should play at

the party?" Eric said. "I'm gonna make a mixtape. I'm thinking maybe INXS, UB40—"

"All the letters and numbers," Jacob said.

Eric slapped him on the shoulder. "See? That's what I mean. Hilarious."

Jacob was startled—again, he hadn't been *trying* to be funny—but he kept it going. "You could play U2," he said. "The B-52s."

"REM," Eric said.

They both laughed, Jacob partly just gratefully.

"For real, though," Eric said. "Tommy Conwell, maybe? Madonna?"

Jacob liked them, and said so.

"Also the Hooters, for sure," Eric said.

Jacob nodded. They were good. They had a song called "Where Do the Children Go" that was deep and sad. And they also had good dance songs.

He and Eric tossed a couple more names around, and the whole thing felt really nice. Pretty soon, though, the bell rang, and they went off to class, which wasn't one they had together. But they saw each other in a couple of other classes that day, and then at the end of the day Jacob went to meet him at the lockers again, and they stayed for a little settling-out time and then went home together. The conversation this time was about that movie *Evil Dead* that Eric had mentioned the other day. He described *Evil Dead* in a lot of detail, because he had recently seen it on VHS and because Jacob, of course, had never seen it at all. Apparently, Jacob learned, *Evil Dead* was full of sexually predatory demonic trees, and a guy with a chain-saw hand, and a lot of other stuff like that.

At one point during the play-by-play, Jacob looked around the subway car, thinking he might see Leron and the guys, but they weren't there, had probably caught an earlier train like usual. Jacob wondered with a jab of guilt if Leron would be wondering where he was, but then realized probably not. And then he tried to go back to listening to Eric.

"Groovy," Eric was saying, wide-eyed, his eyebrows raised, his hand up like a chain saw.

Yom Kippur this year came on the same Monday as Columbus Day, so school was going to be closed, which meant he was available if he and his mother wanted to go to services somewhere. They talked about it over the weekend.

"What do you think?" she said. The two of them were folding the laundry down in the dim basement.

"Do you have the day off?" he asked.

She shook her head. "But I bet I could get Carol to switch with me. Or Linda."

"Where would we go?"

"I bet we could find someplace. Do you really not want to go?"

Jacob thought about it, folding a pair of his underwear in half. He was doing his stuff, and his mother was doing hers, and they were splitting the towels. "Yom Kippur is the sad one," Jacob said. Not really a question so much as just saying it out loud.

"Right. Rosh Hashanah is the happy one and Yom Kippur is the sad one."

There was a pause of a minute or two while Jacob thought about whether it would be dangerous to go. Dangerous because he was actually feeling good for the moment. But was he *that* fragile? And would it maybe be a meaningful experience?

"We don't have to do it," his mother finally said. "All that religion stuff is old-timey stuff anyway."

"Maybe we should at least wait for the happy one to come around again," Jacob said. His mother put one arm around his shoulders and gave him a sideways squeeze.

And so on Monday, October 9th, Jacob stayed home and did his homework and watched TV and played video games and missed whatever people were doing in the synagogues of Philadelphia. Sometimes he thought about what he was missing. Maybe something important and good. And sometimes he thought about the party, which was coming up the next weekend. But his day was a sort of melancholy one in its own way, actually.

Jacob was good at falling into habits, most of which were habits that kept him home and distracted, but he was soon in the habit of going in a little early and coming home a little late, timing both trips to coincide with Eric's trips. His mother noticed and smiled a little mother-who-notices smile. Jacob didn't mind that; it was nice to have a mother who was rooting for him. And it felt—well, strange and unsettling, but also it felt good, after all, to have this little bit of a social life. He looked forward to it.

So far it wasn't very different from his subway rides with Leron and the guys, except that he and Eric had more to talk about, and Leron and Jacob were in different classes because of some randomness but also because of tracking somehow, whereas Eric and Jacob had a couple of classes together where they could continue the conversation, which ranged to different places but came back repeatedly to the party. They talked about ideas for the mixtape, and the guest list—Jacob did know a couple of people in passing that he could probably invite, so Eric gave him some fliers—and they talked about snacks and beverages. It was going to be a chips-and-Coke kind of party. Jacob hadn't known that there even *were* chips-and-Coke parties in high school—wasn't everything supposed to be drugs and sex and alcohol?—but he obviously didn't know anything about parties, so it didn't throw him too much. And it was actually a relief to Jacob, who was pretty sure he wasn't ready for some kind of *Sixteen Candles* drunken blowout.

The whole thing was nice. Jacob wondered why he hadn't already been hanging out with Eric. Well, there had been Canada. And so much not going places and not doing things.

He did also see Leron here and there at school, and they both worked weekends at the zoo, so they saw each other then. On the weekend before Eric's party, Leron asked, "Hey—where you been, Jacob?" and Jacob said he'd been starting to go in a little early and stay a little late, "to settle in, and settle out, I guess." And Leron nodded and told him about the VCR his family had just gotten. Overall he didn't seem to have a strong opinion about when exactly Jacob rode in and out, or who with. That made sense; Jacob had always assumed his presence at things didn't matter very much one way or another.

The following week, Jacob brought in a bunch of tape cassettes so that Eric could use them for the mixtape; Eric had a dual cassette deck. And Jacob did actually ask a couple of people from school—Brian, a kind of quiet guy from his French class, and Robert from astronomy. Also Char, a girl Jacob had once gone on one disappointingly uninspiring date with. And they all said they were going to come. The experience made Jacob feel like a part-owner of the party, which was not a bad feeling.

"You've been really *up* lately," his mother said. She had been too.

The whole thing made Jacob wonder if the inertia analogy extended this far: if a person at rest tended to stay at rest, what about a person who was suddenly in motion?

3

On the night of the party, Jacob didn't spend a lot of time figuring out what he was going to wear. Not because he was relaxed about it, but because almost everything he owned was very old and stupid and ratty and so the previous weekend he had, like the Fresh Prince in "Parents Just Don't Understand," gone shopping at the Gallery Mall. Except in this case his mother *did* understand, and even somehow scrounged together the money for him to buy himself a new pair of jeans and a roomy button-down shirt, white with light blue stripes running down it. It was almost like she had been saving up for his first high school party. So that was what he was for sure going to wear, and that night it was what he put on.

He sniffed himself. Jacob had spent a lot of time showering; he'd worked earlier that day, a Saturday, and the smell of giving pony rides didn't necessarily come off easily. It took effort. But apparently, according to the sniff test, he had managed it this time. Unless he was just used to it. That was something that he worried about at school, and he was going to be worrying about it that night too.

If he went. There was a point in the middle of getting ready where he just sat down on his bed and it occurred to him that he could stay there. He could stay home, watch TV, play video games instead. And why not? The odds that something good would happen at the party were low. Of course, then he would be letting Eric down, and it was awful letting people down, though of course everybody did that all the time, and also maybe Eric didn't really care that much if he— Anyway, the feelings that had been in him quietly all evening started to pile up, as if he were filling with heavy water. And so why not just stay in place indefinitely?

Almost as if she could sense what he was feeling, his mother knocked soon after—he'd been sitting there maybe ten minutes—and opened his door a little. "You getting ready?" she said.

"I guess," he said.

"Come on, Jacob," she said.

"I don't know," he said.

"It'll be fun!" his mother said, her expression concerned. And she stood there with that very concerned look until he just wanted her face to go back to normal, so he pulled himself up off the bed and away from its considerable magnetic force.

Jacob walked the six or seven blocks to Eric's house. His mother didn't love him walking through their neighborhood at night, because West Philadelphia was a high-crime neighborhood and there were a lot of desperate people in it, and at night the streetlights could be inconsistent and you'd be out there on your own, surrounded by plenty of darkness. Shadows. But Eric's house was close and Jacob's mom didn't own a car, so it's not like she could have given him a ride anyway.

And, weirdly, nothing bad had ever happened to Jacob in West Philadelphia—he'd been mugged once in a subway-surface station on the way into Center City, and another time on Olney Avenue, but never in West Philadelphia. Even though bad things happened to plenty of people there. Maybe folks recognized him somehow. And maybe there was an unspoken agreement that you weren't supposed to jump anybody who lived in your own neighborhood. Or maybe they didn't recognize him but you weren't supposed to mug people who looked kind of sad, who looked like they were already expecting to be mugged or something.

When Jacob got to Eric's house uneventfully, it was almost exactly eight o'clock, and he found that he was the first guest to arrive. Eric was still setting up the speakers in the living room; his younger brother watched sullenly while their parents set out big plastic bowls of chips. Right—there was that thing about fashionable lateness. Jacob saw that he was already off to a terrible start.

"Don't worry about it," Eric said. "You can help us set up."

And so Jacob set his embarrassment aside as much as he could and helped. He plugged wires into speakers, got dips out of the refrigerator, moved chairs, and so on, all the while answering questions from Eric's friendly parents; he hadn't seen them in years. His mother, who was some kind of scientist, was sweet and nerdy, and his father, who was some kind of businessman, was chipper and also nerdy. He seemed like the kind of man who would have been happy to say, *Gee, that's swell* if he had the right opportunity. His hair was red too. Anyway, they wanted to know how Jacob was finding school and about his job and his parents and his sister and all that normal kind of stuff. At one point, Eric said, "You two *are* going to be upstairs for the party, right?"

To which his father said, "Cramping your style, are we?" But he had a smile on his face.

Eric's brother, an eighth grader named Greg, broke off his sullen watch to ask if he could stay, and it was clearly not the first time he'd asked. Eric shot a beseeching look at his parents.

"We're going to watch a movie upstairs," his father said. "I rented something good."

Eric's brother crossed his arms and shook his head. *Figures*, his whole posture seemed to say. Jacob understood that thought.

Eric's family stayed downstairs only long enough to help set everything up. It was kind of nice, Jacob thought, that Eric had his whole family around him. Jacob had his mother, but his father was just an occasional phone call. Plus, so was his sister, now that she was off at college. Anyway, when the doorbell next rang, Eric's parents and brother headed up in a hurry. "I hope it's fun," his mother said from a middle step, blowing him a kiss.

"Could you get that?" Eric said, nodding to the door. "I'm gonna turn off some of the lights. Atmosphere."

Jacob went to the door and found Brian behind it. Usually Brian wore sweatshirts, but tonight he was wearing a dress shirt, like something that would normally have a tie with it.

"Hey," Jacob said, and Brian waved a little close-up wave. "Come on in."

Behind Brian he saw other people getting out of cars, including more girls, getting dropped off by their parents. The party was really going to happen. Jacob resisted the impulse to sniff himself again, or to sit on a couch in a corner and not get up.

Brian went inside, and Jacob found himself at the door for a little while—there was a burst of arriving for a few minutes, including a bunch of people he knew by name but not any more than that, a couple he knew a little better, and a few he'd never even seen before, even though he got the idea that they all went to Central High School.

When the rush ended he went inside, and it was a totally different living room, in that now it was a party. The lights were lower, the music was on—"Stray Cat Strut" was playing—and maybe a dozen people or so were talking to each other near the food, seeming to not mind or even really notice that it was a totally PG event. Nobody was dancing, but a couple of people were bobbing a little. It was an actual party underway. His first one.

Jacob immediately didn't have any idea what to do with himself.

But then there was Eric, who swept over and started introducing him to people, and people to him. How could there be so many people he had never met at his own school? It *was* a pretty big school, but still. Anyway, "Do you know Jake? This guy's hilarious," Eric said pretty much each time he introduced him. Each person laughed when Eric said that, as though Jacob had already said something funny, and they didn't seem to require any additional proof, so he just smiled and went with it, trying to catch as many names as he could, beyond the ones he already knew.

Then the doorbell rang again and he turned toward the door, but it opened from the outside. It was a group of girls letting themselves in.

They weren't part of any popular crowd that Jacob knew of—among the group, he recognized only one girl named Alice and also Char, who he'd invited—but the group stood out here, anyway. Char, with her expert makeup and her blond hair teased out and her big gold earrings and electric-blue party dress, altogether looking like she was kind of a grown-up already. The two girls that Jacob didn't know stood out too, in their own ways. One had chin-length dark hair and glasses that didn't make her look dorky so much as extra sharp, like they were X-ray glasses. But the main thing was this incredibly beautiful dirty-blond-haired girl right at the center of the group. She had huge blue eyes, and wavy-curly hair that was like a waterfall. And there she was in front of Jacob, because he had turned to face the door.

"Hi," she said, with an open-mouthed smile. She looked like she was extremely happy to be there, or possibly to be anywhere. "I'm Willow." UB40 was playing just then—"Red, Red Wine"—and that was something Jacob would remember about this moment later.

"Willow?" Jacob said.

"Like the tree," she said, and abruptly she bent at the waist so that her butt was in the air—it was a remarkable butt—and all her abundance of hair streamed down onto and over the floor. Like a willow tree. And then she flung herself up straight again, and her hair resettled all over the place around her. She had really huge blue eyes.

"Wow," he said, feeling the way you might feel if you found yourself unexpectedly in the presence of the aurora borealis or something. "Right."

Char patted him on the shoulder, a sisterly pat. "This is Jacob," she said to Willow.

"Do we need to remind him to breathe?" said the dark-haired girl with the sharp glasses.

Jacob shook himself unfrozen. The girls laughed a little, though not in a mean way, it seemed like—just confident and comfortable. Still, his second-guessing machine launched into motion. Then all of a sudden DJ E-Z Rock and Rob Base came on the stereo—"It Takes Two"—and the girls hooted and streamed around him into the party, Willow giving a finger-wave goodbye as she went.

Jacob spent much of the rest of the party trying to end up next to Willow.

On the plus side, he was able to manage it multiple times, but on the minus side he was apparently not the only guy at the party with that mission. So there was often a circle of guys dancing in her general area—the E-Z Rock and Rob Base had started the dancing—and whenever she left the dancing area to get snacks or a Coke—Eric had gotten the kind in the glass bottles—there were multiple guys present to observe conversationally that the chips were good chips, that the dip was good dip, that the glass bottles were cool. Plus her girlfriends tended to stick with her too. So everything Jacob learned about her that night he learned in a group setting.

At one point he asked her if she was a dancer, partly because she had some good moves on the dance floor, but partly because the way she moved everywhere seemed very dramatic and interesting. Like, she would sort of unroll her arm just to pluck a chip out of a bowl.

In any case, she grabbed his elbow when she answered, but her eyes darted back and forth between everybody who was listening. "Wow, yes," she said. "That's what I am. That's what I want to be."

"Ballet?" said this one guy, Finn, who Jacob had really just met that night. "Or modern dance? Or folk or something?" Finn had his head shaved on the sides, punk-like, and was wearing a white T-shirt that said *The Dead Milkmen*. There was a cartoon of a cow on the shirt, with Xs for eyes.

Willow grabbed Finn's arm and looked at everybody, her eyes even bigger than usual, and said, "I want to do all of it. Everything."

"That's cool," Eric said, nodding.

And right then Jacob had his best moment of the party. He wasn't even trying—it just came to him. He said, "You're gonna need extra feet." And everybody laughed, including Willow, and even the sharp-seeming girl with the glasses, who he had learned was named Tammy. "Nice one," she said. Eric slapped him on the back. And then, when Willow was done re-grabbing his arm, she fielded another question from the crowd.

So things went pretty much like that. Willow wandered the party surrounded by the immediate moons of the girls who had arrived with her, and the more distant asteroids—could asteroids rotate around planets?—of all the guys who were there. Really Willow was more like a sun. Even Brian was quietly orbiting. There were more than twenty people there—Eric knew a lot of people, actually!—but about half of them were centered around Willow. Meanwhile, there was eating, and Coke, and the music was good, and people danced to it, song after mixtape song. And Jacob felt only good feelings. Mostly.

Toward midnight, Finn suggested going outside. It wasn't clear who the exact target of the suggestion was, aside from the general direction of the Willow solar system, but that half of the party ended up in front of Eric's house. Outside, the air was cool. Jacob, standing on the sidewalk at the bottom of Eric's stoop, was a little sweaty from all the dancing. There was still dancing going on inside. He could hear the music, but it was muffled, as if Jacob and the others were beyond the party somehow. It was a successful party, it was still happening, and they were beyond it.

"Wow," said Willow, looking up at the sky and seeing something there. Jacob couldn't tell what it was, but her face made it seem like it was different from what other people saw, and that it was more amazing too.

"Guys," Eric said, "Jake and I have been hanging out in the morning before school, and in the afternoon after school. By our lockers, in the middle hallway. Third floor. You should come by and hang out too."

There was nodding and agreement. "Cool," someone said.

"It's very relaxed," Eric said. "Right, Jake?"

"Practically comatose," Jacob said, and from the laughter he could see that that had been his second-best moment of the night.

Jacob paused to acknowledge it—he was glad to be there.

Then, out of nowhere, standing atop Eric's front stoop, Finn threw his head back and howled. It caught everyone by surprise. His voice filled the air and flew up into the sky over Melville Street.

And then, after a few seconds, Tammy joined in, and Char did, too, a very feminine howl, almost demure, and then Willow offered up her own, and that settled it: now everyone was howling, including even Jacob, whose voice was tentative at first and then a little bigger.

Before now, all the howling Jacob knew about had been internal, and painful, and dangerous. But this was not like that. This was wolf, not coyote, and it was joy rather than tragedy. And it wasn't some trapped thing—it was pouring out of him. Out of all of them. Their voices caromed off the cars parked along the curb, off the line of shoulder-to-shoulder row houses facing each other, even off each other's bodies. The air vibrated. It was like nothing else Jacob had ever experienced.

Pretty soon Finn was going to take things one step too far and shake up his bottle of Coke to spray it up in the air and all over the nearby cars, sparkling sticky on hoods and windshields, and anyway neighbors who had already been irritated by the music were going to start opening their front doors to complain about the howling. Soon after that parents would arrive, and the party would wind down, one person after the next getting picked up or driving themselves away—there was a dramatic crush surrounding Willow when Char announced that the group had to leave—and eventually it would just be Jacob and Eric and Eric's family cleaning up. And then, on the walk home, Jacob would fortieth-guess everything he'd said or done all night, and he would wonder about horse smell and have a lot of feelings, some of which were actually nice.

But that was all a little ways off. For this particular moment, he howled. Surrounded by voices, he threw his own sound into

the air, feeling like he had lungs big enough to hold all the air in
the city of Philadelphia.

4

On Monday, Jacob got to Eric's locker pretty early, full—overfull—of excitement to maybe see people from the party, and especially those girls. Eric was already there—but alone. This was a significant letdown. The two of them had talked on the phone on Sunday about how awesome the party had been and how cool everyone was. Especially Willow. How had neither of them ever seen her before? Well, Central was big. Anyway, Jacob felt really different from normal all that Sunday, in a very, very nice way. Sundays were more likely than other days to be bad days, but this one was a day of no inner howling at all.

Now, though, with nobody else here, Jacob felt his heart do that thing it sometimes did.

At moments like this, Jacob became aware of exactly where his heart was in his body. He could feel it take on extra weight and sink inside him. It was like slipping down into deep water. And all the rest of him wanted to follow on down.

He sat down next to Eric and tried to restart the post-party analysis, basically unsuccessfully, because they were both distracted and at least one of them was sinking internally.

But then Brian showed up, with his small close-up wave and a "hi, Jake," and back in his usual gray sweatshirt. He sat down with them and said how great a party it had been. That was something, anyway. Jacob could feel his heart lighten and rise. A little.

Then Finn showed up, too, clomping down the hall in big black boots and dropping with his army-looking backpack onto the floor. "What's up, guys?" he said. Today his shirt said *Bad Brains*, and there was a picture of lightning striking the Capitol building in Washington, DC. At least Jacob thought it was the Capitol building.

Anyway, they talked about the party a little, but it was pretty clear that everybody had one eye on the far end of the hall, which is where Willow and company would appear if they were, in fact, going to appear. One of the guys would say something and then there would be a pause, and then one of the others would say, "Yeah. Totally." And then there would be another pause. And so on.

It occurred to Jacob that he was the kind of person where nothing good was ever enough by itself. There was always something else he was waiting for.

But then they did show up—four girls, walking down the hall toward them. Willow was once again at the center, already smiling her open-mouthed smile, which you could see from one end of the hallway to the other. And around her was the same group that had come to the party together Saturday night— Char; the glasses-girl, Tammy, who at the party had reminded Jacob to breathe and who said his joke was good; and a girl named Alice, who had a long ponytail and who radiated seriousness like a halo. Jacob had had a couple of classes with her before.

The boys all actually stood up, like it was some formal tea party or something. And not one at a time, copying each other—they all got up at once, together, without any consultation. It just happened automatically for Jacob, and apparently for the rest of them too.

When the girls got to them, there was some standing-around kind of talking for a minute or so—*Great party* and *Thanks for inviting us* and all those sorts of things—and everybody pretended to be talking equally to everybody else. Jacob, meanwhile, was aware of Willow in a way that he hadn't been aware of any other girls before; she really was like strong sunlight. Finally Eric, very smoothly, said, "Well, feel free to have a seat, ladies," indicating the floor as though offering up some very fancy living room furniture. And the girls sat—Willow, in a flowy skirt, descended like a leaf settling through the air to the ground—and the guys sat right after.

"How do you all know each other?" Eric said to them. Jacob realized that Eric was their unofficial leader.

Willow, who was at least the spokesperson of the girls, if not their leader, said, "Middle school. We all went to Jenks."

"Well," Alice said, "I didn't." She spoke very crisply, out of a precise little mouth. She was in Jacob's English class that year, and she always spoke very crisply and usually had the right answer.

"Right," Willow said. She touched Alice's arm apologetically. "Mostly Jenks. But you're in my chemistry class."

"Anyway," Tammy said, eyebrows up over the rims of her glasses, "how do you guys know each other?"

Jacob thought about it. The guys were not a *group* in the way the girls were, but now they sort of were, just in the way this encounter had gotten set up, like two tribes parleying with one another.

Eric shrugged. "Here and there. Classes. Jake and I go way back." He slapped Jacob on the shoulder for that one.

"Prehistoric times," Jacob said, and immediately he was saying to himself, *You don't have to swing for the fences every time*, but people laughed, so it was okay.

So at first it was boy tribe encountering girl tribe, but after a few minutes that broke down just because there were too many people for that, and so the conversation started to bounce around a little more loosely. Willow was still the gravitational center, but now people were popping in comments every which way. As other unrelated kids arrived to go to their own lockers, working around this clump of people in the middle of everything, the group talked about the music that had been played at the party and other bands, too—Finn threw out a bunch of names like Black Flag and Social Distortion and Sonic Youth, and people nodded appreciatively at his advanced knowledge—and people talked about who they had seen in concert, which in Jacob's case was nobody, and then they circled naturally back to their classes. Complaints and eye-rolling and everything, though Jacob could tell that this was a group of people who,

like him, took their classes pretty seriously and had 3.0+ GPAs.
Probably mainly 3.5+ ones. They just gave that off, like a scent.
Still, the deal was that you had to roll your eyes.

When the bell rang, just before they all went wherever they
had to go, everybody talked about meeting up again at the end
of school.

Something had clicked.

In history class Eric leaned over to Jacob—they were sitting
together regularly now—and said, "That Willow girl. Wow,
huh?"

Jacob nodded. "Total wow." He had already been in the middle of thinking about her.

"Yeah," Eric said.

After school, before the group totally gathered, Leron found
Jacob stowing a few things in his locker. "Settling out?" he said.

"Oh yeah, I guess," Jacob said.

Leron looked around at Jacob's new friends—Brian was
there, and Eric, and Alice. In a mock-Caucasian voice, a kind
of Ward Cleaver impression, Leron said, "You've found your
people, son."

"Oh…well," Jacob began, flushing, not sure what to say.

"That's okay," Leron said, smiling and giving Jacob a light
tap on his chest. "I'll see you at work."

"Yeah," Jacob said.

As Leron headed off down the hall, he turned back one last
time. "Stay Black!" he called out to Jacob.

Jacob stood there and watched him go.

After a few minutes the same guys and girls were in the
hallway again, sitting by the lockers. Other kids worked around
them again, and the hall was busy for a while, until the bulk of
the people had done their locker thing and headed off home
and the space belonged to these eight. Though Jacob was a
little distracted, thinking about the movie *Do the Right Thing*.
That's where Leron's "Stay Black" had come from—Buggin'
Out had said it in *Do the Right Thing*. That movie, which Jacob
in fact had seen with Leron, made you think even more about

how difficult things were in the world and had made Jacob 100 percent absolutely cry at the end. He hid it behind a hand, and afterward Leron had pretended that he hadn't noticed.

He tried to refocus himself. Here, now.

"I don't think I've ever been in the school when it's this empty," Char was saying.

"Me, either," Finn said, rubbing the shaved side of his head. "It's kind of spooky."

"I've seen school empty like this, after hours," Alice said. She looked around, her ponytail swaying from side to side. "Debate team."

"Yeah," Tammy said. "I've done a couple of after-school things every once in a while. I was on the track team for about a month."

"Oh yeah," Char said. "Right. I actually did the tennis team for a while."

Brian actually raised his hand, and he added, "French club."

"I have my dance classes," Willow said thoughtfully, "but those are in my neighborhood community theater." All the guys *ahhhed* and *mmmed*.

Hearing all this, Jacob realized that he was a person without extracurricular interests. He liked to read, but he had never joined anything reading-related—the literary magazine or the newspaper, for example, or the literature club, if there was one—or anything else, either. He did like comedy, but was there even a school club for that? He had sometimes had after-school jobs, and other times he had just been in the habit of going home when classes were over. Not even to get a jump on his homework—mainly he watched cartoons and drank chocolate milk, like he was ten years old or something.

"I've gotta get a hobby," he said aloud now. He meant it seriously—was more talking to himself than anyone else—but everybody laughed, and so Jacob laughed too.

They ended up hanging out in the hallway for about an hour talking again about classes and music and the school cafeteria—Willow said you couldn't make it as a vegetarian in there—before somebody introduced the idea of going home, and everybody sighed like old people and said, yeah, it was probably time to go home.

But before they did—Willow had the idea—they got in a real circle and each person took out a sheet of paper and passed it around to get everyone else's phone numbers. They were mostly lined looseleaf sheets and ones ripped out of spiral notebooks, but Finn had one that was from a little notebook that looked like its cover was leather. "Songwriting book," he said, and Jacob saw Willow look at him with wonder. And he saw Tammy roll her eyes a little. From the little he knew about her at that point, Tammy seemed like a person who had strong opinions.

Anyway, they all ended up with all the numbers, and then they went their separate ways. Or somewhat separate. Char had a car, so she set off to drive Tammy and Willow to Germantown and Mount Airy on her way to Chestnut Hill, and Brian had to catch a bus up into Manayunk, while Eric, Finn, Alice, and Jacob ended up on the Broad Street line, and Finn got off at Girard to head east into Fishtown and Alice kept going past City Hall a couple stops further; she lived somewhere on the edge of South Philadelphia. Central, which was a magnet school, really was like a magnet, drawing kids in from everyplace across the city. And at the end of the day letting them go again.

After that, on the subway-surface car that they connected to from the Broad Street Line, it was just Jacob and Eric, debriefing. Willow was still extremely wow, but really everybody was pretty cool, was the gist of the debriefing. "How did we never hang out with these guys before?" Eric said. "That party was the best idea we ever had, Jake." Jacob nodded, not even catching at first that he was being given credit for the party that he didn't deserve; he was feeling very, very conscious of that sheet of paper in his backpack, carrying all those phone numbers, Willow's among them.

5

Jacob did not, of course, call Willow right away. Partly because he was terrified, and not at all confident that anything good could possibly come out of talking to her, but also partly because he realized that it would not be a cool thing to do, calling her right away. And the terror and pessimism helped him keep that in mind.

Nonetheless, the phone had become a bigger part of his life. In the past he had just used it to talk to his sister or his father every couple of weeks. But now he talked to Eric every day, for example. After riding into school with him and hanging out with him and the others before school and then seeing him in a couple of classes and then hanging out with him after school and then riding home together—it took about an hour each way—they still had some debriefing to do. They had to wow about Willow, and wonder what was going on in quiet Brian's head, and laugh about something Tammy said—she really was hilarious—and kind of half-admire Finn and half-be-nervous about Finn—he was the kind of guy who liked to say things like, "Man, I'm bored. Let's break something." Eric and Jacob also talked loosely about plans for a second party.

He talked to Brian a couple of times too. Those conversations were shorter, and less about debriefing. Brian liked to talk about their French class, which was led by a gentle Algerian woman named Madame Lellouche, who Jacob liked pretty well and Brian enthusiastically admired, because she was exposing him to all kinds of French and Francophone literature. He was ahead of everyone else in the class—should have been in French 5, really. He would ask Jacob things like, "Have you read Rabelais? He's really funny—you should read him." Jacob had not read Rabelais, though he took a mental note.

Jacob called Finn once that week too. Finn, who sounded

like he'd been asleep when Jacob called in the late afternoon, mainly recommended music that Jacob had never heard of—though he took more mental notes—while music that Jacob had never heard before played pretty loudly in the background. And there was one phone call with a girl, though that was Char. Not that there was anything wrong with Char—it was just that calling her wasn't a big accomplishment, because ever since they had that one date in tenth grade and realized that they really weren't dating material for each other, the pressure was low. In this conversation she said, "My God, you guys are insane. You've *got* to calm down about Willow." And when Jacob said, "What are you talking about?" she said, "What you're *supposed* to ask is who she's into." And Jacob paused a long pause and then asked that question, and Char said, "Oh, who knows? Everyone. Nobody. You can't tell with Willow. She loves everyone."

After which Jacob had to call Eric to debrief about that.

It was tough talking to Eric about it, though, because of course they were both interested in Willow, so they could talk about how awesome she was, but couldn't get *too* into detail, *too* concrete about plans or possibilities, because that would have made it a competition. Mostly they just had to admire her in a removed way, like she was a comet they had just seen. So when Jacob presented Char's observation, he had to deliver it like *Hey, how about that, huh?* And Eric had to respond with, "She really is a mystery, man." And then they both sighed a *she's awesome* sigh.

Jacob's mother was definitely very interested in this whole new social thing. She had questions.

"Who are these kids? Are they like Eric Strudwick?"

"Like Eric how?" Jacob said. "Red-headed?"

"Nice, I guess," his mother said. "I guess I mean nice." Eric had been by the house once or twice recently, so his mother had had the chance to confirm Eric's ongoing niceness.

"Yeah," Jacob said. And not dismissively—he thought about it, and, sure—everybody was pretty nice. "Yeah," he said again. It was kind of wild that they hadn't all gotten together before now, but Central High School really was huge, and none of them had been looking to hang out with anyone. Jacob for sure hadn't been.

"Okay," his mother said, her forkful of spaghetti sitting idle in her hand, just over the plate. She had worked a bunch of extra shifts recently and looked like someone running on no sleep. She was still in her nurse's outfit from that day. "And?"

"And?"

"And what else are they like?" She made a *go-on* circle gesture with her fork.

Jacob sat back in his chair, chewing on his own spaghetti and his thoughts. What *were* they like?

It seemed to Jacob that you couldn't talk about them in terms of categories the way you were supposed to be able to in high school. There wasn't a straightforward way to classify any of the people who were, believe it or not, becoming his friends. Well, first you probably had to think about the world of Central overall, which was a complicated thing. Maybe it had once been a simple thing, back when there had been only boys there—they had started admitting girls back in 1983, and his sister Deanna had been in one of those first classes, which she said was kind of stressful—but now it was complex. There were different academic tracks and there were electives and all kinds of clubs and things. Plus there really were like two thousand kids at Central, and from all over the city. It wasn't like one of those high schools in *Can't Buy Me Love* or *Heathers* where everybody knew everybody and you knew who was what—jocks, nerds, punks, whatever—automatically. Central was more fluid than that, or messier, or something. It was maybe one of the reasons Jacob had gone undiscovered for more than two years—he hadn't been mechanically sorted into a group the way high school was supposed to do. And he hadn't ever tried to find one of his own.

And that was true for the rest of the kids he was hanging out with, really. Eric had been kind of a loner before the party. Maybe that was because of Canada. And Brian had been a loner too. And even though Char was kind of glamorous and had been on the tennis team and you'd think she'd be in some popular group, she was also really, really smart, which was not a boon to popularity most of the time, and also—Jacob hated to even think this but it was true—not the prettiest; she had a wide nose, and it seemed like all her makeup and hairstyling was engaging with that nose in an epic battle. And meanwhile, among her friends—they were friends, but not a clique per se—Willow was unique and maybe ungroupable; in a way, she seemed to be in her own world, on her own plane, somewhere else from the world of the popular or unpopular. And Tammy, who was definitely pretty and confident but a little frightening with her sharp eyes and her sharp opinions. Alice was so serious. And Finn was kind of punk rock, but he was also in AP Physics and doing advanced math.

And so maybe they were together because none of them fit neatly. If their lives had been a fantasy novel, Jacob realized, they would have been a ragtag band of adventurers. Probably facing insurmountable odds.

To his mother, Jacob said, "I dunno. Just people. They're just like people."

His mother nodded slowly. "My son is befriending *people*. Interesting choice. Well, I guess I can understand that, after those bad experiences you had befriending, you know, wolves and bald eagles."

Jacob shook his head. His mother wasn't too tired for a zinger, apparently. "Thank you, Shecky," he said. "Shecky Greene, ladies and gentlemen."

His mom laughed.

Not that he knew who Shecky Greene was, actually.

On the Thursday of that week he did finally call Willow. It wasn't really his idea.

The thing was that Eric had told him—they were on the subway-surface car on the way home—that Finn had been calling Willow already. Like, maybe a couple of times already. Which explained the way they'd seemed to have some kind of inside joke about avocados that day, and why they were talking about his songwriting that he apparently really did. Which, dammit. And then Eric said, "So I've gotta call her too. Like, *today*. Well, tonight." And so apparently every guy on earth was already talking to Willow, aside from Jacob. Which decided things.

First, though, he had dinner on his own—his mother was working. Only after eating and not tasting anything that he ate did he go to the wall phone in the kitchen and make a call. To his sister. Another girl picked up the dorm-room line but then she got Deanna.

"Hey, bro," she said. She sounded happy. She had never been a mopey person in general the way Jacob was—she was more of a get-things-done type—but her happiness had been particularly big ever since she left for school in the fall. That was a promising thing about college, or at least Cornell. "How's junior year? What's up?"

"Nothing," Jacob said, like a reflex.

"I don't think so," Deanna said. "Mom says you have a *social life*."

Jacob almost protested, again like a reflex, but then he relented. He had called Deanna for a reason. "Well, maybe," he said. "Kind of."

"Okay. 'Kind of' is a start," Deanna said.

"Listen," Jacob said.

Deanna's voice got very pretend-serious. "I'm listening."

Jacob paused. He was bunching up the long, springy spiral cord in his hand. He looked at the linoleum at his feet, which had a weird speckle pattern. He came out with it: "So, say you were a girl in high school."

"You were a girl in high school."

"Deanna, *seriously*," he said.

"Okay, okay," she said. "I'm a girl in high school."

"Okay," he said. "And a guy called you."

"*Ohhhhhh.*"

"Deanna," he said. He was now mangling the spiral cord

in his hand. "So, the question is: what would you want to talk about? What would you want the guy to ask you about?"

"Oh my God," she said. "I'm kind of dying here."

"Just *tell* me, Deanna."

"Okay, okay. But you've had a girlfriend, haven't you? What was that girl's name this summer?"

"Barbara."

"So, didn't you learn anything from that?"

"I don't know," he said. It was completely likely that Jacob hadn't learned anything at all from that.

"Well, start with this: whoever this new girl is, is there anything interesting about her?"

Jacob almost said, *Everything*, which was true because she was so dramatic that she kind of made everything around her interesting; if she was looking out a window, say, you'd want to stand next to her and be like, *What an amazing landscape*; then he almost mentioned how beautiful she was, and all her hair and her huge eyes. But instead he said, "Dancing. She's a dancer. Also, she's a vegetarian."

"I always thought we should be vegetarians," Deanna said thoughtfully. "Well, there you go. Ask her about that stuff. It's really not that hard, you know."

His own sister had blossomed right in front of him in high school. She'd had big glasses and a little afro of frizzy hair for the longest time, and then it was like one of the old movies where the woman—probably a librarian—takes her glasses off and changes her hair, and all of a sudden she's beautiful. That's what Deanna did, and she had boyfriends after that.

"Right," Jacob said. "It's not that hard."

"Jacob," Deanna said, with a lot of love suddenly in her voice, "it seems like you're happy."

The idea of that made Jacob seize up a little. Because if he was happy now, what would he be later? "I guess," he said.

"You can do this, bro."

Jacob took that in—it seemed like she was saying something big to him—and he thanked her.

"How's Mom?" she said in a kind of serious voice. Mom wasn't always good. And it was usually both kids who rallied for her; Deanna would keep the household organized and Jacob brought the humor to lighten things. Now of course there was only Jacob.

"She's okay," he said. "She's doing fine." She really was.

"Great," she said. "Great."

Then Jacob asked Deanna about what was going on in her life, but distractedly, and she told him to shut up and go call this other girl, whoever she was, and so he got off the phone.

Which immediately rang.

But it wasn't Willow, or any of his new friends. It was his father. "Oh, hi," Jacob said, wishing he hadn't picked up.

"Well, nice to hear your voice too," his father said in a voice that was joking but also maybe annoyed.

"Oh—no—I was just watching something. On television."

"Well, can we talk? It's been a while."

"Sure," Jacob said. Why had he chosen *that* excuse?

"So…how are you?"

"Good." He was trying to decide whether to tell his father anything about his new social life. It was a lot to get into. Plus his father was so far away that connecting the dots seemed like it could be pointless. "Good."

His father sighed. "Are we going to have a conversation or are we not going to have a conversation?"

"Yes. Yeah," Jacob said. And he updated his father about his classes one by one—possibly-cool Mr. Nowacki, strict Ms. Hudson, patient Ms. Terrell, and so on. Test scores and grades on papers. The usual stuff. His father made listening noises through it all.

"Sounds like everything's going well," his father said, and Jacob said that, yeah, it was. After which Jacob almost forgot to ask, but luckily didn't, "What about you?" And his father updated him on his work—an insurance company, doing something involving a computer. Jacob had heard about it many times but still didn't have a clear idea what his father did. "Cool," he said when his father had finished.

"I'm going to see you for Hanukkah this year," his father said. "You'll come out to Chicago."

"Oh—cool," Jacob said. His parents must have worked that out between the two of them.

"Your mother's going to get Thanksgiving this time and I'm going to get Hanukkah. Or at least part of it."

"Great." He and his father fought a lot, but hopefully it would be an okay visit this time.

"Okay," his father said. "You can go watch your television show. But I'm glad you made time to talk with me. I think that's important."

"Sure," Jacob said. "I'm sorry."

Afterward, he leaned against the wall and wondered if he was a bad son in general or if it was just some particular thing with him and his father. It took him a few minutes standing there, feeling this and feeling that, and wondering if he should bother to try Willow, before he got that under control. And then he picked up the phone again.

It took a few tries to reach Willow, because her phone was busy for a while. Each busy signal felt like someone put weight on him, or in him, and he almost gave it up. But then he finally got through. Willow herself picked up.

"Jake!" she said. She sounded really excited. "Oh my gosh! It's *so* good to hear from you."

Before he could stop himself, Jacob found himself saying, "Really?"

"*So* good," she said. Even on the phone it felt like she was reaching out and grabbing his arm. That was one of the things about Willow. When she focused on you, it was like you were completely *there*. All the busy signal weight was gone.

"Well, it's really great to talk to you," he said.

"Wow. I've been on the phone for like two hours straight!"

That was not the best news for Jacob, but he fielded it as well as he could. "Me, too," he said.

"Really?"

"Yeah. I was just talking to my sister. She's at college."

"Wow, college," she said. "That's got to be really fun. Where does she go?"

"Cornell."

"For sure," she said. "New York."

"Right. Ithaca. It does seem really fun," he said.

"Yeah."

He said, "I guess that's going to be us in a couple of years." At this point, realizing with terror that he was way off-script, Jacob was turning and turning, binding himself in the spiral phone cord.

"Yeah, wow," she said. "Can you even imagine?"

"I bet you want to go somewhere where you'll be able to dance," Jacob said. He stopped turning; that segue had been brilliant.

"For sure," she said. "Sometimes I think I maybe don't even want to go to college. Maybe I just want to go dance. I think that could be what I'm meant to do." She paused for a second, before adding, "Is that crazy?"

"No way," Jacob said. Though in fact skipping college was not something that would have occurred to him, and actually he thought maybe it *could* be a little crazy for a person to not go. But maybe not when Willow said it, because she was operating on that other plane and everything. "It sounds cool."

"Thanks," she said, with a sigh.

There was a moment of silence, so Jacob charged in with "So you're a vegetarian?" because it was all he had.

Luckily, Willow was happy to talk about that. She had been a vegetarian since she was four, apparently—her parents had read her a book about farms and somehow that one book woke her up to the fact that these were *living creatures*—and didn't even remember what meat tasted like, though she was pretty sure, from looking at it, that it tasted disgusting. "Like, hamburger?" she said. "I can't believe hamburger."

"Yeah," Jacob said. He liked hamburger.

"Because that was *alive*, and now it's chopped up into bits. Do you know what I mean?" She sounded almost tearful. When Willow got sad, he saw, it was because of some real thing in the world, not because of nothing.

"For sure," Jacob said. That notion—alive to chopped up—really was kind of profound, when you thought about it. "That's a good point."

From there they talked a while longer about meat having once been alive, and she talked a little about factory farms, which definitely did sound like horrible places, and he talked about working at the zoo and the different animals he liked, and she laughed at some of his stories, which was like being showered with flowers or something, and then in the background there was the sound of Willow's mother's voice, asking her to get off the phone, so she said, "Jake, I have to go, unfortunately—it was *so* nice to talk to you, though!"

"Yeah—totally," he said. "See you tomorrow?"

"Definitely!" she said, and then they said goodbye and hung up.

Jacob sat down right where he was, in the kitchen, next to the wall phone, only partly tangled in the cord. His whole body was on high alert, like he had just survived a tornado or a shark attack—barely. *It was so nice to talk to you*, she had said. *It was so nice to talk to you.* He replayed that line a few more times in his mind. It was like music.

But of course he remembered the dumb things too. Why had he told that story about the bossy parent who stepped in the pony poop? Why didn't he know enough about dance to ask even one real question about it? Despite himself, Jacob could feel those thoughts piling up. But he forcefully shook himself free of that, because he really didn't want to go in that direction. She liked his stories. It had been *so* nice to talk to him. That was the point.

Jacob sat on the speckles of the linoleum and repeated the music of that for quite a little while, holding on to it for as long as he could.

6

That weekend they all went dancing. Or they tried to. The plan was to go to this one club in the suburbs that was open on Sunday nights to people under twenty-one. When he asked his mother about it, she said, "On a school night?" She looked at him. "Is this important to you?"

"Yeah," he said. It really was.

"Oh, okay," she said, kind of grudgingly. "Well, I guess we'd better talk curfew, then."

Jacob had never needed a curfew, but his mother, who already had the precedent of Deanna, came up with one pretty readily: eleven on school nights, and midnight on other nights. "And I won't be able to fall asleep until you're back, so definitely don't be late."

Jacob knew she had an early morning coming on the Monday after when he wanted to go out; it was cool that she was giving him permission since it meant she'd have to stay up. "Thanks, Mom," he said. And he gave her a little kiss on the cheek. She smiled from a little way away.

Both of the days of the weekend Jacob was at the zoo, giving pony rides. Jacob knew the season was coming to an end—by November, there wouldn't be many customers around, and the full-timers could handle the ones that did show up—but it was a good-weather weekend for late October, so there were families there, and they still wanted rides, and they still wanted to complain that the rides were too short for the money. So things felt normal.

Leron and Ty were there, too, along with a couple of the other usual guys and girls, the ones who hadn't just had this for a summer job. For Barbara, for example, it had been just a summer job. Her plus, Jacob realized, all the other girls who had thought he was cute.

The people who were there today each had particular ponies that they led around the track. Ty was with Daisy, the miniature horse, who was only for the smallest children. Leron had Buster, who walked fast. The customers complained a lot about that pony. But still it was better than trying to lead Delilah, who was a mule, and never wanted to do her job. The customers liked her because she walked slowly, but the workers didn't, because you had to spend the whole time basically dragging her along. Jacob had Delilah both days, because the other workers had grabbed the other options first. And Leron and Ty looked back at Jacob behind them and mimicked her slow, unwilling steps and cracked up at him. But that was normal too.

It was the kind of job that gave you a lot of time to think. Walking along with Delilah after lunch on Sunday, he thought about how he used to spend every afternoon and most mornings riding the subway with these guys. And now he mainly saw them only at work—they ate their lunches together, usually, and talked about video games and stuff—and even that was coming to an end.

Delilah stopped and Jacob dragged her back into motion. It was weird, wasn't it, just swapping out some friends for some other ones? Especially, maybe, if you were a white person who was leaving your Black friends behind to hang out with white people. But Leron himself—there he was, laughing at something Ty had said farther ahead on the track—didn't seem to think it was so weird.

Maybe this was just more of Jacob's usual readiness to make things more problematic than they really were. He sighed and got a tighter hold on Delilah's reins. The toddler in the saddle was bouncing up and down as though he was on a racehorse, wildly galloping. *And why not?* Jacob thought.

Transportation for Sunday night had been a complicated thing to work out. Everybody was scattered all over the city, so even if they could have all fit in one car it would have been too much for one person to drive all around to get the rest of them. Luckily, Eric got permission to borrow the family car, and he volunteered to grab Jacob—shotgun—and then circle down into Center City for Alice, who turned out to live on this little secret cobblestone side street not far from South Street, and then up into Fishtown for Finn, and then into Manayunk, where Brian lived. "Thanks, man," Finn said when he got into the back seat of Eric's family's Volkswagen Golf. "I'm saving up for a bike." And when Alice asked more about what kind he was saving up for—she liked precision—it became clear he was talking about a motorcycle. "I think there are a lot of good used ones out there," he said.

Fishtown looked like South Philly, the kind of South Philly that was down further than Alice's place: kind of stoic brick row houses with a door on the left and a window on the right and then two windows above for the second floor, everything simple and plain. You could tell that the people who lived in them had to work hard, like his mother did. And normally that recognition would start a small howl in him, but tonight, he noticed, it didn't. Tonight he was pretty much just excited.

Finn handed a tape forward to Eric, and they played it on the way to Char's place—the Ramones. It was pretty good. Jacob had never heard "I Wanna Be Sedated" before, but it was pretty good and more upbeat than you'd expect from the title.

"What kinda club are we going to, anyway?" Finn asked. But nobody really knew. Char was the one who had found it.

On the way up to Char's house—the plan was to gather first in Chestnut Hill, where Char had a car of her own, get a sense of where they were going, and then caravan their way to dancing—they picked Brian up in Manayunk. He lived on this steep street with houses that were paired off like Siamese twins, instead of one continuous row of homes, and facing a bunch of trees on the other side of the street. Not quite pastoral,

but different from West Philly. It was amazing how little of
Philadelphia Jacob had ever seen. Let alone beyond.

At his door they met Brian's father, who turned out to be a
soft-spoken man himself. "Do you want to come in?" he said,
his voice as gentle as a librarian, but then Brian zipped past him.
"Not now, Dad," he said. It was the most aggressive Jacob had
ever seen him. And then they all got back into the car, Jacob
up front—shotgun privileges, by unspoken decree, lasted the
length of a one-way trip, and then would have to be reclaimed
for the return—and Brian and Finn sat on either side of Alice
in the back. It was tight, and Jacob definitely hoped he didn't
still smell like horses. It occurred to him with a small pang:
whatever he did smell like, somewhere in the city was Leron,
smelling like that too.

When the Ramones were done, Finn replaced them with another group Jacob didn't recognize but that was pretty intense,
screaming about how someone's head was like a hole. "I just
got this," Finn said. "Like, today."

Finally they made it to Char's house, which Jacob hadn't yet
seen. It was a revelation. Meaning it was big. Meaning it looked
like some characters from a Victorian novel should come
walking out of it. Well, maybe not that huge, definitely not a
mansion, but still—nothing like what you'd ever see in West
Philly or, apparently, South Philly or Fishtown or Manayunk.
The nearest house was like a quarter of a block down, and everything else around the place was lawn.

"Wow," Jacob said.

"Nice," Eric said.

"Shit," Finn said.

They got out of the car slowly, tentatively, and then stood
still on the sidewalk. They had parked the car along the curb
even though there was a half-circle driveway in front of the
house. More than half a circle. "This is the right place?" Jacob
said.

But then, just as Alice confirmed that it was the right house, three girls burst out of the front of the place, and they were the expected girls. "Bye, Mom, Dad!" Char called back over her shoulder as she slammed the door. The three of them came down to the sidewalk like a flock of birds landing. Willow was in a denim jacket and a dress that had flowers all over it. On her, it almost seemed like they were real flowers.

"Hey, guys," Char said. "You ready?"

"For what—your house?" Jacob said. Laughter.

"Shut up," Char said. "It's a house."

"It's like a house-plus," Jacob said. "Like a house-a-rama."

Tammy laughed. "Funny man," she said. She was a person who, when she looked at you, always seemed to be thinking mysterious thoughts. Coming to conclusions about you. Maybe it was the glasses.

"Hey," he said, a little flushed from the compliment.

"Listen," Char broke in, "did I give you the address of the club?"

Eric nodded. "I looked it up. I know how to get there." Jacob reflected on the fact that, for a guy who had spent two key teen years in Canada, Eric really knew his way around Philly. For that whole trip, picking everyone up, he had never looked at a map once.

"Okay—well, and you can follow us, too, if you want. Come on, Alice."

There was a tense moment when all the boys, Jacob could tell, thought about the fact that they had each anticipated being in the same car as Willow, and as they now adjusted to the fact that apparently none of them were going to be in the same car as Willow. *Well*, Jacob thought, *better none than some*.

So the boys all got back into Eric's car, and the girls got into Char's, which was parked in the driveway circle, and everybody headed off. The mood in Eric's Golf, against a backdrop of screaming and grinding and pounding music, was muted.

It took half an hour to get to the club, which looked like a big suburban block of cement and had a big parking lot—Jacob had never been comfortable in the suburbs, where it seemed like there was all this space and nothing real *in* it—and then everybody got out and mixed in together.

The mood unmuted; they were going *dancing*. Together.

Or at least that was the plan.

The big guy who was at the door stopped them before they even quite arrived in front of him: "We have a dress policy," he said in a growly voice.

The group came to a crash landing. "A dress policy?" Char said.

He nodded his head, which made his blond heavy metal hair bob. "No sneakers, and no jeans," he said, "among other things." This last one he said while looking at Finn.

Jacob looked around. Char was okay, obviously, in high heels and a dress, and Willow and Tammy were both wearing non-sneaker girl shoes and girl going-out clothes, both of them really pretty, actually, and Eric and Brian were wearing slacks and penny loafers, but Jacob and Alice were in jeans and sneakers—her T-shirt said *NOW*, which was an organization and not a time, she had told them in the car—and Finn was in really torn-up jeans and army boots. Plus a leather jacket and a shirt that said *Social Distortion*.

The bouncer pointed to the well-dressed ones among them. "You can come in if you want," he said, "but not the others."

Eric stepped up. "You know, we're good kids," he said in a kind of salesman voice. "I can vouch for everybody here."

The guy at the door just laughed, which was also like a growl. "Can't do, red," he said.

Tammy, glare from a streetlight flashing off her glasses, said to the man, "You're wearing jeans—and boots."

He laughed again, but this time in appreciation. "You want my job?" he said.

She shrugged. "How much do you get paid?"

He gave one final big laugh—Jacob was pretty impressed with her, too—and then waved the group away in order to field some other folks who *were* getting in.

The nice thing was that there wasn't any discussion of whether the better-dressed folks should go in and leave the rest behind. Instead, everybody just shuffled around dejectedly while Char apologized—it hadn't even occurred to her to think about how everybody was going to dress—and then Finn said, "I know a club in Center City we could definitely get into." And then there was a little discussion around that, but it felt like too much at that point, and Eric spotted a diner across the highway, and that settled it.

They ran across multiple lanes, laughing as the cars honked, and went into the bright light of the diner. The diner, of course, had no dress code at all. And inside they joked about the heavy metal bouncer—Jacob did an impression of him growling *Can't do, red*, which everybody liked—and they speculated about the music they were probably playing in that club, Milli Vanilli or something, and they laughed and laughed and ordered three orders of French fries and eight waters and made enough noise that people at the other tables were looking over them. That felt good to Jacob, being part of a larger problem. Maybe an electric, edgy kind of good. Meanwhile he tried not to think about the fact that Finn and Willow had ended up next to each other and were trading little side comments throughout. That was edgy in a different way. Instead he just kept talking and joking, even after the waitress plunked the three orders of fries down among them and shook her head, looking as tired as his mother sometimes did. When Finn did an impression of her glum, heavy face, Jacob laughed, too, but he felt tight inside as he did it.

"They're gonna throw us out of this place too," Tammy said. She shook her head, her dark hair shiny in the light.

"They should," Alice said.

"Pack of no-good hoodlums," Jacob said in a growly voice. It sounded more old-man than like the bouncer, but as he did it he felt a surge of desperate need for people to like it—which luckily they did.

In the end, they didn't get kicked out. They finished their

fries and waters and after a long while headed loudly back out
to the highway and across to the club parking lot. And there
they couldn't come up with anything else to do, so they did a
lot of very long goodbyes, each guy trying to get the last one in
with Willow—Jacob thought he had it, but then Finn yelled out,
Avocados! to her from the car door and got a final smile—and
then they all got back into their cars the original way, with Eric's
car holding all the boys plus Alice. Jacob got shotgun again. On
the way out of the parking lot they honked and waved at the
bouncer, and then they yelled at each other, one car to another:
"Pack of hoodlums! Criminals!"

The mood in the car was complicated on the way back, because on the one hand it had been kind of a cool night, with
these friendships really happening, and on the other there was
the Willow problem, and every one of the guys was there in
the car. And it looked like Finn had a lead on the rest of them.
Songwriting and motorcycles, Jacob thought glumly. *What are you
supposed to do about songwriting and motorcycles? And avocados?*

By the time Jacob got home, it was pretty close to eleven
o'clock. He got out of Eric's car—the last drop-off—and went
up the steps to his porch. He was charged with complicated
energy. Inside, sure enough, his mother was still awake. But she
went to bed as soon as he was back, and he was left with his
energy, off to his own bed, lying in the dark, chewing on his lip,
his heels bouncing on the mattress. Along with everything else,
some questions kept coming up for him. Was it a good thing,
this new life of his? It felt good. But what kind of down might
come from an up like this?

Jacob didn't fall asleep for a long time.

7

The next day, Monday, they were calling themselves the Pack, as in, *You hanging out with the Pack this afternoon?* That kind of thing.

And that evening Jacob called Willow again. With the chummy way she and Finn had been on Sunday and then on Monday he was beginning to feel kind of low, but then whenever he'd be sitting there next to Willow and feeling sure it was time to give up on her altogether, she would reach out and touch his arm in response to something, and he would get a surge of hope again. And so he decided that he needed to call her as soon as possible and just make some kind of decisive move.

Before that, though, over dinner—meatloaf—he said to his mother, "I wonder if we should become vegetarians."

His mother said, "Your sister used to say that sometimes."

"I just wonder if it's cruel."

She poked at her meatloaf with a fork. "The truth is, those farms *are* apparently pretty cruel. The factory farms."

"For sure," he said. "That's what I heard."

She shrugged. "Well, let me think about it. I can see if I have any cookbooks with good recipes. You sure it's not just that you're sick of my famous meatloaf, specifically?"

He smiled. "Of course not," he said, though he actually was a little sick of it. "I just wonder about the bigger principle."

She nodded. "Well, I'll think about it."

And then they finished the meatloaf, their silverware clinking in the small space of their dining room.

After dinner, Jacob dialed Willow. She picked up and again seemed to be more or less delighted to hear from him. "Oh, *Jake!*" etc. But then: "Listen," she said. "I just have to make one phone call, and then I'll call you back. Give me your number?"

"You have it, I think," he said.

"Well, just in case I can't find it or something," she said.

So he gave her his number, and then hung up. He dragged the upstairs phone into his bedroom, though—the wall cord was just long enough—so that it would be right there next to him as he worked on his homework, which he proceeded to do, but in total distraction. The history chapter in front of him on the bed seemed almost blurry, no matter how much he tried to focus on reading it.

Five minutes went by like that, and they were not great minutes. And then it was fifteen minutes. He checked the phone for a dial tone a couple of times, very quickly. There was a dial tone. And then it was a half-hour. And then an hour. It all passed very slowly. Throughout that hour, Jacob felt things shift inside him; at first, right after the call, the feeling had been jittery, panicky, but over time something else started to take over. The thing was that it could get worse than howling for Jacob. Sometimes it was more like drowning. Sinking to the bottom of a swimming pool, heavier and heavier, further and further from the surface; and so he needed this Willow thing to go in a good direction. There was a way in which, when she was focused on him, it seemed like the world was going to turn out to be a more amazing place than he usually found it to be. But what if she wasn't focused on him? It was almost like his lungs were starting to fill with water instead of air.

"Hey, honey," his mother said from the door. "I know it's early, but I think I'm going to go to bed, okay?" She was already in a nightgown.

"Sure," Jacob said. It felt like he said it very slowly.

Her face creased. "Are you okay?"

Jacob used all the strength he could rally to sweep the sadness off his face. Tried to speak more briskly. "Sure," he said. "Just bored from homework."

She scrutinized him, though her eyes were tired and she didn't scrutinize for long. "Are you sure?" she said. "You would tell me?"

That last question actually almost brought unexpected tears

to his eyes—his mother had been there for him through some pretty sad moments in his life, when he was very, very bummed out for no good reason, and was this going to be one of those moments?—but he controlled his facial expression and his voice, and he said, "I'm sure. You should get some sleep, and I'll try again with this chapter." He tapped the open book with his hand.

She paused for a moment, and then kissed him on the top of his head, and rubbed his hair some, and said good night. After she was gone, Jacob felt one tear come out. Why was he even so upset? Over just a phone call? His mother used to tell him he had an artistic temperament, by which she meant the way he would get so bummed out and what she called his "lump nights" and everything else.

But this wasn't going to go bad like that.

Jacob picked up the phone receiver and dialed Willow again. Busy signal.

Steeling himself, like trying to seal off the openings where water was getting in, he waited five more minutes, and tried her again. Busy signal.

Jacob, he told himself. *There's no reason to be upset. Stop it. Stop being stupid.*

He thought about the summer, working at the zoo, when all those girls liked him. When he'd had a girlfriend. "Look who's too smooth," Leron had said. But of course that just showed that Leron was shocked too.

Jacob tried to force himself back into the history chapter, which was now made of some impenetrable substance that refused him altogether. Still he stayed at it, as long as he could.

Busy signal.

Busy signal.

Then, even when he wasn't trying her, it was almost like he could hear the busy signal anyway. And each buzz dragged him further down and away.

He had been here before, sinking like this. He didn't want to be here.

It didn't even make sense to him.

But when it was ten o'clock and he still hadn't managed to reach her, and she certainly hadn't called him, he just turned out the lights and slept. He was in his clothes, fully underwater, and the book was still open on the bed.

Tuesday Jacob stayed home. He didn't exactly fake sick; the way he was feeling was almost flu-like—exhausted, heavy as stone—and his mother put the back of her hand on his forehead, testing for fever. Not finding any, she sat quietly next to him on the bed. After a long while of looking at him she said, "You can stay home today. If at the end of the day it doesn't look like it's a bug or something like that, you can't stay home tomorrow. Okay?"

Jacob nodded.

"You'll have to go to school tomorrow if you're not sick. Okay?"

He nodded again.

After a minute or two, his mother abruptly hugged him and then left. "You know how to reach me," she said.

Jacob looked around his room. His walls still had stupid kid stuff on them—posters of dragons and spaceships. He got out of bed long enough to tear down all of the kid posters and leave them on the floor, and then he got into bed again and went back to sleep. There was no reason why he really would need more sleep, but it was better than feeling the things he was otherwise going to feel.

The day, hour by hour, passed over him and all the other unmoving things.

8

On Wednesday Jacob woke up still feeling bad, but his mother decided that he needed to go to school. And in any case his bad feeling had shifted slightly, to a little less sad and a little more irritable. *Stupid Willow*, he said.

Eric had called the afternoon before, and Jacob's mother told him—and Brian, who also called, and Char—that Jacob was "under the weather." It was nice that they all checked in on him. It was not nice that Willow didn't, but *Stupid Willow*, he tried to tell himself.

On the subway-surface car that morning, Eric asked if Jacob was feeling better, and Jacob said he was, though he honestly felt like a bad mixture of heavy and combustible. "Well, it's good to have you back," Eric said, with a clap on the shoulder for emphasis.

That was also nice. *Look*, Jacob said to himself. *That's nice.*

At some point, in the middle of their conversation, he asked Eric if he'd talked to Willow on the phone recently.

"No," Eric said. "All I ever get is a busy signal."

"Me, too," Jacob said, in an unintentionally bitter tone. "Woman of mystery."

Eric looked at him with a question in his eyes, but he didn't voice whatever that question was. That was the kind of thing that had developed because of Willow; neither one of them could say what they were thinking. Jacob forcibly changed the subject by asking Eric if they could talk about the history chapter. Eric had gotten through it—*It's not like it's a hard textbook or anything*, Jacob thought—and so Eric explained everything. Jacob sort of took it in.

When they were at the lockers that morning, with everyone gathered again, one thing was clear: Willow was pretty focused on Finn, and Finn was definitely pretty focused on Willow. He was telling stories, talking about things he knew about, smiling. And she looked like he was telling her things that positively amazed her, even if what he was mainly talking about was people who played guitars and other people who played drums.

Jacob felt his inner balance shift back to more of that sinking heaviness. He watched the group's conversation from a distance, to the point where most of it—Eric, Char, Brian, Alice, and Tammy—was blurry like the history chapter. They made sounds and moved around and everything was vague. Even Willow and Finn were sort of distorted, though her laughter and her touching his arm came through well enough.

Who were these people, anyway? Why was he with them?

Once or twice he tried to channel himself into something better than heaviness, like humor, but it didn't come out right. At one point someone said something about gym class and he made a joke about how his gym teacher was kind of fat, but his timing was off, a little late, and it felt mean when he did say it, so he ended up just looking at the ground for a little while after that. And then, another time, in the middle of whatever, Willow said, "Finn's writing a song about that"—Jacob hadn't caught *what* he was writing a song about—and Jacob responded by saying, "Oh, really?" but in the floaty voice of Willow, and with her big wide eyes too. And everybody pulled up short and stared at him for a moment. Tammy actually gave him a backhanded slap in the chest.

"Sorry," Jacob said. "Not enough sleep." Though it had also felt a little good, lashing out.

The conversation went on without him. He wondered if his mother would let him stay home again, maybe just one more day.

When the bell rang, he grabbed his stuff and took off with only a quick goodbye to everyone else. He didn't know why the gloom had to be so thick for him, but it was.

Around him were dozens of people he didn't know and who didn't know him. Maybe that was just the deal.

But then, at the end of the hall, someone caught up with him and grabbed his arm. In the instant before he turned around, he managed to hope it was Willow. But it was Tammy.

"Oh," he said. "Hey."

"What's going on, Jake?" she said. "You're not acting like you."

"What?"

"Are you okay?" she said. All the random people were roaming past them on both sides, everybody off to class one way or another.

Jacob opened his mouth but couldn't figure out what to say.

"This is the part where you speak," she said.

Jacob surprised himself by laughing. Not a big laugh, but a surprise chuckle.

"I guess I'm tired," he said.

Tammy looked at him with her sharp eyes. It really was like she had X-ray vision or something. "Listen. Don't let those two get to you," she said, pointing back over her shoulder with her thumb.

"Who?" Jacob protested feebly.

She raised an eyebrow. "Please."

Jacob sighed.

"I know," Tammy said. "It's kind of, like," and she made a pretend puking gesture.

He smiled. "Yeah. I guess it is."

"I think they're just gonna be like that from now on," she said, with a shrug. "Kids today!"

"Right. Kids today."

She nodded. "We're all just gonna have to learn to ignore it."

He tried out a low chuckle. "Yeah. I guess maybe so."

And then—he didn't see this coming—she leaned in abruptly, pretty close, which, maybe because it was so unexpected, shot volts through Jacob's nervous system. Like sudden lightning in the gloom. "Anyway," she said, not quite whispering because he couldn't have heard a whisper in a crowded hallway like that one, but still softly, "You could do better." After which she leaned back out again, overhead light flashing off her glasses as

she straightened, a one-sided smile on her face. She left behind
a slight scent of coconut shampoo as she turned to go.

Jacob stood there with his mouth open again, watching
Tammy go down the hall. The air was still foggy, but there were
also some little sparks of lightning in it.

9

Things really changed then.

First of all, Jacob didn't call Willow again that week. She didn't call him, either, though some mornings she did look at him in a questioning way, as if she were wondering why he'd backed off.

Meanwhile, he and Tammy were spending more time talking in the mornings and afternoons—still there among everyone else, but breaking off sometimes for side comments. Tammy was sharp with the side comments. Plus she had pretty lips, and her eyes held you; she just seemed so sure of herself somehow. But he didn't do anything, didn't call her or anything; he was still tired and slow—it always took a while to wear off—and maybe he felt a little burned too. Instead they just talked in person. But he learned things about her—for example, she lived in Germantown, which he knew could be kind of rough in the same way West Philly was, depending on where in Germantown. And she had a single-parent situation, too, actually—her mother had died when she was in middle school. There was a soft howl in him when she told him that, but it was for her, and so in a way it felt okay.

Really they had a lot to talk about and a lot in common. But he didn't call. He wasn't ready yet.

The next weekend, the last in October, was Jacob's last one working at the zoo until the spring season started up again. He mainly sat around. You couldn't do that out in front of everyone, but you could sit inside the stables and wait for something to happen, so Jacob did that throughout Saturday, and Leron did too. They hung out.

There was something easy about it. When Leron was alone— Ty wasn't at the zoo that weekend, for whatever reason—there wasn't the whole group dynamic to deal with, which for Jacob had always been like standing next to some people doing double Dutch, trying to figure out a way in. Just the two of them was simpler. And because Leron was really funny, there wasn't any pressure for Jacob to be. It was more optional. And even if they didn't have exactly the same interests and didn't ever get into deep topics, they had plenty in common—they both came from the same neighborhood, they both had the same job, and they both smelled like horses. Easy.

"What you gonna do for work now?" Leron asked. They were sitting on the floor in between the horse stalls. You couldn't be squeamish if you worked at the zoo; Jacob had touched uncountable different species of shit since he'd started there.

Jacob shrugged. "I dunno. I thought I was gonna try to coast on what I've already made, but now I feel like I need to make some more."

"Yeah," Leron said. "You got that active social life."

Jacob blushed. But that was the reason. "Yeah," he said.

Leron again put on that Ward Cleaver voice. "You can't be living beyond your means, Jacob," he said.

"What are *you* gonna do?" Jacob said.

Leron shrugged. "I might see about bagging at the Pathmark. I got to have my spending money, especially now with Latia."

"Latia?" Jacob said. Latia worked the ticket booth at the pony track, and Leron had been after her for a year.

"Yeah," Leron said with a little smile. He picked some hay off the ground and dropped it again.

"That's cool," Jacob said. "Latia. She's cool."

"Yeahhhhhh," Leron said in a drawn-out way. "But that means I need some *finance*."

Jacob nodded.

"What about you?" Leron said. "Girls."

Jacob thought about that. He looked up at one of the little windows in one of the stalls, the late October light streaming in. "I dunno," he said.

"You're surrounded by girls these days, smooth."

"I guess," Jacob said. The ground was damp under his butt, he was realizing. He shifted a couple of inches to the side, which didn't make any difference.

"Any nice Jewish girls?"

"Huh?" That took Jacob by surprise, Leron remembering that he was Jewish. "No. Not really." In fact, none of the people in the Pack were at all Jewish. Not at all.

"Who's that big-eyes one?" Leron said. "She's fine."

"Willow," Jacob said with a little sneer. "She's too much trouble." He didn't know he was going to say that, but he realized the truth of it as he was saying it. "Huh," he added. "She maybe really is."

"They always are, the big-eyes ones," Leron said.

Jacob laughed. They sat there quietly for maybe a minute. And then he said, "There's this other one. I don't know."

"Glasses?" Leron said.

Jacob looked at him, surprised. "Tammy Bocek? How did you know?"

"I know," Leron said.

Jacob took that in.

"So, you gonna bust a move, or what?"

"I don't know what I'm gonna do," Jacob said.

Leron laughed. "You better figure that out," he said.

That night the Pack met up at the club Finn had told them about. It was in Center City, which meant that transportation was a little different this time; Char grabbed the Mt. Airy and Germantown girls and then Brian, and Eric took Jacob in from West Philly, and Alice and Finn came separately, each their own way.

Eric found a spot a few blocks off, and then he and Jacob walked over to meet the others.

They heard the place—beats, noise—before they saw it.

When they rounded the corner, Jacob stopped in his tracks. He realized he'd been expecting an anonymous door in the wall

of some alley—some sketchy, secret place. But Revival was in
this huge stone building, with pillars and everything, which
looked like it used to be a bank or even a monument. Thunder-
ous music pounded at them even a half-block away. Meanwhile,
coming in and out were heavily pierced people in black and
some with hair in different colors and shaved in various ways.

"Whoa," Eric said. "You think that's because of Halloween?" Halloween was on the coming Tuesday.

"I do not," Jacob said.

Finn had warned them to dress *down*. Eric hadn't really
listened, was still in slacks and penny loafers, but Jacob had
worn his black sneakers—the only pair of shoes he owned, in
fact—plus some older jeans and a T-shirt. The shirt didn't have
anything on it—just plain red—but he was glad he wasn't wearing the button-down shirt Eric was wearing, anyway.

Alice was already in front, waiting for them—"Do you think
this is because of Halloween?" she asked—and Char's contin-
gent arrived soon after. Char just didn't have it in her to dress
down too much, but everybody else was fairly casual. Stupid
Willow was in jeans and a T-shirt herself, and Alice, Jacob saw,
had on a black T-shirt that had *All oppression creates a state of war*
written on it—and Tammy—Tammy was wearing a dark turtleneck that fit her in a very flattering way. And everybody was full
of nervous energy, because most of them were on completely
unfamiliar ground. Nobody but Finn had ever even heard of
this place before. Plus, hardly anybody at Central dressed the
way these folks around them did—punk, new wave, whatever
exactly it was.

"Did anybody already make the Halloween joke?" Tammy
said.

Jacob thumbed at Eric and Alice. "They weren't kidding,
though."

"Yup," Tammy said. "I called that."

"I bet you did," Jacob said, appreciating.

Finn showed up last, and grinning. "Hey," he said. "Isn't this
place so fucking cool?"

And, yeah—it was. They all, Jacob saw, had open mouths. Including Willow, who had already fluttered over to Finn. The whole Pack was like an illustration for the word *amazement*. Honestly, Jacob was kind of scared of the place, but he was excited too. Everybody going in and out looked so intense, so *happy*. Well, angry, actually, but like they were happy to be angry. Jacob remembered how it had felt good to lash out even a little bit. Felt a lot better than sad did.

"Let's go," Finn said.

The guy at the door was very different from the one at the suburban club—super-skinny and with his hair dyed sheet-white and plastered back on his head, lots of piercings everywhere. And he seemed to know Finn. "Hey, man," he said. And then he waved them inside to the window where they paid and got stamped with the too-young-for-alcohol stamp. It cost less than Jacob had expected, and definitely less than the last club they had tried to get into.

If outside there had been thunder, being inside was like being in the storm cloud. Lights were strobing against the dark and smoke, and the sound was all crash and bang and boom rebounding off the walls and their chests. Or into them—Jacob could feel it deep in his body. It felt good.

Finn led them upstairs, further into the cloud. And by the time they got to the second floor Jacob was already dancing a little, moving his arms and shoulders. He was feeling too good to not move. And it seemed like the others were having the same experience, because the Pack went right out onto the floor in this dark, flashing room, the sound growling and grinding out so loud from speakers somewhere, and without any hesitation they just let themselves dance. It was like a whole other thing from dancing at Eric's place. In comparison, that had been like a dance at a nursing home or something. Here, people were stomping and punching the air and screaming—you could barely hear them over the music but you could see their open mouths, their teeth. They were headbanging and even shoving a little, to the point where after a while the music cut out abruptly, and as everyone crashed to a stop the DJ's voice came on, loud: "No *fucking* moshing in here, motherfuckers." And the music came back on and people stopped shoving but kept thrashing.

Above all of them was this giant railway clock on the wall, running backward.

One song went into the next, and the next, and Jacob's friends were all dancing. Finn was right at home, pounding the ground with his boots, and Char was using her arms to swim in there, and Willow was twirling with her eyes closed and her mouth open, and Tammy was jumping and playing drums in the air, and Brian and Eric and Alice were hopping in place. Alice's long ponytail was flying all around.

And then that same song came on—the one from the car the previous week—screaming about how someone had a head like a hole and Jacob was just eating it up, just really agreeing with everything that was coming out of those speakers. The singer really hated that head like a hole, which somehow felt great rather than terrible. Jacob closed his eyes and started jumping, jumping, jumping—

Suddenly he accidentally crashed into someone.

"Oh, sorry," he said, loud, the music still drumming forward all around, before he realized it was Tammy. He'd crashed into Tammy.

He stood still. Tammy had a look on her face that he hadn't seen before, or maybe he'd seen it in the movies, but not in real life. It was a very serious look, very alert, looking right into him.

"Klutz," she said. Quiet, but he could read her very pretty lips.

The music and the strobe and everything all kept going, but the two of them were standing in one place.

And then they were kissing, and this time Jacob didn't have to wonder what to do with all the parts of his face. This time it just made sense. Over the drums, the lyrics screamed at the two of them. Tammy tasted a little metallic somehow. Overhead, the clock kept rolling backward, like they might even get to do the night over again, the exact same way.

10

The weird thing was that people were mad at Jacob for a few days after that. On the way home from Revival that Saturday night, Eric seemed happy for Jacob. "So—you and Tammy, huh?" he said. But then they talked on the phone on Sunday and this time Eric said, "You know, it sounds like Willow's really upset about the way you and Tammy were all over each other at the club." And Eric sounded a little upset himself all of a sudden. Char called to tell him the same thing about how Willow was feeling. It didn't make a huge amount of sense to Jacob.

"She wasn't into me," he said to Char.

"I told you," Char said. "She's into everybody."

Jacob thought that that was kind of messed up, but still, the news made him anxious. That night at Revival had been big; maybe a turning point. All day he'd been feeling a lot better than before, and what he really didn't need was something lousy coming in and dragging him back down.

Luckily, he was very distracted by Tammy. The two of them talked twice on Sunday at great length. Some of it was about getting to know each other more. He learned, for example, that she wanted to study psychology in college, "because people are lunatics," and also that she was really into biking—like on a bicycle, not a motorcycle—and she talked about her two younger brothers, "a whole house full of boyness," she said; and he talked about his own family, and the fact that he had no idea what he wanted to study in college, and how he needed to find a job now that the zoo had wound down for the season. "You like working, don't you?" she said. He didn't explain that he basically had to work, because of the money. They talked about random things, too, like music and classes they were taking and teachers who were crazy, and the funny things about the other people in the Pack. They talked about how the guys were mad at Jacob for hurting Willow's feelings. "Don't worry about them," Tammy said. "They're just trying to get in with her. You're like the only guy who's got it together." Which was a really remarkable thing to say.

But really, even as they did get to know each other, even as they went back and forth about a thousand things, asking questions, telling their stories, laughing a lot, the conversation felt to Jacob as if, underneath the spoken words, they were secretly saying the same things over and over to each other. It was as though they were saying:

"We kissed each other at Revival."

"We really did kiss each other at Revival."

"We, like, made out at Revival."

And so on.

Monday was tense because of Willow's agitation, and the fact that the guys all seemed to be on her side about it, for their individual reasons that were—Tammy was right—all about each of them still wanting to end up with her. Everybody still sat in the hallway together, but now there was more clumping—Willow and all the other guys clumping here; Jacob and Tammy mini-clumping just a few feet away, admittedly a little cozily, Tammy lying with her head in Jacob's lap; and meanwhile Char and Alice just tried to fill in the cracks, pretending there was only one group, like what was happening was one totally mutual conversation.

"Maybe I should study sociology," Tammy said in a side comment to Jacob. "Because people in groups are even bigger lunatics."

Jacob stroked Tammy's hair a little. It was very smooth and dark and shiny.

Tuesday was Halloween, which wasn't Jacob's favorite.

School, first of all, was stressful; were you supposed to wear a costume or not? Some of the dorky kids did—superheroes and sci-fi—but then also some of the most confident kids did too. Like at least vampire teeth for the boys and cat ears for the girls. There was this one group of wealthy kids in Jacob's grade—they called themselves the Tribe, even though they were all white, and they had fake "Indian" stuff on this year—feathers and face paint. They went around the halls whooping. That was confidence, which was actually kind of cool, at least when it didn't come out racist.

Jacob didn't get dressed up, and neither did anyone else in the Pack. Whether because they weren't secure enough or because of tension in the group, they just dressed like normal.

Then there was night, at home. His mother had a policy that they wouldn't give out any candy to anybody who wasn't wearing a costume, even though that was kind of standard in West Philadelphia, teenaged boys coming to the house just wearing normal jeans and a white T-shirt or something and saying, "Trick or treat" like it was a command, brown grocery bags thrust out in front of them. The Black guys at school hadn't dressed up either. There were a couple of Neneh Cherrys and Rhythm Nation Janets among the girls, but none of the boys did anything. Anyway, because his mother was working—the hospital always needed extra people on Halloween—she left Jacob in charge of saying no to the kids without costumes, some of whom looked like they probably could have beaten the crap out of Jacob, and might have wanted to, even *with* candy. Jacob's front door had a glass window on it, though. So he could see what the situation was before he unlocked the door, and he could tell people his mother's policy through the locked door. It helped. Still, he did feel his heart going when one of the guys left muttering, "Fuckin' white people," to his friends.

The Willow situation stayed weird for a few days. For one thing, Eric had stopped taking the usual subway-surface car in the mornings that week, and though he and Jacob both took the Broad Street line from Central in the afternoons, making small talk that was pretty small, Eric all of a sudden wasn't getting on the subway-surface at City Hall with Jacob; he was walking home instead. It was like a three-mile walk. So that was uncomfortable.

But things resolved themselves on Thursday morning. That was when Willow officially made Finn her selection, a selection that became clear to everyone when she started lying in the hallway with *her* head back in *his* lap. It was like that was the international signal of dating, Jacob thought.

Willow did stop him in the hall that day once the Pack had gone in its various directions toward class. He was walking along, sort of saying to himself *Tammy, Tammy, Tammy* when someone grabbed his arm, and it was Willow. "I was hurt when you stopped calling me," she said. Her eyes were a little narrowed, which made them seem less enormous than usual.

Jacob went through a strange cascade of feelings. There was a bit of automatic recognition that Willow was a very pretty girl, but that was quickly washed out by guilt, and that was quickly swept away by irritation. "I'm sorry," Jacob said, with fading sincerity. "You didn't seem like you were interested in talking to me."

Willow searched his face for something, and apparently didn't find it. "Well, everything's good now," she said brightly, and she gave a big smile and touched his arm again and kind of flounced away down the hall. Jacob watched her go, shaking his head. He could imagine Leron shaking his head, too, and saying something about big-eyed girls—and he could imagine Tammy saying something about lunatics.

Things got back to normal with Eric immediately; as soon as Willow's head hit Finn's lap the subway-surface car was back in business. They rode home together debriefing about various things. Mostly they talked about classes and other minor things, but eventually Eric said, "Boy. Finn and Willow, I guess, huh?"

"Yeah," Jacob said. "It seems like it."

"Yeah." Eric looked out the window at the subway walls going by. And then, after a minute, "Do you think everyone's gonna keep hanging out?"

Jacob felt a jolt of anxiety at that question. "Why not?"

Eric shrugged, still looking out the window. It was like he was trying not to make eye contact. "I dunno. I mean, maybe those two are gonna do their thing, and you and Tammy are gonna do your thing, and—but I guess Tammy and Willow are friends, so there's the four of you, anyway, now that Willow's not upset anymore. And maybe Willow's other friends. The girls. But everybody else?"

"What are you talking about?" Jacob asked. Though—he realized as he asked—he already knew.

Eric finally did make eye contact. He blushed a little and said, "About this week. I mean, the way I was...." He gestured with his hands at the thing he was trying to say.

Jacob did feel annoyed about the whole experience, but he looked at Eric's obviously sorry-for-real face, and he shrugged it off. "Big-eyed girls," he said. "What can you do?"

Eric laughed gratefully and clapped him on the shoulder. "My man," he said.

It's funny, Jacob thought, *what it means for things to go back to normal.*

The next Saturday the Pack went back to Revival, but only after going to South Street first. Finn had the idea that they needed to gear up, and also that they just needed to make South Street part of their lives.

First they went into Mystic Market, which was kind of isolated over near Broad Street. Jacob had never been aware of the place. What it turned out to be was this funny store with shelves full of potions and elixirs and stuff—but all of the labels admitted that it wasn't really magic. Like there was "alleged invisibility formula," and "so-called truth serum," and "purported love potion." There were curses and magic powders and protective runes and all kinds of other things, and they were all covered in disclaimers.

"It's like someone was running a perfectly good fake stuff shop," Jacob said to Tammy as they browsed the shelves, and then she finished his thought: "But then a lawyer showed up," she said.

"Totally," he said.

She waved at him with a supposed monkey's paw. "I might or might not be waving at you," she said. "I have to consult my attorney."

Jacob wondered what it'd be like to work at Mystic Market. The guy behind the counter seemed like he was tired of everything, and particularly tired in advance of this group of teenagers who were now picking up all the stuff in the store and not buying any of it. Jacob did think about getting the "possible happiness syrup"—his mother had been kind of down for the last week, like she sometimes was, particularly in November—but knew it was silly and wouldn't have wanted to talk to the others about why he was getting it, so he put the bottle back on the shelf.

Tammy noticed. "That one's probably booze," she said. And he laughed.

After Mystic they roamed east, to the busier part of South Street, which was jammed with cars cruising one way slowly alongside the foot traffic and people going in every direction on the sidewalk. The air, Jacob felt, was full of momentum. Why hadn't he ever come here at night before? Because of his habit of never going anywhere or doing anything. But maybe that had been taken care of now—new friends, maybe a girlfriend, even. Was that his happiness syrup? He put his arm around Tammy as they walked, and she bumped his hip with hers in a fun way. Up at the front of the group were Finn and Willow, also in an arm-around situation, and between the two couples were the other four Pack people.

"Who do you think's next?" Tammy said, nodding at the rest of them.

Jacob shook his head. "What do you mean?" he said.

"For a pretty clever guy," Tammy said, "you sure can be a doofus. Well, it's going to be Eric and Char, for sure, and it's going to be Brian and Alice."

"Really?" Jacob said. He looked at them, all those theoretically loose parts, but actually there was something in those pairings—Brian and Alice were talking seriously about something right then, and Eric and Char were making plans. And Tammy had been able to see it. For her, loose parts didn't have to stay loose. He held her closer.

"Definitely," Tammy said. "I just don't know which one's gonna happen first."

"Huh," Jacob said.

And so maybe that was the answer to Eric's question about whether they were all going to keep hanging out. If four disconnected guys all ended up dating four girls who had already been friends, did that make a group? Jacob, his arm tight around Tammy, hoped it did.

They went into a couple of shops—Zipperhead and Skinz—where the music was loud and rough and immediately there was that same atmosphere of possibility, where bad feelings could become active and angry. Also where there were long jewelry cases of spider earrings and skull necklaces and spiked leather bracelets, and a thousand black T-shirts of different kinds. And in these places they did buy things. Char found a black dress and she and Willow picked out boots, and Brian got a black bandanna that he tied around his head. Alice bought a plain black T-shirt, and Eric got one, also black, with a picture of a bust on it, colored all kinds of colors, under the words *New Order*. Jacob, meanwhile, fretted for a minute about money—he was really going to need another job—but eventually chose a *Joy Division* T-shirt (again black) with a kind of mountain range on it, because it wasn't very expensive and looked cool even if he didn't know what *Joy Division* was. But Finn saw it and said, "Yeah. Definitely."

At the counter, looking at Jacob and Eric, the cashier said, "You guys are like before and after."

Jacob didn't know what to make of that, so he said, "Yeah."

Tammy came up to him, holding spiked hoop earrings up to her ears. "What do you think?" she said.

Jacob thought she was the cutest person he had ever seen. And then he said it. "You're like the cutest person I've ever seen."

For that, she kissed him right there in the store. "You sap," she said. When she was done, she said to him, "You should get your ear pierced, too, while we're here."

Jacob only thought about that for a second. Or more it was like he took a second to savor it, to enjoy the fact that he was definitely going to get an earring. He did still have money from the zoo in his pocket, after all. Then he went to the right counter, where it said you had to be eighteen or have parental permission. He knew his father wouldn't have approved of something like this, and he wasn't sure about his mother. The guy who had the hole puncher, or whatever it was, looked Jacob over suspiciously. "I can vouch for him," Tammy said, even though she was actually a few months younger than Jacob was. And the guy shrugged and took the money for the ear-punching. It wasn't too bad, the price. The man used a ball-point pen to put a dot on Jacob's left earlobe, and said, "Is that where?"

Tammy gave a thumbs-up.

Jacob expected it to hurt, but it really didn't. And Tammy nodded with satisfaction when she looked at it, her spiky earrings wobbling in the light. "Very cool," she said.

He checked himself out in the mirror. "I look like a badass."

"You *are* a badass," she said.

They all put their new stuff on as they got it, so that by the time they were done with both shops, they were completely ready for Revival. They hit the street and headed up toward the club. Jacob felt electric.

"Yo, Jake—what was that 'before and after' thing?" Eric said to him as they walked. This time everybody was all mixed together, rather than two couples and the rest.

"I don't know," Jacob said.

"You guys don't know these bands at all, do you?" Finn said.

Eric and Jacob had to admit they didn't.

Finn laughed. "Well, Joy Division—" he pointed at Jacob's

shirt—"became New Order—" pointing at Eric's—"when the lead singer of Joy Division killed himself."

"Seriously?" Eric said.

Jacob was too surprised to say anything.

"Yup," Finn said. "He checked himself out. Ian Curtis. He was like twenty-two or twenty-three."

Before and after.

Jacob—he put one foot in front of the other and thought about the fact that he was wearing a shirt from a band called Joy Division whose lead singer had killed himself. Knowing that thing about the guy—Ian Curtis—changed things. In a way, the way it felt, it was almost like he wasn't wearing a shirt at all, but was naked instead. But everybody around him kept walking, and he did too. The conversation moved on. Tammy found him and put her arm around his waist. That was nice. That was definitely nice. They all kept walking, off toward the club, toward the storm cloud.

At Revival, in the middle of the thunder and lightning, he stomped and threw himself around, tried to become the storm cloud, and kissed Tammy whenever he got the chance. Also from time to time he touched his pierced earlobe, which had become a little tender after the fact.

11

His mother was surprised by the earring. It took her a while to notice at breakfast the next morning; she seemed slow and tired and distracted as she got them both Kix cereal and bananas. "Oh," she said, spotting the earring. She went to the refrigerator and came back without anything, as if she were confused, even though milk would have made sense. And then, "Aren't you supposed to ask my permission before you do something like that?"

"You have earrings," he said, though her ears were bare right then. She was dressed plain for work.

"But you're my baby," she said.

Jacob got up to get the milk for both of them and smiled what he hoped was a charming and childlike smile. "Can I, Mom?"

She reached out and touched his ear. "My baby," she said. "There's a hole in my baby."

In general, November was always a difficult month for his mother. She said it was the light, the way the days got short. She said it seemed like there were fewer possibilities. And things hit her harder, and she was more tired. Exhausted, sometimes. It was in November when his mother was especially likely to say to Jacob, "Tell me something funny." And he would roll out jokes and funny stories from his life, and things he made up—it didn't matter as long as it got her to smile a little. Which sometimes it did and sometimes it didn't. There were times when November was just stronger than he was.

By the middle of the school week, everything was the way Tammy had predicted: Eric and Char were together, and Brian and Alice were together. The new couples didn't do heads in laps, though; Eric sat leaning back against the lockers and Char sat in front of him and leaned back on his shoulder. And Brian and Alice just sat next to each other. There were multiple ways to do it, as it turned out.

"We should go on a date, Jake," Tammy said one morning. She was looking up at him, playing a little with the stud in his ear. "Like, just the two of us."

"Yeah," Jacob said. "That sounds great. Like the movies or something?"

Tammy nodded, satisfied. "Maybe Sunday," she said. She turned her head a little, sat up, and looked at Jacob's legs. "You should get some new jeans, by the way," she said. "These ones are really tight on you."

Jacob blushed. He wasn't wearing the new jeans that he got for Eric's party, and these old ones didn't fit that well anymore. Only the one new pair really did.

"It's like you're wearing spandex," Tammy said, and then she settled her head back down.

That comment made him feel pretty stupid, but he managed to come back with, "Well, that's what superheroes wear."

"Ooh," she said. "Good response there."

That was the one thing about Tammy: she definitely had an edge. Like, she was hilarious, and she had a sharp eye for funny things around her, but sometimes when it was pointed at him, Jacob felt the sting of it. If his hair was a mess, for example, which it often was, she might say something about that. Or if one of his own jokes fell flat, she'd point it out with a "nice try, babe." That kind of thing. Usually he would find a way to banter back, which she definitely liked, but sometimes he would protest, and she would say, "What? It's just a joke." And he would try to find words for what bothered him exactly, and all he could come up with is, "I guess I'm just sensitive."

Which he was. It was strange: even in the midst of all the good stuff that was going on in his life, Jacob still had these moments—maybe he would be up alone, studying, and hadn't

talked to any of his friends for a few hours, and he would feel a
keen howl of loneliness; or he would walk down his street and
suddenly wonder whether he belonged there; or he would just
wake up feeling a sense of being disconnected from the world.
That lone coyote again. These moments happened unexpectedly, and not because of anything big—maybe he'd see a broken
window as he walked down the street or he'd see somebody
get shamefaced after they got an answer wrong in class and he
would just find himself wondering why things were the way
they were.

The moments really were just moments, instead of—well,
looking back, he could see how he'd lived a lot of his life before
the Pack with these kinds of feelings. Weekend nights, where
feelings like this would creep up whenever the TV show he
was watching went over to commercials. Long stretches that he
couldn't get out of. But maybe there was an antidote now—if
stuff like that hit him, he could just make a phone call or get a
call, or see one of these awesome people in his life, and all the
questions would probably fly away for a while. And Tammy,
who seemed like someone who wouldn't put up with feelings
like that if they happened to her, could especially help, at least
when she wasn't being *too* sharp.

The weekend started with Pack nights. On Friday they went
back to Revival and danced until they were exhausted and
sweaty. In a way it was him and Tammy alone—there was some
significant making out—but also it was the Pack in full force.
Even though everyone was coupled up, the group danced close
together, grinning at each other, teeth flashing in the strobe
light, hooting and hollering. It was like the opposite of being
at the bottom of the swimming pool; it was like fighting his
way to the top. And afterward they spilled out onto the front
steps, practically steaming they were so overheated, and laughing about nothing in particular, or just the fact that life was
good. Jacob kissed Tammy under the streetlight, his hands in
her damp hair.

On Saturday the Pack met up in Old City to see the movie *Henry V* at the Ritz. Jacob had read some Shakespeare for school, of course—they'd gone through *Macbeth* in Mrs. Hudson's class that fall—but he'd never actually seen any, and he was surprised at how exciting the movie was. When the main character—Henry—gave the St. Crispin's Day speech to rally his troops, Jacob almost wanted to grab a sword and join the battle himself. And then during the courtship scene between Henry and Kate, he and Tammy snuggled up together over the armrest.

"Good sir Jacob," Tammy said to him in a kind of British accent.

"Fair lady Tammy," he said back.

Afterward, full of energy, they all walked and then ran through the streets of Old City, yelling out lines from the movie that they were probably remembering wrong, bothering the various respectable people strolling, at one point running out onto the lawn across the street from the Bourse—a big open field right there in the city!—and flung themselves down in the grass, looking up at the clouds that were sharp and real in the moonlight. Jacob, panting, held Tammy's hand, feeling like there was something deeply important about being there under clouds that you could see at night.

"Amazing," he said.

"I know I am," Tammy said in her joking voice. "But thanks for telling me."

And then there was some making out under the clouds.

The next day, Sunday, Jacob took public transportation down to Center City to meet Tammy at the Roxy, which was a movie theater that Jacob had been to once or twice; like the Ritz, it showed high-brow films.

He got there a little before Tammy, and he looked up at the low clouds for a while. It was a cool fall day. Winter was on its way.

Tammy showed up on her bicycle, looking really cute in

jeans and a striped black-and-white shirt. And she was wearing the spiky loop earrings.

"You look great," he said.

She did a half-curtsy and locked her bike to a pole. "You too."

For his part, Jacob had been sure to put on his better jeans, and a nice maroon sweater. His style was caught these days between the preppy thing he had tried to build up over a year or two and the Revival style that he hadn't been able to accumulate yet. It was just going to have to be one item at a time. And he really did need to get another job. Leron had stopped him in the hall the other day to say that Erol's Video was hiring.

"I think it's date day for everyone," Tammy said, giving him a little pursed-lips kiss hello and then putting her arms around his neck and standing close to him. "Char and Eric are going to the movies too. And I think the other couples are doing things. Like maybe Willow and Finn are going to go check out motorcycles? Just for fact-finding purposes? Something like that."

"We're all grown up," Jacob said, in a mock-wistful voice, though inside it did actually make him feel a little wistful.

"Ha," Tammy said. "Nice." There was some wind down Sansom Street, and it was a cool November day, but it was already a little warm between him and Tammy.

"Yeah." He thought about how the math of it worked out so neatly—an even number of people in the Pack, matching numbers of boys and girls.

"Oh—except Alice and Brian. She went down to DC by herself for a march."

"A march?" he said. "Oh yeah—pro-choice." She had mentioned something about that earlier in the week.

"Right."

"Wow." Jacob was impressed.

"Yeah. Probably we all should have gone." She shrugged. "What are we seeing again?" Tammy glanced over at the door to the Roxy.

Jacob reoriented himself. "It's called *Valmont*. It's supposed to be French and romantic. It's based on a book from this eighteenth-century French novel."

"Oh, right. Brian said something about it, right?"

"Right," Jacob said. Brian was basically the repository of anything that had to do with French.

Then, in a flash of inspiration, he stepped back and put out his arm in a showy way for her to take.

"Well, what a gentleman," she said, taking his arm.

They strolled in like royalty.

As it turned out, the movie was really more about sex than romance. There was a whole plot of various seductions and bets about seductions and things like that, and so at first the whole thing was a little embarrassing—what kind of maniac brings a date, kind of a first date, to a movie like this?—but then it got both Jacob and Tammy going; their hands started roaming around.

Tammy looked behind them. "Do you want to sit in the back?" she said.

Jacob nodded. There weren't that many people in the theater, but it would be better to be behind the ones who were there.

So they missed most of the movie that afternoon, but they did get to know each other physically about as well as they possibly could without any clothes coming off or even opening. For Jacob it was like an experience of chasing an animal or being chased by an animal, but the capture never happening. When the movie ended he felt as alert as he ever had in his entire life. All of his senses were buzzing.

"Is there anywhere we can go?" he said.

Tammy was breathing kind of hard herself, and her hair was uncharacteristically all over the place, but she said, "There's nowhere we can go. That's gonna have to be enough for today."

"Really?" he said.

"Don't beg," she said.

That stung a little. "I'm not begging," he said.

"I'm just kidding," she said.

Letting themselves lapse into quiet, they sat there in the now fully lit theater long enough that the guy came in to clear trash from the aisles. And then they got up and left, dazed.

Afterward, they walked, cooling themselves down in the November air, and then they found an ice cream place a couple of blocks away to cool themselves down further. As they ate from the little Styrofoam bowls, they were almost bashful with each other.

"What?" Tammy said when he looked at her. She straightened her already straight hair.

"I dunno," Jacob said.

"What?" she said.

"I like you a lot," he said.

"You sap," she said. And then she saw his face fall a little, and added, "I like you a lot too. You sap."

Jacob sighed and dipped into his ice cream again. It was basically nice.

12

It was true that there was something about November. Even in the midst of all the good things happening in his life, Jacob felt it, maybe the same way his mother did. It didn't make logical sense, obviously, but he still felt it. Before the Pack, he had been particularly likely to have a bad night or a bad weekend altogether in November—or, actually, any of the darker months.

Luckily these days he was distracted. And between South Street and Revival, it did seem like the darkness had more possibilities than it used to. On South Street he spent what was left of his zoo money on black T-shirts with band names on them and a black bandanna, like Brian's, to tie around his head. At Revival he studied all those people who seemed to be able to make sadness into anger and to make anger a happy thing. While the music pounded, he'd throw punches into his own dancing, the way the guys around him were doing, and stomp his sneakers as hard as he could. "Watch it, Rocky," Tammy said more than once when his thrashing got too wild on the dance floor. But of course he wasn't aiming at anyone. He was just trying to push those feelings into his fists and then maybe out into the world. And it helped.

Still, though, he watched his mother get off-and-on more irritable and anxious and tired in the face of the advancing winter, and drink a little more gin. She spent more time sleeping, more time complaining about work and then housework. Which Jacob really wasn't doing enough of. So he tried to do more—garbage, dishes, laundry, keeping the bathroom clean. And he tried to tell her funny stories from his life—she loved his imitation of his teacher Ms. Hudson's Boston accent. But also—and he felt bad about it—he was gone a lot. In a way his mom's mood felt dangerous, contagious, so it was hard to be

there. Plus, he had an actual social life. Still, whether the month
or contagion or something deeper, he could feel November
inside himself, in flashes and moments.

Tammy felt it too. When Jacob got negative, she'd say something like, "What's with the mood swings?"

Jacob didn't know how to explain.

One night they were on the phone and he got lost in himself
looking out the window across the street. The low yellow light
of the streetlamp hung over everything. "Where'd you go?"
Tammy said.

"Oh. I was just looking at Spark Park outside."

"Spark Park?"

"It used to be a building," Jacob said, "but it burned down,
right in between two other row houses, and after a while they
just demolished what was left of it and put down some wood
chips. And they call it Spark Park."

"You sound like that's a sad thing."

"I dunno. You can hardly see what it is in the streetlight."

Tammy sighed. "You know, you are not always the barrel of
monkeys I thought you were gonna be."

That brought him around and he made a joke about being
a tortured park artist, which got an appreciative chuckle out of
her. But he still felt it a little. It was like the season was partly
inside him.

Plans for a second party got underway. Things crystallized
when they were all hanging out at Char's the Saturday night
after Jacob and Tammy's movie date. Char's house was just as
impressive inside as it had been on the outside—big and full
of rooms and space and nice furniture. Or maybe *shocking* was
more the word than *impressive*. When Jacob first got there he
spent a few minutes wandering around, counting the two eating
rooms—casual and formal—the handful of common spaces,
plus bathrooms. And that was just the first floor. There was so
much furniture. And it was dark inside, but not the gray dim of
his own house; instead it was a warm brown darkness. Stately

or something. Eric had warned him—"Wait until you see this house, Jake. These Wests have unbelievable money."—but even with the warning, Jesus. Maybe the right word was actually *up-setting*. As hard as his mother worked, why didn't *she* get to have a house like this one? He thought about her—she was at work then, maybe lifting a patient onto a bed, maybe running an IV, maybe cleaning a *bedpan*—and he winced.

He had calmed down, though, mostly, since those first minutes of astonishment, because he was with Tammy. In this particular moment he was on a couch in the living room, sort of lying on her while she was also sort of lying on him too; it was physically complicated. The Cure was playing on the stereo. Everybody was just listening, in lazy mode. Then Eric, who was in a big loveseat with Char, said, "You know what we were thinking?"

The others looked over at them, ready.

"It's time," Char said, "for Pack Party number two."

"*This time, it's personal*," Jacob said in a movie trailer voice. Tammy smacked him an appreciative smack in the chest. That was a definite girlfriend thing, Jacob had observed. Even Willow did it. Maybe not Alice, though.

"We're thinking my place." Char spread her arms wide as if to somehow encompass the whole thing.

This caught Jacob by surprise. He had, without even fully realizing it, and obviously without having done anything about it, been assuming that they'd do the next party at *his* house. Since the whole thing had started with him and Eric. Well, Eric and him.

Finn looked around as if he were seeing Char's place for the first time. "Swanky," he said dubiously.

"Well, it wouldn't be swanky," Char said. "It would be a party, like last time."

"Yeah," Finn said, "because I'm not up for some kind of old-people party."

"Old-people party?" Alice said, in her *I require clarification* voice.

"You know—one of those parties where you stand around with food on a plate in one hand and a drink in the other hand"—he pantomimed those hands—"and just *talk*." The way he said *talk* was the way you might say *get hemorrhoids*.

Willow—she and Finn were in their own complicated physical mesh in an armchair—giggled and bounced the heels of her black boots off the oriental rug.

"What about my place?" Jacob said, his face feeling a little flushed.

Char wrinkled her nose a little. "Well, we already did West Philly, though."

"Plus, Char's house is…" Eric said. "I mean, look at it." He spread his arms wide too. "It's seriously nice."

"The neighborhood's really safe too," Willow said, and then said, "What?" to Finn, who was looking at her sideways. "It *is*."

"There *is* a lot of space here," Tammy said, mostly to Jacob; Tammy, who hadn't even *seen* his house yet.

"Right. And we're planning to invite more people this time," Eric said.

"Okay," Jacob said. "So better stay out of the ghetto, then."

"Dude," Eric said.

Tammy rubbed circles on Jacob's chest. "Come on, Jake."

"We were also thinking," Eric said, "that maybe it could be kind of a sleepover too."

"A *sleepover*?" Finn said. "Like, with footie pajamas?"

"Oh my God," Char said, rolling her eyes. "Would you just *listen*?"

Finn put his hands up. *My fault*, his hands said. His face said other things.

Eric continued. "That way people could just keep hanging out as late as they want. And eventually we could have breakfast for whoever was left. Your mom wouldn't go for that if it was your place, would she, Jake?" he said, trying to make it okay.

Jacob shrugged. She probably wouldn't.

Tammy looked over at Char. "Are *your* parents gonna go for that?"

Char nodded. "They already said it was okay. You know how they are."

Tammy nodded, made a *fair enough* face.

"Two Saturdays from now, everybody?" Eric said. "The Saturday after Thanksgiving weekend?"

Jacob saw that everything had already been worked out. And maybe Char's place *was* better. Which itself didn't feel great. "We can call it the Jeffersons party," he said. "Movin' on up."

Uneasy laughter.

"What about your parents?" Brian said to Alice. They were on the other couch, side by side. She shrugged, her hands busy with her ponytail that she'd pulled over one shoulder, her small, precise mouth closed. So Brian said to the group as a whole, "Her parents have been getting a little nervous about this." He gestured at the group.

"Nervous about *this*?" Tammy said.

Jacob wasn't expecting that either. By high school standards, he got the sense that his group was a kind of unbelievably un-dangerous group.

"They don't know any of you," Alice said, spreading her arms wide. She was wearing a T-shirt that said *Penn PIRG*, which was not a meaningful thing to Jacob. "They don't know if this whole thing is such a good idea. In terms of my schoolwork and so on."

Jacob had noticed that Alice hadn't made it to all their afternoon settling-out sessions that week. So that was why.

"And now a sleepover?" Alice added.

Somehow this line of conversation agitated Jacob again. If they were going to do this, they couldn't lose Alice, or anyone, because maybe that would be just the beginning of something worse. So he jumped in. "Well, you *do* have to sleep that night," he said. "So that would be on your to-do list anyway." Everybody laughed.

"What if they talked to Char's parents?" Eric said. "That could be reassuring, knowing that someone would be watching everything."

"They would definitely want to do that," Alice said.

Char rolled her eyes. "First of all, my parents are pretty much not going to be watching over any of it. My parents aren't the *interfering* type." That was true—they were home, but hadn't been visible the whole time that the Pack was there. "I don't think my parents would reassure anyone."

"Well, I could just come for the night portion, and not do the sleepover," Alice said. "They *might* let me do that."

"No," Willow said. "You *have* to be here for the *whole thing*. We neeeeed you."

Tangled up, Jacob felt Tammy sigh in frustration at the situation.

"Hang on," he said. He extracted himself from her and the couch and went over to a phone that was in the living room.

"What?" Alice said.

Jacob dialed her home number—he had everybody's numbers memorized by then—while everybody watched him. He wasn't thinking about what he was doing; he was just doing it, feeling a strange kind of energy in him.

When Alice's father picked up, Jacob put on a voice that wasn't Ward Cleaver but that was only a couple of houses away from Ward Cleaver. "Hi," he said. "Doug?" He was pretty sure that was Alice's father's name. Out of the corner of his eye he saw Alice cover her mouth with her hand.

"This is," Doug said.

"Hi, hi—my name is Mark West. I'm the father of Charlotte West. Charlotte is one of Alice's friends?"

Everybody in the room was staring at Jacob in pure, frozen silence. He felt the energy pulsing inside him.

"Oh, sure," Doug said. He had a thick voice, as if he had a cold.

"Well, I'm just calling around to all the parents because our Charlotte's planning to have a little get-together at our place two weeks from now, and I want to check in with the invitees' parents."

Char was up out of her seat by then, her mouth and eyes open wide right in front of Jacob's face.

"Oh, okay. That's thoughtful. Two weeks from now, you said?"

"That's right—a Saturday night, a week after Thanksgiving. I'm just making calls because I want to let everyone know that we're going to be here keeping an eye on things."

"You're going to be there?"

"Start to finish," Jacob said. "Now, I should say," he added, in an extremely responsible-sounding voice, "they're planning on a sleepover component."

Everyone in the room was still staring at Jacob, some of them smiling and shaking their heads. Tammy's eyes were wide with excitement, her mouth a little open. In a way, he felt like that was how he was looking at himself right then. Meanwhile, he realized that the voice he was doing was actually his father's voice, more or less. His father's voice got things done.

"A sleepover," Doug said. There was a pause. He sniffed, cold-like. "Can I be honest with you, Mr....?"

"It's Mark," Jacob said. Char hit him very lightly in the chest, his chest that was buzzing.

"Mark, sometimes I wonder if this friend group is getting a little out of control. Not that any of them are probably bad kids, obviously. It just takes up so much of Alice's time."

"I hear you," Jacob said.

"She's got the political stuff, already, and her schoolwork."

"I hear you."

"It's just that there's an intensity to these friendships that we haven't seen with Alice before."

"Well, that's why we think it's a good idea to have some of their get-togethers happen in our home," Jacob said. "We're the type of parents who like to keep an eye on things." As crazy as this felt, he managed to wink at Alice, over Char's shoulder. "And it probably goes without saying, but we obviously draw a hard line about anything illicit. Alcohol, drugs, even smoking.

Not that we have to worry about that with these kids. They're absolutely great kids. Honor-roll kids. They'll probably spend the night talking about calculus."

Tammy clapped a hand over her mouth to muffle her laughter.

"Well, I hear that. That's all good, obviously," Doug said.

"You know how *some* kids are," Jacob said.

"Absolutely."

"These are not those kids, thank God," Jacob said.

"Listen—this is very reassuring."

"Sure. That's who we are, Doug," Jacob said. Char hit him lightly in his buzzing chest again. She didn't mean it aggressively, maybe, but it felt a little aggressive. And actually he felt a little aggressive himself. "And this is a *very* nice neighborhood," he added, looking straight into Char's eyes. "Chestnut Hill. A nice house in a nice, safe neighborhood."

Doug thought for a moment and then said, "You know, I'll talk to my wife, but I think it sounds okay."

"That's great," Jacob said. The energy was still in him, making quiet suggestions. He felt how easy it would be to take things too far. "I know Char will be thrilled. Details to come, Doug."

"Sounds good, Mark," said Alice's father, sniffing again. "I sure appreciate it."

Jacob looked around at Char's stately living room, where some of the furniture was probably older than his mother. "And let's have you over for dinner at some point," he said. This time Char actually punched him, pretty hard, in the arm. Definitely aggressive.

"Sounds good. Sounds good," Doug said.

"Do you want to look at calendars now?" Jacob said. Char's face was genuinely horrified. She squeezed his arm tightly. Everybody was sitting bolt upright at this point, or on their feet like Char. He really could take this pretty far—right over the edge.

"Well, I'm a little under the weather," Doug said. "I'm sure we can work something out later."

"Sure, sure," Jacob said. "Well, I hope you feel better soon. You take care."

And then they said goodbye and hung up.

Jacob looked over at Alice. "You're in," he said.

The room stayed silent for another few seconds, a few seconds in which Jacob wondered how that whole thing had even happened. It was so unlike him. Wasn't it? Just thinking of something and then going right ahead and doing it? And what had been driving him?

Finally Tammy said, "What...was...that...you...*crazy*... person?" but with an openly admiring look on her face.

"*That*," Finn said, "was legendary. That was the stuff of legends. That calendars thing was *hilarious*."

"No," Char said, "it was not."

Eric shook Jacob's hand, and then he put his arms around Char, who was still shaking her head at Jacob. Frowning. "Very cool," Eric said.

Alice, in her corner of the couch, had a mix of scandalized and happy on her face. "Maybe my parents *should* be worried," she said.

"Really," Char said.

Jacob stood there, grinning, his teeth slightly gritted until Tammy tugged his arm to get him back into a tangle with her. "My hero," she said. "My crazy boy hero."

And, as for Jacob, he couldn't help feeling that he was still very much getting to know himself, and that there was probably a lot more to come.

13

The other thing happening was that Jacob had finally found a job. Well, not that he had really been looking. He had thought about putting an application in at Erol's Video where Leron was working, but he couldn't seem to get himself motivated to do it. But as it happened, another job fell into his lap instead.

His mother had tried to talk him out of it. "You've got a lot going on already," she said, standing at the door to his room, wearing her nurse clothes.

Jacob shrugged from where he'd been studying on the bed. "That's why I need the money."

"I know," his mother said, her face creased with worry, leaning against his doorjamb. "But your schoolwork."

"I can handle it," he said. He lifted the book he was reading—physics. "See?"

"Maybe I can give you more of an allowance," she said.

That didn't seem at all realistic to him. "Come on," he said.

She looked off over his shoulder at the window and crossed her arms. "You'd probably be better off if you were living with your father, wouldn't you? *He's* done all right for himself." Sometimes she was very bitter about his father.

"I don't even like Chicago," he said, rallying for her. "Dey have dose ridiculous ak-sents dere."

She breathed a little laugh over her crossed arms.

"It's okay, Mom," he said. "I was fine when I was working at the zoo this fall, wasn't I? And last spring?"

His mother chewed on her lower lip. "But that was before you had this social life of yours."

"It'll all work out," Jacob said.

"I don't know," she said.

He stood up and went over to her. "Hey," he said. "You

want a cheese wit' *nuttin'*?" He was doing an impression of a person in a commercial they had both seen. It involved him squinting up his face and it always made her laugh.

This time too. She hugged him, and partly she was crying, but partly she was laughing. They stood like that for a while, the feelings going back and forth between them.

One reason Jacob was confident about things working out was that the parts of his life were connected. For example, his friends from the Pack—and his girlfriend—were people from his school, which is where he had to be all week anyway. And now the job was actually tied to his girlfriend too.

It had come together when, after the Pack broke up the morning settling-in to head to class, Tammy walked Jacob down the hall and said, "My father wants to know if you know how to put things into boxes." Her father ran a shop in Center City that was some mix of a thrift store and an antique shop, and he apparently did a fair amount of business by mail—so, as she explained now, he needed someone to pack boxes.

"Wait—you told him I was looking for a job?"

She shrugged. "You're always talking about it."

"That's nice," Jacob said, feeling a happy warmth in him. He gave her body a sideways bump with his body.

She bumped back. "Well, that's me—the nice girl."

Something occurred to Jacob. "Why doesn't he just get you and your brothers to do it?" he asked. "Put stuff in boxes?"

She laughed. "We're not *willing* to do it," she said.

It wasn't like Tammy *never* worked. She had a job most summers, apparently, doling out ice cream or some such thing. But even that seemed kind of optional, and during the school year she was completely off the hook. Jacob didn't completely understand it.

Anyway, Jacob had taken the subway down with Tammy to meet her father in his store, which was down on Pine Street on Antiques Row. It was the Tuesday before Thanksgiving. Eric and Alice and Finn were on the subway, too, on their own ways home—and the guys were giving him joking advice on how to get the job. Eric said, "Be sure you really squeeze his hand when you shake it. He's only going to respect you if you break a couple of fingers." And Finn said, "Don't steal anything. Not until you've been there for a while." Alice and Tammy shook their heads.

"Thanks, guys. Really," Jacob said. He was feeling good.

And maybe that was why, when he saw the subway map on the wall and saw the name Fern Rock on the top of it, he found himself talking about his secret vision. "Have you guys ever been up to Fern Rock?" he said.

Nobody had.

So Jacob said, "I dunno. I just have this nice image in my mind of that stop." And he described it—the meadow, the occasional trees, the ferns, the river. The peaceful, wide-open landscape. He felt his heart beating a little fast as he finished talking, looking around at his friends' faces. He'd never shared this vision with anyone before.

Finn said, "That'd be cool. Like an oasis."

"Huh," Eric said.

"I don't know if that's too likely," Alice said. "We're talking about North Philadelphia."

And Tammy snuggled into Jacob a little deeper. She said, "We should go see it sometime." Which was really, really nice, and almost made him want to cry. They watched the concrete of the subway tunnel walls rush by.

Finn got off first, and then Eric, and then Tammy and Jacob, leaving Alice to finish the trip by herself. She looked like she was concentrating. Maybe like she was trying to picture something.

Tammy's father's shop was jammed with all kinds of stuff—old mirrors and free-standing stained-glass windows, china dishes, dark-wood chairs and cabinets—armoires was probably the right word—dolls from forever ago, jewelry in cases, and even a few rugs. Everywhere Jacob looked there was more stuff, and not any of it the kind of thing he had in his own house. Light bounced all around, off the many reflective surfaces. Mr. Bocek, meanwhile, was a gruff guy with a large mustache and military tattoos on his forearms. He seemed too big, too brawny, to be in a store full of objects that might break. "My kids don't believe in work," he said to Jacob right away. "Do you believe in work?"

A little startled, Jacob said yes. "I have a job every summer and usually during the school year too. I don't know if Tammy told you"—Tammy was sitting off to the side on a painted wooden stool, like a spectator—"but I just finished the season working at the zoo. I worked there last summer too. The one before this past one, I mean."

"The zoo, huh?" Mr. Bocek said. "I guess you know a lot about shoveling."

Jacob smiled. "Yeah. A lot." But then Mr. Bocek wasn't smiling—he hadn't been making a joke—so Jacob stopped smiling too.

Mr. Bocek looked him over, pausing to study the earring with a sour look on his face—Jacob's own father had sometimes looked at him like that for one reason or another—and finally he shook Jacob's hand, testing it. Jacob didn't attempt to break any fingers, but he stayed in there.

"Yeah, okay," Mr. Bocek said. "Okay. We'll see."

He offered five dollars an hour, under the table, for a chunk of hours on the weekends, plus afternoons as needed. "It may get in the way of your social life a little," he said pointedly. Jacob wondered if he was being hired just so that Mr. Bocek could keep his eye on him.

Outside the shop, Tammy said, "Nice *work*, Mr. Man. I was pretty sure you were gonna get it as soon as the handshake."

"The handshake?"

"You looked him in the eye while you were shaking his hand. That's huge with my father. So he's probably sort of okay with you now." She took his arm in an old-fashioned way, like on their first date, and they went down the sidewalk together. Almost like solid grown-ups.

14

Deanna came home for Thanksgiving, grabbing a ride with a Cornell friend who was also from Philly. It felt like Jacob hadn't seen her in a year, even though it had actually only been a few months. She looked a little different—extra confident, bouncier, her big hair sloppy in a having-fun way, and she was always in a school sweatshirt if she could help it. She bounced around the house talking about the dorms and the crazy professors and her new friends and how hard classes were and going to parties. She started a lot of her sentences with "At Cornell, we…." With all her excitement, it would have made sense if she'd woken up and painted her face half red and half white each morning. The energy level in the house—which Jacob realized had been kind of low recently—surged. And Jacob joined right in, chattering about his own new life. His mother got back into a laughing and joking mode. "It's good to have you back, D," she said a bunch of times.

Thursday night—Thanksgiving—it was just the two kids at home. Their mother was at work to get time-and-a-half for holiday hours; the family holiday was going to be on Friday instead of Thursday. Deanna and Jacob were in the kitchen looking for something easy for dinner.

"So Mom's been doing her usual November thing?" Deanna said.

Jacob turned to look at her. He had been checking the fridge even though he knew it was probably going to end up a frozen dinner night. Deanna had a cabinet open, scanning the shelves. "Yeah," he said. "Pretty much."

"Man. You know, I should for sure be taking psychology." She picked up a can of something and put it down again. "Are you guys really eating vegetarian now?"

"What do you mean, psychology?" Jacob said.

"That woman needs *something*. I wish I knew what it was, is all."

"She just gets sad."

Deanna turned around and gave him a searching look. "*Very* sad," she said.

"Okay," Jacob admitted.

"And you do too."

In the face of that searching look, Jacob felt like he was pinned to the refrigerator. It was true that he was different from his sister in that way, more like their mother. Deanna's personality was like their father's; they got angry, but not really *down*.

"I'm sorry I left you with—with all this," she said, gesturing around loosely.

Jacob didn't know what to say.

"But you seem much happier now, with your new friends. And—what's her name?—*Tammy*." She winked at him and turned back to the cabinet.

"Yeah," Jacob said, opening the fridge again to hide his face in there.

"Hey—is it true your new friends call you *Jake*? Because *that* is crazy."

They did Thanksgiving at their uncle's house in Northeast Philly—their mother's brother. Since they didn't have a car, they took a cab, which was a total luxury for the Wassermans. "It's just once a year," their mother said. And then, in a quieter voice: "And anyway your uncle is splitting the cost with us." So they rode over on Friday afternoon, with the smell of their mother's dish, just out of the oven, rising up to fill the vehicle.

"What is that?" the cabbie said at one point, when they were stuck in some traffic. There had been snow over the previous couple of days and it was slowing everything down.

"It's called a nut loaf," their mother said. "It's vegetarian."

"Nut loaf?" the man said. The back of his neck was substantially hairy. "Well, it smells pretty good all the same."

Eventually they pulled up to their uncle's place. "Over the

river—of cars—and through the Roosevelt Boulevard," Deanna said. They looked out the window at the little brick house. Uncle Joe was already standing at the open front door, grinning through his beard. He came down the shoveled walkway and paid the cab driver.

"Ah, nice," he said, kissing their mother on the cheek and taking the casserole dish from her. "Now we can feed *everybody*."

With Jacob and his mother being vegetarian all of a sudden, it was a more complicated holiday, foodwise.

"Happy Thanksgiving," he said. "And Shabbat Shalom! Come on in out of the snow." He was an extra-hearty guy, pretty much what you'd expect from a bearded man who was a little fat. To Jacob he said, "Getting pretty big, kiddo! Have you joined the wrestling team yet?"

This was a recurring joke. Apparently there was a story in the Bible about Biblical Jacob wrestling an angel, which made Philadelphia Jacob picture something out of the WWF—Hulk Hogan with wings, maybe. Or maybe the angel would be one of the bad-guy wrestlers, hitting you with a folding chair? Anyway, in this moment Jacob just chuckled and told his uncle no, not yet.

Inside, everything was all hellos and hugs and kisses. The big sound of family. Though it wasn't a huge gathering; there were the three West Philly Wassermans, and then there were the four Northeast Blauers—Blauer was Jacob's mother's maiden name—who were Uncle Joe, Aunt Sheryl, and cousins Seth and Rebecca. Plus Seth, who was in his early twenties, had brought his girlfriend Yael. She was blond and very skinny.

It was a pretty nice house—Jacob noticed that each time he was there. Not big or anything, but it seemed like the furniture had all been picked out on purpose and they had multiple large TVs and nice pictures on the walls, and in general things seemed bright and cheerful. He also always noticed that there was a lot of Hebrew around—on the spines of books on the living room shelf and written artistically in frames on the wall.

Jacob couldn't read any of it, but the framed letters looked a bit like flames.

For a while everybody sat around in the living room catching up. Grown-ups asked kids about school—"What grade are you in now?" Uncle Joe asked Jacob—and kids talked among themselves about what was new, which was generally also about school. What else was there to talk about? Jacob didn't get into much detail in his answers. When you thought about it, a person's life was a long story, even at the age of sixteen. And you could either tell the whole story, try to unpack all the details about nights of trying to distract yourself from being sad and that not totally working, but then this new group of people, and the Willow thing, which was bad, and the Tammy thing, which was good, and then Revival, and all the different people in your life, and what it all meant, and how it all felt—the whole big giant mess of yourself and your life that you don't even remotely understand yourself—or you could just say, "Things are good." So when Uncle Joe asked him what grade he was in, Jacob said eleventh, and he nodded when the follow-up question was whether it was a good year so far.

Meanwhile there were lots of refreshments. Food everywhere, all over the coffee table and end tables, and beverages. The adults had alcoholic drinks—them plus Seth and Yael, who were possibly adults themselves, depending on how you looked at them. It was hard to know where the line was. Jacob, though, was the youngest of all the cousins, and Seth even tousled his hair at one point as Jacob reached for the bowl of chips.

Then it was mealtime. As it turned out—Uncle Joe announced this as they were putting out plates of food—the Blauers had actually cooked the turkey the day before and ate some of it then. "Well," Uncle Joe said, "we figured it was the actual day. And we needed an excuse to watch football." Which explained the lack of the big dead-but-still-in-one-piece bird, replaced instead by plates of sliced dead bird. Everybody at the table laughed at the situation, though Jacob's mother was obviously a little hurt. "You couldn't wait?" she said. She lifted her wineglass and took a big drink from it.

"Don't take it like that, Miri," Uncle Joe said, patting her wineglass hand when it was back on the table. "That was just a sneak preview. *This* is Thanksgiving. Not to mention Shabbat. Let's light the candles."

It surprised Jacob a little each time, the way that these Blauers were more religious than he and his sister and mother were. It wasn't hard to be more religious than the Wassermans, for sure—they never did anything for Shabbat, even though it was theoretically there every Friday, and they usually missed High Holy Day services in the fall. The only holiday they ever observed at home was Hanukkah, and Jacob gathered that that was so that he and Deanna wouldn't feel cheated during the overwhelming Christmas season. Beyond that, they went to his uncle's place for Passover, and sometimes for a Rosh Hashanah lunch or something, but that was about it for Judaism. He had not remotely done the bar mitzvah thing, for example.

Watching his aunt light the Shabbat candles—they were right at the center of the table in these pretty silver candlesticks, kind of rectangular and modern-looking—and watching the Blauers do the blessings over the food and the wine, Jacob felt something he'd felt before at his uncle's house: like he'd been missing out on something. It was nice, this whole family doing these things together, things they found meaningful. Jacob and his sister didn't know the words, so they just sat and watched. Their mother tried, partly successfully, to stumble along with her brother.

Jacob felt a particular longing—familiar but new each time it happened—when Uncle Joe put his hands on Jacob's cousins' heads and said a specific blessing for them. He palmed their heads like basketballs, but it was gentle, until the end, at least, when he tousled them quite a bit. It wasn't the first time Jacob had ever seen that blessing. On this occasion, though, it stuck out to him. He had talked to his own father the day before, like he usually did every other week or so. They caught up, tried not to argue about whether Jacob was focused enough on his studies given his new social life—"A lot of times I call and you're not even home," his father said—and wished each other a happy Thanksgiving. "Remember, I'll see you at Hanukkah," he said. But these blessings were something else.

He was also aware of Yael, his cousin Seth's girlfriend. She was a chatty, friendly girl—or woman, maybe?—though not necessarily super-interesting to Jacob; she mostly talked about celebrities. Like, "Can you believe Milli Vanilli isn't even for real?" was one question she had. But it made him think about Tammy and he wished she were there with him. Tammy was busy this weekend, her family hosting out-of-town family of their own. Would he have brought her if she were free, though? Was that the kind of thing they had, boyfriend-girlfriend-wise? He didn't think any of the other Pack couples were together for Thanksgiving.

Jacob chewed on all that throughout the dinner, along with the nut loaf—which was really good, actually, and had a sauce called bechamel that was fantastic. Not everybody there tried it, but everyone who did gave it rave reviews, and that seemed to cheer Jacob's mother a bit; she told a funny story about work at some point during the dinner. Still she did go through a few glasses of wine. And Jacob didn't really get into the joke-telling that had become his thing lately, because he felt like that was a new version of him that these folks wouldn't recognize; he just quietly chewed on his thoughts.

"You okay over there?" Uncle Joe called to him from down the table.

"Yeah," Jacob said. "Thanks."

Meanwhile, his sister spent the whole time talking to their cousin Rebecca, their heads close together. They were the same age, and both in their first year of college. So it was probably Cornell this, Brandeis that. Jacob thought about how Deanna was going to be leaving again soon.

Jacob left the dinner with this weird mixed feeling. Physically full, of course—to dangerous levels—but also empty in an unexpected way, as if things were scattered. At the door, with another cab waiting outside, there was a bunch more hugging and kissing and noise, and he saw his uncle slip his mother some money for the ride home too. The Wassermans left the house and stepped into the cold and dark. Uncle Joe waved from the door. Jacob was so aware of things that weren't happening, things that were stopping or absent. Why? He wished he could go to Revival with the Pack and turn this weak feeling into something stronger. Were they even open on Thanksgiving?

On the way home their mother wanted to know if they had *really* liked the nut loaf.

Deanna left on Sunday. *Another missing piece*, Jacob thought.

15

Jacob was definitely a little off after Deanna left town. The house had gone back to November quiet, and the season continued to progress outside him, and inside him too. Tammy kept reacting to his moods. On the phone one night, she said, "What's going on *this* time? You seem like you're upset about something."

Jacob sighed. "Sorry," he said. "I'm not upset about anything. There's nothing to *be* upset about."

"So what's wrong, you nutcase?" Tammy said. And that was supposed to be funny, of course, but it wasn't actually that funny to Jacob. Still he tried to pick his end of the conversation up and brighten his voice. And Tammy seemed to buy it. Or at least she seemed to want to.

On the plus side, his job was turning out to be okay. Sunday of Thanksgiving weekend Mr. Bocek set Jacob up in the back room and showed him the stack of newspapers and other packing materials and outlined some tips on how to protect the delicate things—porcelain figurines, mostly—that were going into the boxes. Every once in a while, he said something like, "My daughter says you're funny," or "My daughter says you like French movies," or "My daughter says you're a good dancer," but in a gruff way that made Jacob want to deny whatever Tammy had claimed.

Just put the things in the boxes, Jacob told himself. *Just put the things in the boxes.*

It was easy work, really, and—as he discovered that week—if it did leave him too much time for his thoughts and moods to wander, at least there was no shovel involved.

A couple of times that first week Tammy—who apparently hadn't, before Jacob's interview, been to the shop in years—

visited while he was working; she went on the Broad Street Line with him after school. Her father said, repeatedly, "Don't distract the kid." In response to which Tammy settled on a three-legged stool a few feet away from Jacob and tried to be as distracting as possible, giving him sexy eyes or asking when they were going to go to the movies again. The light flashed off her glasses. She made kissy lips. During Tammy's visits, her father stopped by the back room frequently. Sometimes he crossed his muscly, tattooed arms over his broad chest and just watched the two of them as Jacob made sure he was working in a very focused way.

Still—the whole thing was fine. Jacob was making money, and for some reason he liked Mr. Bocek and his gruffness as much as he was afraid of him, and it felt like a big, nice thing that Tammy had set it up.

Meanwhile, the sleepover party came together. That was kind of energizing.

One of the interesting things was the guest list, because in a way they had forgotten about everybody else at Central High School as they had gotten closer to each other, but if it was going to be a party, they wanted to invite more than just the eight of them. In fact, Char and Eric were trying to make it a *lot* bigger.

But Central had changed around them too. The fact was, some people now knew who the people in the Pack were. They even knew the *name* "Pack." Not everybody, obviously—the school was too big and complicated for that—but in Jacob's classes, anyway, his group was a visible entity, and maybe beyond into some of the rest of the eleventh grade. Again, you couldn't really talk about *popular* at a school like Central, not when you had so many people and points of origin and ethnicities and groups, but you could talk about *existing*. Lots of groups existed—the mostly white stoner-types who hung out on the south lawn, the mostly Black cheerleaders, the cluster of completely white wealthy prep-school-looking kids who called themselves the Tribe and were pretty much jerks, the Vietnamese girls on the badminton team, and a hundred more—and Jacob's group was now one of those groups. So, when he talked to folks about the party at Char's house—they were calling it an *All-Nighter*, rather than a *Sleepover*—the answer he always got was, "Really? Cool." Some people were going to come for the whole thing, and some were only going to be able to come for the pre-sleep part, but everybody said, "Really? Cool."

His own mother had made an actual call to Char's parents and spoke to the real people, because this party broke the original idea of a curfew. But although Char's parents were low-interference types, apparently they were reassuring enough for her. Also, Jacob had stressed that Eric was one of the organizers, and he was still filed under *Nice Boy* in his mother's internal filing system. So she ultimately didn't give him a hard time about it. Plus she was a bit distracted.

And the truth was that the party prep was still very PG. There really wasn't going to be any alcohol or drugs, or anything like that. For some reason nobody in the Pack ever even brought up the possibility. Just music and snacks and Coke in glass bottles and hanging out. Jacob knew that other parties happened among the kids of Central High School that were more intense, but this wasn't going to be one of them. He wondered what those other parties were like, and if they were worse, or better, or just some whole other thing altogether.

One person Jacob invited almost by accident was Leron. He and Leron had run into each other in the hall and were comparing jobs when Jacob brought it up.

"Erol's is cool," Leron was saying. "Mostly it's a lot of nothing to do."

"Cool. Mine looks like it's gonna be pretty busy," Jacob said.

"Working for your girl's father? Could be dangerous."

Jacob laughed. "Maybe so."

"Well, you got to make that money, right?"

"Right." Jacob smiled. It was nice talking to Leron right

then, and so he found himself saying, "You know, we're having a party this Saturday."

Leron nodded. "I heard something about that."

"You want to come? You and the guys?"

Leron looked surprised. "For real?"

"Yeah," Jacob said.

"What kind of party?"

Jacob shrugged. "Dancing."

"All right," Leron said, after a pause, clasping Jacob's hand. It was different from an Eric handshake. "Bet. I'ma try and be there."

"Bet," Jacob said.

On the night of, Jacob drove out to Char's early with Eric to help with setup. Eric had been noticing Jacob's mood too. On the drive over, he asked, not for the first time, if anything was wrong. "You and Tammy are okay, right?"

"Yeah," Jacob said. He didn't know how to put into words what was going on with him. It seemed like it was disconnected from the actual facts of his life somehow. Because those facts were good, right? They definitely were. Well, except his mom. When he left for the party, she was alone in the living room with a drink and what looked like heavy thoughts. Some of which followed him out the door.

"You just haven't been cracking the jokes as much recently," Eric said. "It's just been different."

"Huh," Jacob said. He resolved internally to get back to the jokes. They were sort of his job, after all.

"But it's party time, right, Jake?" Eric said.

"Party o'clock," Jacob said forcefully.

"That's my man," Eric said.

The whole Pack was there early. It was like the pre-party party. And Char's parents were around this time, looking amused at everyone, remembering aloud what their high school experiences had been like. They were tall and fit and confident people. He had never really met grown-ups like them before.

"My parents would never have gone for this," Mr. West said, sitting on the couch with his wife. He didn't sound very much like Jacob's phone version of him, and Jacob blushed when he even thought about that phone call.

"Oh, mine either," Mrs. West said. They each had a glass of something brown and alcoholic, and they looked very cozy.

But they made themselves scarce when things got started. And it was easy to be scarce in a house this big. Jacob was still dumbfounded any time he thought about it. Char was an only child, and yet they had all these *rooms*. Her parents, meanwhile, always referred to the house as "this old place." Like, "This old place has her creaks and groans," or "This old place has a few good years left in her." It was ridiculous. You were supposed to laugh, but it was ridiculous. Anyway, they disappeared into the back somewhere.

And pretty soon the lights were dim and the music was very loud and people started to show up, wave after wave—a lot more than at the first party. Like maybe forty or fifty; Jacob lost count fast. And there were people from all over school this time. People he knew from one class or another; people he'd seen in the hallways; people he wasn't sure he'd ever seen. The rooms set aside for the party were filling up. Jacob even ran into a guy and a girl who were part of the Tribe when they converged at the chips and soda at the same time. Jacob remembered that Char knew some of them. They knew each other through richness, maybe.

The guy spoke to Jacob, loud over the Depeche Mode on the stereo. "Soda, huh?" he said, disapproving but conversational.

"The 'rents are home," explained the girl, shrugging. Leah. She was in his English class and usually seemed bored but sometimes she said surprising and interesting things. They had never spoken to each other. At the moment, one of her hands was playing with her halo of dark, curly hair; with her other one, she picked up a single potato chip and ate it whole in one exact bite.

Jacob didn't really know what to say to these people, so he shrugged like Leah had.

"So, Wassermann," Mike said, "you're Jewish, right?"

Jacob was caught off guard, but he nodded.

"So what's it like being the only one in the Pack?" His brown eyes narrowed at Jacob.

Leah stopped playing with her hair to smack Mike in the chest. Were they dating? He was a lot taller than she was. In any case, Jacob was reeling from the question. "Huh?" he said.

"This guy's supposed to be the witty one, isn't he?" Mike said—practically bellowed—to Leah.

"I'm just more used to doing my chitchat in Hebrew," Jacob said, feeling flushed.

They both laughed. "See?" Leah said.

It suddenly occurred to Jacob that Mike was Mike Berman and Leah was Leah Shaffer, and that other folks in the Tribe were Jessica Roth and Noah Lieber and—Jacob realized that the Tribe was all Jewish. Well, plus Stacy Adams. And probably that Oscar kid wasn't. But almost all Jewish.

"Totally," Mike said. "Aaaanyway, I'm just saying." He grabbed a soda like it was about to get away from him. "Stay Jewish." And then he went off back into the crowd. Leah rolled her eyes at his back, maybe apologetically and maybe not, and then followed him with hair twirled around her finger.

Jacob shook his head, as if he were trying to shake off that weird interaction. What was that question even supposed to mean? What was it supposed to mean if he was the only one or wasn't? He shook his head again, harder. Then he went back to where people were dancing and found Tammy, and soon he was busy trying to keep his hands from being all over her. His attraction to Tammy was extra strong right then. It was almost as if he wanted to merge with her or something. U2's "Desire" was rolling out of the speakers, and Willow had borrowed a blacklight from the studio where she danced, which meant that the mountain range on Jacob's Joy Division shirt glowed brightly, the same way Tammy's whole white shirt was also glowing.

They made out pretty intensely on the dance floor, which was to say the living room.

Leron actually did show up, with Latia, Omar, Ty, and Derrick, plus Derrick's girlfriend, who Jacob had seen around school but didn't know. He found out they were there when Eric poked him. "Your friend Leron," he said, thumbing back over his shoulder toward the front of the house.

Jacob separated himself from Tammy, who looked a little stunned from all the making out—"I'll be right back," he said—and weaved through the crowd, searching. After a minute he found them, not too far from the front door, jackets still on even though the room was hot by then.

"Hey," Jacob said loudly, clasping Leron's hand.

"Hey," Leron called back. He had a wary expression on his face, his eyes wide. The others with him were looking around at Char's ridiculous house, and out into the crowd that was— Jacob saw it now—almost all white, and just a little Asian and Middle Eastern. Nine Inch Nails hammering from the stereo. Some of the people thrashing a little. Finn was not far away, stomping his big black boots hard, Willow flutter-dancing next to him.

"Welcome," Jacob said.

"Yeah," Leron said. "You know, we wanted to stop by." Jacob had never seen him look so thrown.

"Yeah," Omar boomed from next to Leron. "Stop by."

"Hey," Latia said. They hadn't seen each other since working at the zoo.

"Hey," he said.

"We can only stay for just a minute," Leron added.

"Oh," Jacob said. "Totally."

"We gotta go somewhere else," Omar said.

"You got that right," Ty said. Not meaning to be audible over the music, probably, but Jacob heard it.

"I'm sorry," he wanted to say to all of them, but especially Leron. Instead he just nodded his head and clasped Leron's hand again.

"See you," Leron said, and they turned to go.

Derrick's girlfriend said, "Nice house," on her way past Jacob.

"It's not mine," he said, but maybe too quietly.

When they were gone he turned and looked at the party, seeing it like—or at least something like—Leron and Jacob's other old friends had seen it. He stood there for a minute like that, until he felt clear that, mood-wise, he couldn't afford to stand there like that any longer. Not unless he wanted to start howling inside. He pushed himself back into the party and found Tammy. "Hey—where are—" she started.

"Let's dance," Jacob said. It helped, having his hands on her again.

In fact, as the night went on, there was a lot more of that, especially once the people who weren't spending the night had left, and by that point it wasn't just Jacob and Tammy but basically everybody who was coupled up, and some people who were coupling up for the first time that night—people would get physically wrapped up in each other on the dance floor and then they would fall into a couch or a loveseat and get a little more involved or they'd leave the room altogether. Jacob even saw couples leave the house; it was too cold to be out on the lawn or something, but some people did have cars.

Pretty late, Jacob, hot from dancing, said to Tammy, "Let's find someplace."

It took some doing, because kids were everywhere, and they needed a place where people wouldn't be looking at them. So they did the thing that theoretically was off-limits for this particular party, which was to go upstairs. Jacob had been upstairs once, had seen Char's big bedroom with its fashion photos torn out of magazines and taped to the walls, but Tammy took him in another direction, tiptoeing across the carpet to another room. "Guest room," Tammy said, closing the door behind them. "They have three of these." Jacob could hear the beat from what sounded like Fine Young Cannibals coming up through the floor, muffled.

One of the things about being a teenager was that you could

hardly ever find a way to be alone. So Jacob had not even seen Tammy completely naked yet. The intensity of wanting to merge with her, which had been building all night, somehow ratcheted up even higher as she started to pull her shirt off, and his too. And then they got down on the carpet instinctively, so as to not mess up the bed, and ran their hands over each other in a desperate, rough way. Particularly Jacob, who was keenly desperate and rough inside.

When they were like this with each other, for Jacob it was like being in a fever state, like he didn't totally understand what was happening or who he was or who she was. Though this time it seemed like there was a sound in the background, a rising sound that he couldn't distinguish yet.

And there were moments of clarity. At one point Jacob emerged from the fever somewhat to say, "So you…you…what do you think about sex?"

At which point Tammy emerged completely from the fever, though her black hair was wild and her face was a bit wild too. "What?" she said. "Sex?"

"Yeah," Jacob said. "Are you…do you…?"

Tammy's face clarified. "I'm not ready for that," she said with certainty.

"Okay," Jacob said. "Totally." He kissed her again, put his hand on her breast, and then pulled back again. "Wait—is it because of me? Because it's me?"

"What? You? Are you stupid?"

"Well," Jacob said.

"*Please* don't get like that right now. Come here. It was really getting nice."

And they went back to it—hands and breasts and all this warm skin—but Jacob was only partly there, because another part of him was thinking that maybe it was because of him that she didn't want to have sex. Or maybe another part of him was somewhere else completely, like thinking about staying Jewish even though he wasn't much of a Jew, or staying Black, even though he wasn't Black at all. And it *was* all stupid, and most of him got that, but it howled, low, in him—that was the rising sound—distracting him. He felt his hands slow down. He felt himself gradually, steadily, lose his erection.

"What's wrong?" Tammy said. "What's wrong?"

And somehow hearing that question again—it did something to him.

Jacob was going to look back on this moment with real misery. What happened was that, before he knew it, he was fighting tears. It was as if it had been waiting there under a tiny protective layer, like a soap bubble that had popped, but inside was all this sadness. And so suddenly he was almost crying, and fighting hard against it. And it happened so suddenly that they were still on top of each other, almost in the middle of making out and groping each other, and then there were his eyes, clenching shut, his whole face clenching shut as tears tried to punch and kick their way out. He was already deeper than howling; this was already more like the drowning thing.

"Jake?" Tammy said, sitting up and pushing him to sit up. "What's happening? What's going on right now?"

"I don't know," Jacob said, slamming his fist down on the carpet, like he could *force* the sadness to become anger. "I don't know."

"Are you really this upset about not having sex? Because you know that's my choice, right?"

"I know that," Jacob said, wiping his face, which he'd managed to keep dry, leaning back against the bed. "Of course I know that."

"There are other things we can do," Tammy said. "Like, we were already doing some of them." She gestured at the floor.

"I know," Jacob said. "It's not that. I don't think it's that."

"Then what *is* it?" she said. "We're at a party, with all your friends. We're up here and I'm half-naked."

"I don't know," Jacob said. "I'm just sad."

"Jesus, Jake," Tammy said. She just put a hand on his knee, watching him. Her eyes were X-ray even without her glasses on. And then she put her shirt on and moved over next to him to lean against the bed too. And they just sat there like that for a long while. He wasn't sure how long it was. But they sat there until he felt normal again. Which for the moment just meant not drowning. And eventually they fooled around a little more, but not much, and then they went back downstairs to dance. But before that, as they sat there, Jacob heard the Ramones come on below him. It wasn't "I Wanna Be Sedated"—it was "Pet Sematary," it sounded like—but it made him think of "I Wanna Be Sedated," and he wondered what *he* wanted.

16

When Jacob woke up Sunday morning it took a minute to orient himself. He was stretched out on a rug, one of those Persian-type rugs—right: he was in Char's house, and it was probably from actual Persia. The next thing he realized was that Tammy was not next to him. They had eventually fallen asleep in a tangle, but now she was gone from the rug altogether; it was just Jacob and, a few feet away, a kid named Kenny who had stayed over, too, and who was still sleeping. Jacob sat up. There were a few other non-Pack people in the living room—armchairs and couches—but where was everyone else? Where was Tammy? An anxious pulse went through him.

Feeling hungover, or what he imagined hungover felt like, even though he wasn't hungover, obviously—could caffeine and fitful sleeping on a rug on a hardwood floor do that to you?—he stood up and walked over to look into the next room, which the Wests called their den. A few kids were sleeping there, including Willow and Finn, who were intertwined on the couch. Then, in the sunroom, there was just one girl—whose name, he thought, was Freddie—who looked freshly awake, stretching her arms up over her head.

"Do you know where Tammy is?" he said.

Freddie did not.

As Jacob looked around the first floor, the events of the previous night came back to him one at a time. *Only Jew in the Pack. We can only stay for just a minute.* And then Tammy—that situation came back to him as he entered the giant kitchen and saw her. She was with Char and Eric, all of them talking in low voices.

"Oh hey, Jake," Eric said, spotting him at the door.

"Hey," Jacob said, but, feeling panicked, looking only at Tammy.

Tammy had a spatula in one hand and a plate in the other, the plate piled pretty high with pancakes. She gave Jacob a small smile. "Hi."

"You were gone when I woke up."

Tammy held up the pancake plate. "Making breakfast," she said. Her eyes seemed to be saying something too. They seemed to be saying *Don't*.

And so Jacob put a smile on his face and took a breath. "I hope this is one of those all-you-can-eat places," he said, rubbing his not-very-hungry stomach.

That afternoon he had a shift at Mr. Bocek's shop. There was no way that Tammy had given her father anything like a play-by-play of the party, but still he watched Jacob more fiercely that afternoon. It made sense; his daughter had just spent the night with Jacob, in a sense.

"Have fun?" Mr. Bocek asked, like a warning.

"It was okay," Jacob said tentatively.

Mr. Bocek grunted.

"I'd better get back there," Jacob said, pointing at the room where he did his work.

Mr. Bocek nodded soberly.

Just put things in boxes, Jacob told himself.

But while he was back there, wrapping a china teacup in newspaper, he had too much time to think. He wished Tammy was there, but maybe the Tammy from two days ago. Or from the first week they were together, when everything was promising and they were the best, most excited, most confident versions of themselves; when they were like royalty. Everything was completely happy then. He thought about his first girlfriend, Barbara, and the way they had broken up in August. She had left her zoo job to go be a counselor at a sleepaway camp somewhere, and after a week she'd sent him a letter that said, *I like you and maybe even love you, but I'm not in love with you*, and that was the end of things. "Girl is crazy," Leron said back then—Jacob felt a pang of regret or embarrassment thinking of Leron now—and Jacob hadn't minded the breakup *too* much. Well, he'd had a couple of pretty bad days, but that was more because of the experience of being broken up with generally rather than anything specific about Barbara. For his part, Jacob *liked* Barbara, but he didn't love her and wasn't *in* love with her, either, whatever the difference was. With Tammy, though… with Tammy a breakup would be a very bad thing. He could feel in advance how bad it could be.

Jacob put the wrapped teacup in the box and picked up another one to wrap. His hands were dark with newsprint.

When they were back in school on Monday, the rumor was that it had been an orgy, the party at Char's house. People who had been there for part of it heard that it was all sex after they left, and people who hadn't been there at all had heard that it was all sex pretty much from the beginning. The fact that there were any rumors at all was incredible—as far as he knew, nobody had ever, in his whole life, talked among themselves about what Jacob Wasserman had done over the weekend—but on top of that, that the rumors were about an orgy was downright astonishing. Also embarrassing, or something worse, given that episode between him and Tammy.

They had talked on Sunday night. It was normal or at least it seemed pretty normal. She was attributing his breakdown to the result of too much dry humping and blue balls. "We'll get creative," she said to him. "Because we can't have you losing it again over *sex*."

Jacob felt a little resentment at that. "No," he said. "You wouldn't want a guy with *feelings*."

"Come on," she said.

He did like the sound of *getting creative*, anyway. And maybe it had just been some kind of overreaction to the sex thing. His desire to have sex with Tammy was at times pretty overwhelming.

Even Leron and the guys had heard the rumor about the party. "I heard you got your freak on," Derrick said to Jacob on Monday in the hallway. Leron and Ty and Omar were with him.

"I dunno," Jacob said—he wasn't sure what to say—and they all laughed, but in a respectful way.

"See?" Leron said to his guys. "That's how a gentleman behaves."

"That's the truth," Omar said.

Leron and Jacob shared a look that was full of a lot of things. Jacob wasn't sure he knew what most of those things were.

And then they all went on their way, leaving Jacob to wonder how he was supposed to handle a question like Derrick's. He didn't want people to think *Tammy* was at an orgy, but it was possible he wouldn't mind people thinking *he* was at an orgy. Maybe *with* Tammy.

He saw people from the Tribe that day, too, at a distance. Mike was there, and Leah, standing together in the hallway with some of their friends. Probably they knew the rumor. Maybe they'd even started it, for all Jacob knew. They laughed at something one of them said, and even the laughter sounded obnoxious. It was not clear to Jacob what he was supposed to have in common with any of those people.

Mike noticed him from that same distance, through the students wandering between them. "Jake," he called out. "Come here a second."

But Jacob just pointed at his watch. "Gotta go," he said, and he went.

Eric didn't have any advice on the subject of the rumor. He was too excited about their new status. "We made it, Jake," he said, when they were on the last leg of their trip home on Monday. "We made it."

"It's kind of cool, yeah," Jacob said, though he didn't know if that was true, or even what *made it* really meant, when you thought about it. "But it wasn't actually an orgy."

Eric put his hands up in a *Don't look at me* pose. "I don't know what was happening in every corner of that house. There was a lot of stuff happening, though."

"I guess that's true," Jacob said.

What stuff *did* happen?

Meanwhile, at home, which was like another planet somehow, he asked his mother about Judaism.

"What does it mean?" he said. "That we're Jewish?"

"What does it mean?" she repeated, looking up from her lentil burger. She was experimenting with a recipe for lentil burgers. So far they were terrible. But of course why wasn't *Jacob* cooking? Wouldn't a responsible kid pitch in a little more? Especially since the vegetarian thing had been his idea in the first place. "I don't know," his mother said, sighing. "I mean, it's more or less random. I was born into it. You were born into it."

"Okay," he persisted, "but now that we're born, what does it mean to *us*?"

"*I* don't know," his mother said, with a hint of bitterness in her voice. But a lot of what she said came out that way in the dark months. "I usually think religion is kind of silly. I thought you did too."

"Yeah. Maybe." He picked up his lentil burger. A piece crumbled off the edge and landed on his plate. "It just seems like it means something to a lot of people. Uncle Joe and Aunt Sheryl, for example."

"I don't really understand those two," his mother said. "He's changed a lot since he was a kid."

"Okay—so what was it like when you were growing up? With Grandma and Grandpa?" They had both been dead for a few years—his grandfather for maybe ten years. Jacob remembered them mainly as quiet people.

"Well, you know the Passover story, right? From Uncle Joe's? And basically you know the Hanukkah story?"

"Basically," Jacob said. "Sort of." He took a bite of his burger. Dry.

"People trying to kill us. Sometimes I think being Jewish is supposed to be about suffering."

Jacob sat back in his chair. "Really?"

She held her burger with both hands, resting partly on her plate. She was looking off away from Jacob. "Still—I do feel drawn back to it. Like this fall. I would have gone to High Holy Day services."

Jacob remembered that they had only skipped because he had been worried that Yom Kippur would make him sad.

"You never really let go of it," his mother said.

17

That week Eric and Char organized everybody into a Dirty Santa thing. It was Jacob's first, and not at all what it sounded like. The way it worked was everybody had to buy two gifts that were terrible gifts, things you wouldn't want to have, and then there was going to be a party where the gifts got distributed one by one and each person tried to trade theirs for other ones they disliked less. Something like that.

There hadn't been a lot of gift-giving in the Pack so far. Brian's birthday had happened a month earlier, and they had gotten a couple of slices of cake at the South Street Diner, but otherwise that hadn't been a very big deal. But maybe that was because it was Brian. Not-big-deal-ness seemed to surround things having to do with him.

"We should really be calling this something else. Like… Dirty…Gift-giver, or something," Jacob said, when they first talked about it in the hallway. "Because we don't all do Christmas."

Tammy, who was nestled up against him, rolled her eyes and gave him a light, back-handed smack to the chest. "Don't be oversensitive," she said. Which was pretty annoying; he was just stating a fact.

"I think it *is* a Christmas tradition," Char said, breaking off from fixing the cuffs of her pegged jeans.

"I'm not sure about that," Alice put in, her hand half-raised as if she were in class. She was sitting next to Brian, both of them leaning against the lockers. They were not snugglers. "I always heard of this as something called a White Elephant. And that the tradition goes back to Asia."

"Cool," Willow said.

"Oh, Alice," Char said.

"Okay," Eric said, running a hand through his red hair. Where he and Char were sitting, it was like they were at the head of a big conference table, running a business meeting. "But we were thinking of doing it at our Christmas party."

"Christmas party?" Jacob said.

"Christmas soiree," Char said. "Just the Pack this time."

"Well," Eric added, "Christmas and birthday." Char's birthday was December 22nd.

"Is this thing on?" Jacob tapped an invisible mic. "Are you guys not hearing the part where I'm Jewish?" He wasn't sure why he was making such a big deal out of this, actually. Maybe just to see what it felt like. Maybe because *oversensitive* was an annoying thing to call a person.

"Kind of all of a sudden," Tammy said.

"I was *born* Jewish," Jacob said. "I'm just saying, what about Hanukkah?" He didn't know what the exact date parameters of Hanukkah were that year, but it was going to be somewhere around then, anyway.

"My cute, sensitive Jewish boy," Tammy said, smiling up at him. Which was better than what she'd said before, anyway.

"There's also the solstice," Alice said, quite serious.

"Right. The solstice," Jacob said. "New Year's. Um…Kwanzaa?"

"Kwanzaa?" Char said. "Do you celebrate Kwanzaa now?"

"You never know," Jacob said, feeling like he wanted to drop the topic at this point. Like he was out on a limb for no especially good reason. "I'm just saying there are a lot of holidays."

"There *really are*," Willow said, nodding at him.

"Well, I don't care *what* we call it, as long as I get *presents*," Eric said, and then Char smacked him lightly in the chest.

"Just everybody come to my house on Friday the 22nd," Char said.

"For the party that has no name," Finn said, and then he turned to Jacob and raised his fist in the air. "I'm with you, Jake. Fuck Christianity anyway."

Willow gave him a girlfriend smack.

Meanwhile, Brian said, "Is there a maximum? For spending?"

Which Jacob was very glad someone had asked.

"Maximum?" Char said. "Oh, sure. Of course. What do we think? Twenty dollars total?"

That seemed like a lot to Jacob, but everyone else more or less nodded, and twenty dollars was the deal. In any case that was the maximum, not the minimum. "Do you want to go shopping together?" Tammy asked Jacob. Her breath smelled nice—a little sweet.

"Yeah," Jacob said. "White Elephant date."

"I dunno," Tammy said. "I kind of like the idea of *Dirty Santa*."

Which did sound okay when she put it like that.

"We can go to the mall or something," she said. "But you can't buy *my* present while we're there together. I want it to be a surprise."

Oh, Jacob thought. *Right*. People who were dating each other got each other Christmas gifts. Or holiday gifts. Or whatever.

Everything ticked along from there. Jacob kept working at Mr. Bocek's shop—Mr. Bocek didn't ask questions about the party, but he continued to watch Jacob closely, while reluctantly acknowledging once or twice that Jacob was doing a "decent job"—and the Pack kept meeting mornings and afternoons during the school week, and they also went to their classes. It was easy to forget about the school part of school, because it felt less real than all the things that were happening in and around it, but classes and homework continued, and Jacob kept up with all of it well enough.

On Friday they went back to Revival, where everything was loud and like a storm but so good. The Pack danced and stomped and Jacob threw his punches in the air. Afterward they walked down to South Street, just up and down the street in the cold, not even going into any shops, until they were too ravenous to hold off any longer.

There was one place—the South Street Diner—where they regularly went and where Jacob was forced to order the Hungry Lady Special instead of the Hungry Man Special because the Lady one had French toast instead of pancakes, and who doesn't prefer French toast? Tammy liked to joke about that, calling him *Hungry Lady*.

On this night, per usual, they came in carrying lots of noise and energy. Jacob was sure that they annoyed the hell out of the waitresses—not to mention the other customers—but he was in such a good mood for the moment that he tried not to think about that. And everybody ordered food, unlike the times when it was eight waters and two orders of fries. So they were legitimate customers.

At the end of all that they retreated to cars, parked a few blocks down into South Philly. Char, Eric, Finn, and Willow went off to Char's car, and Jacob, Tammy, Brian, and Alice headed to the family car that Brian had borrowed. None of it made much sense geographically, but the point was that it made sense couples-wise, because nobody was going home right away.

At first Alice tried to make some conversation from up in the shotgun seat—was Trent Reznor yelling at a girl, or at money, or at God in "Head Like a Hole"?—but it didn't catch on, and soon there was just a lot of making out. Doing that in the same car as another couple could have been strange, and maybe it was, but mainly Jacob was so interested in being with Tammy physically that the strangeness flew off and away pretty fast. They were all covered up in coats because the car was cold even with the engine running, but in the back seat he and Tammy burrowed into each other as far as possible. It was farther than Jacob would have expected. Pretty soon it was like they were fully clothed, but inside those clothes together, bare, or close to it. At one point they pulled apart and they saw that Alice and Brian were eyeing them from the front seats with wide eyes.

But then everybody snuggled back in, and time went by in a delirious spin; Jacob couldn't say how long they were there, but a lot happened. Tammy was right about being creative.

After a while, Brian drove them home. First Alice, who was right nearby, and then Jacob. By the time they got to West Philly, Tammy was actually asleep on Jacob's shoulder. They had stayed in the back seat, leaving Brian up front like a chauffeur.

In front of Jacob's house, before Jacob woke Tammy up to say goodbye, Brian said, "You two are really…intense."

"What? What do you mean?"

Brian shook his head. "Individually, you're intense. But then together…."

Jacob felt a flush go through his face. "I dunno," he said.

"You really are."

"Okay," Jacob said.

"Okay."

They got quiet for a minute, and then Jacob woke Tammy. Outside the car he kissed her, kind of self-consciously this time, and went up his stairs as the car drove off.

His mother was waiting up for him, like she usually did. "It's 12:30," she said. She was sitting in the living room in her night-gown, just one table lamp on. The TV was off and she didn't have a book in her lap.

"I'm sorry," Jacob said.

"I just can't wait for the days to start getting longer again," she said, looking out the window at the dark. "And for your sister to come home. Of course, then you're both going to leave and go to your father's." She got up and went up the stairs as Jacob tried to figure out what to say.

That Sunday Jacob and Tammy did their shopping date. Jacob had work that afternoon on Antiques Row, so they met in Center City at The Gallery, which was a mall that was mostly underground. Jacob hadn't been there since he'd bought that shirt and jeans for the party at Eric's house. It was unbelievable how much had happened since then.

"This is so different from the suburban ones," Tammy said, as they walked hand in hand down the corridor between all the shops and all the people. "It's darker," she said. "And more city."

There were not this many Black people at suburban malls, Jacob was willing to bet. For that matter, there were not this many Black people at the shops they went to on South Street either. Philadelphia was one city, but with a whole lot of different parts. Everywhere, different parts.

They looked in store after store, looking at possibilities for White Elephant gifts—ridiculous hats that were mostly too expensive and thick books about economics and ugly reading glasses and so on. At times they got a little handsy with each other, and then they'd go back to shopping.

Eventually they ended up in a place that mostly sold joke gifts, and where the jokes got more sexual toward the back. Like an apron for grilling that read *Want to try my meat?* Tammy said, "I am *definitely* getting *that*," and slung it over her shoulder. And there were drinking glasses with nude drawings on them, a couple of sex-oriented board games, and T-shirts that said things like *Hangin' and Bangin'* and *Don't Mess with PMS*. Jacob held up a little plastic box—the kind you might keep jewelry in—and he said, "I don't get this one." It had a picture of a rainbow on it, and on top of the rainbow was a red heart. "It seems innocent."

Tammy studied it for a second. "Rainbow with a heart on," she said.

Jacob heard it when she said it aloud. "Rainbow with a *hard-on?*" he said. "This poor, innocent rainbow? Wow. Sold."

By the time they left the store, they had gotten everything they needed—Jacob already had a werewolf back scratcher from an earlier shop—and they were both feeling a little heated up from the sexy gag stuff they had just seen, goofy as it was.

"That place was hilarious," Tammy said.

"Completely," Jacob said.

And in a minute they were in the part of the mall that was connected to the Market East train station, mashed up against each other and a wall. Everything hands and bodies, and especially hands, and especially bodies.

"Jesus," Jacob eventually said, pulling apart for a second.

"No, I'm Tammy," she said, putting a hand on her chest. "Easy mistake. But I thought you weren't into that guy."

"Is there somewhere we can go? Your house? My house?"

Tammy shook her head. "No time." And she pulled him back in.

"Here." Jacob took them over to a corner that was a little more secluded, behind a pillar. And then they went back to it. There were people around, but not that close, and on their way to other places. Every once in a while, Jacob would say something like "There's gotta be *somewhere* we can go," and Tammy would say something like "Shut up," but otherwise they focused on doing everything they could where they were.

At one point Tammy's hand was in Jacob's pants and his hand was in her pants—and pretty soon he was cumming into her hand. And his underpants.

Tammy pulled a few inches back from him, some mix of scandal and delight on her face. "You didn't," she said, extracting her hand and balling it closed. They had gone this far a few times, but never out in public. Not even in that dark car with Brian and Alice. "Now we're going to need napkins."

Jacob was in a state of shock himself, in the way he always was after cumming. It was like *Is this the world? This is the world?*

There they were in a corner of Market East, both of them panting. Tammy dug one-handed into her purse for tissues.

"Thanks?" Jacob said.

"Oh God," Tammy said.

Jacob got to work slightly late, in his now-uncomfortable underpants. Tammy dropped him off on the corner with a little kiss and the words "I guess that was your Christmas bonus," before getting on her bike, which she had walked along with them on the sidewalk, and riding away.

In the store Jacob said, "Hey, Mr. Bocek," maybe louder and more cheerful than he'd intended.

Mr. Bocek, who had been putting some picture frames on a display shelf, nodded at him suspiciously.

Jacob ratcheted down the cheer. "I'll head to the back," he said.

Soon enough he settled into the work. For sure Jacob was glad he had a job, with all of this gift-giving. And it was a quiet and peaceful job, almost like meditating or something, crumpling up the newspapers and tucking them around whatever semi-antique thing had to go out in the mail from Mr. Bocek's shop. Maybe it was a lamp where the base was a ceramic Dalmatian, or maybe it was a clock with a glass front, or maybe an old doll with a porcelain face. Whatever it was, it was Jacob's job to make sure it had all the right padding around it—the right amount, crumpled correctly, put in the right way—to get wherever it was going safely. These things got shipped all over the country.

He didn't even let his thoughts wander to anyplace bad.

In no time Jacob's hands were smeared with newsprint again, and it was sort of like a nicer version of the pony-track smell—a tangible proof that Jacob was working.

Around closing, Mr. Bocek caught Jacob smiling into a box that he was packing, and said, "You like this work, don't you?" His voice wasn't as gruff as usual. More like surprised.

Jacob was startled by the suddenness of the question, but he said, "Yeah. I guess I do." He held up his newsprinted hands.

Mt. Bocek nodded. "If only *my* kids liked getting their hands dirty." His voice was back to normal.

Still, somehow Jacob found himself asking a question he hadn't been expecting to ask. "Mr. Bocek," he said, "what do you think I should get your daughter for…for Christmas?"

Mr. Bocek looked over at Jacob sharply, as though looking for a trick. And then he looked again at Jacob's dirty hands and back at Jacob's face. His own features softened a little. "You like my girl," he said, crossing his arms over his chest. One of his forearm tattoos was of a wolf.

Jacob smiled. "I do," he said. "She's great."

Mr. Bocek nodded thoughtfully. He nodded for a while. Finally, "Could be worse," he said. And then he went back to his own work in the back room—sorting through some items that he had just received in the mail himself—without answering the question. Or at least not right away. After a minute, once Jacob had decided that the conversation had ended, Mr. Bocek spoke up again. "I'm no good with gifts," he said. "I always just get her whatever she asks for."

"Huh," Jacob said. "Thanks, Mr. Bocek."

Mr. Bocek shrugged his big shoulders.

When Jacob got home, he found a note from his mother on the dining room table. She had gone off to work herself for an extra shift. The note said only *Call Brian*. Which was not a note Jacob usually got; they talked on the phone sometimes, but it was never a *Call me* kind of situation.

"Hey—what's up, man?" Jacob said when Brian picked up. "You go shopping today too?" He looked out his window at the block that was already dark. The sun had gone down before five o'clock that day.

"No," Brian said, and even in that one word Jacob could hear that something was off.

"What is it?"

"Alice…Alice and I broke up today," Brian said.

"*What?*" It felt like an electric shock had gone through Jacob's chest.

"Yeah," he said. "Today."

"But—" Jacob's heart and mind were going fast. He knew this wasn't about him but it immediately felt like it was *in* him. Like a crack.

Brian was saying more things. Jacob was trying to listen. He looked at Spark Park across the street, or tried to. His heart and mind were going very fast.

Jacob called Tammy as soon as he was off the phone with Brian. Well, after a few minutes of sitting and thinking about everything feverishly.

"Hello?" she answered.

"Hey," Jacob said. "Listen—have you heard about Brian and Alice?"

She sighed. "Yeah."

"It's crazy, right?" Brian hadn't really been able to explain what happened. Just something about it *not working out.*

"I dunno. Alice has had some questions for a while."

"Wait," Jacob said. "You knew about this?"

"Well, I knew a little."

"Why didn't you tell me?"

"I don't tell you *everything,*" she said. "This was a girl thing."

I don't tell you everything echoed in Jacob's head some. "I think we *should* tell each other everything." His eyes roamed nervously around his room, like a person looking for a life preserver, landing on the mostly blank walls, which used to have that kid stuff on them—dragons and sci-fi—and which hadn't been fully replaced by things that reflected his current world. One wall had caution tape stuck to it in the shape of an X—the Pack had seen it flapping over a hole in a lot next to South Street one time, and he had grabbed it. So that was the main new decoration. And otherwise there was a fair amount of blankness.

"Some things are private," she said.

Jacob tried not to think about that. "What's going to happen now?" he said.

"What do you mean? They're going to stop dating."

"I don't know what I mean."

"Well, Alice told me they're going to try to stay friends," Tammy said.

"Huh," Jacob said. "Brian didn't mention anything about that."

"I guess we'll see how it goes."

"How come you don't sound more upset about this?"

"I *am* upset, obviously. But like I said, I'm not totally surprised."

Jacob got up and went over to a poster of the Beatles that had survived his burst of tearing things down. But why had it? Why did he have a poster of the Beatles up?

"What does this mean for the Pack?"

"I don't know," Tammy said. Her voice was more sober. "Hopefully nothing."

"*Hopefully?*" Jacob said, his own voice going higher and a little wilder. "What does that mean, *hopefully?*"

"Jacob, you're doing it again," she said. "You're worrying about something that isn't even happening. It's not a great situation, but we just have to wait and see."

"How do you know it's not happening?"

"How do you know it *is*? Because you're crazy," Tammy said.

Jacob just stood there with the phone against his ear.

"I'm kidding," Tammy said after a while.

18

The next morning, Monday morning, Eric was on the subway-surface car in the usual way—they talked about the break-up, mainly—but half of Jacob's mind was caught up in wondering who would show up in the hallway for settling-in. And he was thinking about one other thing that had occurred to him overnight: had he had anything to do with this? That time when he called Alice's parents pretending to be Char's father? Had something come out about that? He was afraid to even bring it up with Eric, but it was on his mind.

Meanwhile, Eric seemed worried too, about what this meant for the Pack, but he kept saying things like, "I'm just going to hope for the best," and "Probably it'll all work itself out," and so on.

Hope, Jacob thought. *What even* is *that?* All he could feel was that weight building, pulling him down.

The settling-in time turned out sort of like the Monday after the original party. First it was Eric and Jacob, alone. Then Brian showed up with his small wave and his "hi, guys." And Finn right after. They talked about the situation with Alice very briefly and then they didn't talk about it anymore. And they waited to see what would happen.

It wasn't long before the girls showed up—all four of them. Seeing them, it was like Jacob was released, abruptly free to lunge toward the surface of the pool. *Maybe it's going to work itself out*, he said to himself as they came down the hall. *Tammy's right that I'm crazy.* He almost jumped to his feet in excitement. But then Brian got up instead and said, "You know, actually, I don't think I can do this after all." And he started to walk off. But he had to pass the girls to do it, and Alice said to him, "You don't have to go. I can go."

"You don't have to," Brian said. "I will." And he did leave.

Everybody was standing now. "Damn," Finn said.

"You know," Alice said, "I think I'm going to go too." And before anybody could stop her, she was gone, back the way she'd come.

"Stay here," Char told everyone else. "With all of us, it's just too much attention on her." And then she went off after Alice.

Jacob was feeling each leaving person, right in his body. He could feel his whole body sinking.

"Okay, I'm gonna be right back," Tammy said, not seeing that Jacob had just reached for her hand.

"I'll come with you," he said, desperate.

She put her hand up like a crossing guard. "No. Alice really does hate all the focus on her. It would be too much. I'll come back."

But she didn't come back. Instead it was just Eric, Jacob, Finn, and Willow, and Finn and Willow were wrapped up in each other. For a while she was snuggled up into him like into a blanket, and then he tried to restart conversation by backhanding Jacob's arm and saying, "Shit. Girls suck, huh?" And that started a fight between him and Willow that pretty fast sent them off down the hall to finish it.

Jacob sat with Eric. They talked a little. Eric was doing the stiff-upper-lip thing. "Char'll cool it all down," he said. But Jacob was thinking about what his life had been like before the Pack. He knew this wasn't about him, no more than the shrinking light of the season was about him. Still he couldn't shake what was *in* him. The really bad nights—and days—the idea of going back to that, to the full-on drowning that he'd been trying to ignore—the feeling was a mix of fear and thick, certain dread, and it had started to fill his chest.

Jacob missed the next day of school. He just couldn't go. He slept instead. According to his mother, he got some phone calls from his friends that night.

She made him go to school on Wednesday; his mother basically had a one-personal-day policy. "You have to shrug it off," she said.

And so he went in, meeting up with Eric on the subway-surface, giving an "under the weather" excuse. And Eric said, "Nobody's really hanging out before or after school. Like, we'll probably see Char, and Tammy, I bet. But I think the idea is that people are still figuring out how things are gonna be. Everybody's working it out."

"Okay," Jacob said, watching the concrete walls go by the window. He didn't know why he was out of bed. Either way he was under water.

When they got to school, Char and Tammy were there. "Where'd you go?" Tammy said.

"I don't know," Jacob said.

The rest of that week people mostly got to school later and left earlier, and there was no settling in or settling out. Jacob used the extra afternoon time to buy gifts. Hanukkah was coming, in terms of his family, and there was Tammy, too, even if, or especially because, things felt so fragile between him and her right now. Every sarcastic or exasperated comment from Tammy sounded like *It's not working out* to Jacob's ears.

The family stuff came together in a couple of days. Fairly mechanically, he bought a tie for his father, a New Order tape for his sister—she had said she liked them when she overheard him playing *Technique* during Thanksgiving break—and some new slippers for his mother. Her current ones were really ratty. And, also for his mother, he went in with Deanna on a new bathrobe. The current bathrobe was ratty too.

Jacob hoped everybody would like their gifts, even if he was buying them like a robot.

A bunch of times that week he thought about calling Brian or Alice. A better person would have, he knew. But whenever he thought about it, he would look at the phone and it seemed like the phone was going to weigh a hundred thousand pounds.

He saw each of them at school, individually in classes or the hallway, but he didn't know what to say then either.

He also wasn't sure what to say when he ran into Mike Berman and other folks from the Tribe one day just after last period.

"Hey, Wassermann," Mike said. As usual, Jacob couldn't tell whether his tone was friendly or not friendly. "How come I can't find the Pack around anywhere?"

"Hibernation season," Jacob said without even really meaning to. Auto-joke. They laughed.

"Okay," he said, running a hand backward through his hair. "But can you spread a message?"

"A message?"

"Yeah. We're having a party on Saturday the 23rd. Like nine o'clock."

"Okay," Jacob said. It occurred to him on some level that a few months ago he would have been astounded to get an invite like this; this was definitely a "cool" party. But all he could really focus on was that it was really something—here was this group, humming right along with nothing wrong.

"It's at Jessica's house," Leah said, pointing at Jessica—who gave a finger-twinkle hello, her turquoise bracelets bright—and then she said the address. "Her parents are going to be away overnight."

"Yeah," Mike said. He put a hand on Jacob's shoulder. "So we should probably warn you delicate types that this is going to be more of an aaa-dult party." Whether his hand was meant to be friendly or not, Jacob felt a surge of anger, of wanting to shove Mike off him.

"I don't know," Noah put in. "Sounds like they got pretty *adult* at Char's house." Laughter.

"Well, I mean beverages," Mike said. "Okay, Wass?"

Mike let go of Jacob's shoulder just before the urge to shove became irresistible, and the group turned to go. Jessica called out the address one more time.

"Spread the word," Leah said, giving Jacob a little wave before she went. Her nails were silver and they flashed.

Jacob did not spread the word.

Later that week when work at Mr. Bocek's store was done, before Jacob went home, he spent a few minutes looking in the jewelry cases just to get a sense of what things cost, at least in an antique store. Thinking about a gift for Tammy was a little less robotic than looking for something for his family; it felt more like hope. So he checked the cases out. Necklaces, earrings, bracelets. He even looked at rings, though that seemed like a pretty big move. Mr. Bocek had some stuff that looked very old-fashioned, like the kind of thing one of his grandmothers would have. But there were also simpler things, like this one silver necklace that looked like a chain but with thin, circular links about as wide as a dime, or like these earrings that dangled down gold threads, or one bracelet which was just a simple silver cuff. In any case, everything was pretty expensive. But maybe there were cheaper versions of these kinds of things somewhere.

"What you looking for?" Mr. Bocek's voice came unexpectedly behind him, making Jacob jump a little. For such a big, grumbly guy, he moved like a deer in the damn woods.

"Oh, nothing," Jacob said. "Just looking."

But Mr. Bocek was sort of staring him down, as though searching inside Jacob through Jacob's eyes. The man's big mustache twitched. "You're going to get something for my daughter for Christmas," he said evenly. Jacob couldn't tell whether it was said in curiosity or anger or possibly rage.

"Well. Yeah, I am," Jacob said. "But probably something simple. These are…I mean, they're beautiful."

"And expensive," Mr. Bocek said firmly.

Jacob nodded, a small howl inside. "For sure. Definitely. I'm just looking." He turned back and looked at the necklace with the circular links. He could picture it on Tammy, and in his head it was a nice picture. For whatever that was worth.

"That one," Mr. Bocek agreed. "She would like that one."

Jacob nodded, and then sighed and stood up straight—he'd been bent down to see it better—and said, "Well, when do you want me to come back for more packing?" There was a bit of a holiday rush going on.

"You didn't get paid yet, kid," Mr. Bocek said. There was no pattern to when Mr Bocek paid Jacob—sometimes at the end of one day, sometimes the end of a week, sometimes in the middle of a week. But it was always in cash. The whole thing was under the table. "How many hours do I owe you for?"

Jacob looked up at the ceiling as though to calculate, though he definitely already knew. "Three and a half," he said.

"All right," Mr. Bocek said, nodding. "Take the necklace instead."

Jacob's mouth fell open. For a moment he just stood there like that, but then he could hear Tammy in his head from the first time he met her—*Do we need to remind him to breathe?*—and then he said, "Wait—that's not even close to how much that costs."

Mr. Bocek kind of sneered at the necklace. "I've had it here a while, and it doesn't sell. People don't have any goddamn taste anymore. Just take it."

"Are you—are you sure?" Jacob asked, but Mr. Bocek was already unlocking the case, and then he was putting the necklace in a nice box very delicately with his big hands. And then he was handing it over to Jacob. "I always wanted Tammy to have it, to be honest with you."

Standing for a moment on the sidewalk outside the store, the necklace deep in his backpack for safekeeping, Jacob felt like a thief and like a hero and like he wanted to cry, but in a nice way.

That Friday the Pack didn't go to South Street or Revival. They did couples dates, each one separate. There *was* no Pack, maybe.

Jacob felt like staying home and burying himself in television and video games and trying not to feel things, but instead he and Tammy saw a movie—*Glory*. Which was not an upbeat choice of movie, unfortunately, in spite of the title. It was about the Civil War, and a group of Black soldiers who were fighting for the Union, but really it was about how unbelievably, astronomically fucked up slavery and racism were. There was a scene where Denzel Washington was being punished for a military infraction that wasn't completely his fault, and the punishment was whipping. So they were whipping him, but he already had all these whipping scars on his back from when he was a slave, and Matthew Broderick, who was in charge, watched it happen. Ferris Bueller! By that stage of the movie, Jacob couldn't take it anymore. He turned to Tammy and said, "I've gotta go." Matthew Broderick tried to make things right for the soldiers, but could you really make something like that right? How could you take *anything* wrong and make it right?

"What? Are you serious?" she said.

"Yeah. I've gotta go," he said.

"Are you okay?"

Jacob shrugged, his fists clenched.

"You need to go?"

He shrugged again.

"Okay—we'll go," she decided, and she led him out of there and into the lobby. They stood near a wall of movie posters. "Jake, what can I do?" she said.

"I don't know," he said, everything in him tight, everything straining, his face damp with sweat. Drowning.

"I don't either," she said. "I really don't know what to do." And they stood there together, waiting.

19

Deanna got home from school Friday night while Jacob was out seeing *Glory*, and then she went out, too, so that by the time he got home, earlier than expected, she was gone. But their mother was excited, or at least agitated. She had cleaned up the living room, dining room, and kitchen—the whole first floor—and had even gotten out the family menorah a week early. It was gold-colored, but of course not actual gold. "Everybody's here," she said, even though Deanna was out. "How was your night? You're home early."

"Fine," Jacob said. Although he felt a little numb, he pointed at the dining room table. "This is clean enough to *eat* off."

"Oh, get out of here," she said, but with a proud and nervous smile.

He saw Deanna the next morning—or, really, it was noon by the time he was up. He found his sister downstairs reading a newspaper at the dining room table. She had an old pair of her glasses on, instead of the usual contact lenses. And she was wearing a Cornell sweatshirt, of course.

"Hey!" she said. She jumped up for a hug. Then, when she pulled back, she said, "What's wrong?" as though his hug had delivered an accidental distress call.

"Where's Mom?" he said.

"Grocery shopping, I think." For some reason that made him sadder. His mom always had *some* chore or work that she had to do. Why didn't *he* do more? Deanna led him to a chair. "What's wrong?"

Jacob rubbed his face. "Nothing. Well, my friend group is falling apart."

"Falling apart? I bet it's not falling apart." Deanna sat down across from him.

So he told her about the breakup and people not hanging

out in the mornings or afternoons, and the individual couples dates instead of everyone being together.

"Wow," Deanna said. "That's hard. How are you doing with it?"

"Not great," he said. "I've been down." He left out the part of the weird fit at the movies.

"Oh well," she said, "you know, maybe it's not as bad as it looks. Like, breakups happen. It just means everyone has to adjust. I'm sure it's going to sort itself out."

"I dunno," Jacob said. This wasn't how he wanted to be greeting his sister, but he couldn't seem to control it.

"But you and Tammy are okay?"

"I guess." He shrugged. "But who knows, right?"

"Now, come on."

"Deanna," he said. "Do you ever feel like the whole world is underwater? Like...like you're drowning?"

"Oh, Jacob—that's just normal teenager stuff."

He shook his head. "There isn't anything normal about me."

Deanna leaned forward over the table and reached like she would have taken his hands, but they were under the table. So she just put her hands on the placemat. "Jacob," she said.

He looked her in the eyes.

"You're doing it. That thing you do. Trust me that this is all normal teenager stuff and it's going to pass and you don't have anything to be sad about."

"Then...why am I so sad?" He started to tear up, just a little, halfway through the question.

Now Deanna came around to his side of the table and pulled a chair close so that she could put her arms around him. "I don't know," she said. "I wish I had taken psychology. But I think you're just kind of depressed right now."

Depressed. What did that mean? Wasn't that just another word for the same thing?

They sat there for a minute, him getting his tears under control and her holding him. And then she said, "But you've been so good this year, it seems like."

Jacob nodded. It was true. "I had these friends."

She rolled her eyes. He wasn't even looking at her and he could tell that she had rolled her eyes. "You *have* these friends," she said. "But I think it was more than that, anyway. It can't just be friends. That'd be like a Band-Aid. Don't you think it was *you*? Like, *you* changed?"

"I dunno."

"I think you have to get on top of this," Deanna said, letting go to look at him. "Be the person who *isn't* depressed."

Jacob straightened up a little. "What—like don't worry, be happy?"

"I don't know," his sister said. "Just be the person you've been lately. He's still here, isn't he?"

Jacob thought, *What did it mean to be a certain kind of person?* He thought about Revival, which is where his life really started to get good. He thought about kissing Tammy there for the first time, and other times. He thought about the storm cloud. He thought about people who were angry instead of sad. About there being better ways into darkness.

Be the person who isn't depressed.

That afternoon the family went to the movies—a comedy this time, called *Blaze*. It went down a lot easier for Jacob. Well, it was uncomfortable because it was about a stripper—"I didn't really know what this was about," their mother whispered in embarrassment at one point—but it wasn't *sad*. There were so many possible feelings. In any case, Jacob was somewhat distracted, chewing on how he could be the person who wasn't depressed. It seemed to him, after what Deanna said, that maybe he had a choice about it. That maybe it was about choices.

That night he called Eric.

"I think we really need to get everyone together," he said. "Do you know if Brian and Alice are planning to come to the White Elephant party on Friday?"

"I don't know anything," Eric said. "Char was even thinking

we shouldn't have the party. The soiree. Like maybe we wait until winter break is over and see where everything is then."

"She wants to cancel the party?"

"I dunno," Eric said. "It's not a bad idea, right? Just let everything cool off? I think that'll make it easier for things to get back to normal after."

"I think it's a *terrible* idea," Jacob said, and then he just hung up.

After a few seconds he called Eric back and apologized—Eric seemed more confused than anything—and got off the phone with a regular *goodbye.*

When Jacob called Tammy, she said more or less the same thing Eric had, but she also quickly turned the focus back on Jacob. "You can't get so worked up about this," she said. "It's not helping."

His voice got a little loud. "I just don't understand why I'm the only person who cares that the Pack is falling apart."

"What? The only person? What? Of course I would care if I thought that was happening, but I think we're just in a rough patch. Temporary. Nothing has to fall apart, Jake," she said, snapping, "except maybe you."

"What?"

"I just can't deal with you right now," she said. "I have to go."

"Wait—are you—?" He felt himself panicking.

"I'm not doing anything," she said, snapping again. "I'm just saying I can't deal with you right now. Get yourself together and I'll see you tomorrow."

After they both hung up, Jacob sat on the bed in his room, getting angrier and angrier, thinking that this *was* him together.

Without a doubt Jacob was off, going into the week. He alternated between that bottom-of-the-pool feeling and a feverish, flailing state of thought where he was either trying to come up with solutions or picking at himself—he was being crazy, obnoxious, totally self-absorbed, but how was he supposed to be the person who *wasn't* depressed? On the subway with the wall blurring past, in the press of people in the Central hallway, in classes—drowned or trying to flail his way to the surface. In Monday's history class Mr. Nowacki had to wave his hand to get Jacob's attention. "Earth to Mr. Wasserman," he said. And then: "*Somebody* really needs Christmas break." Jacob felt Eric's eyes on him from the next seat over. But he didn't correct Mr. Nowacki, didn't tell him he should be saying *Winter* break. Because why did that even matter?

Break *was* coming, and Jacob was going to be spending a lot of it in Chicago with Deanna and their father. He tried to picture it but couldn't, even though he'd been to Chicago to visit his father plenty of times. In his mind he just saw snow and ice.

Philadelphia, meanwhile, was itself plenty cold. That afternoon he got off the Broad Street Line at South Street so he could go to Mystic Market before work, and the wind was hard all down the street. He was wearing an old military jacket he'd gotten at a thrift shop back in November for practically nothing, and ever since, with how the wind ripped right through the jacket, he understood why.

In Mystic Market, Jacob stood a long time in front of the "Possible Happiness Syrup." He remembered the first time they'd been here, how fun it had all been. Tammy and the supposed monkey paw. He had seen her in school today, and they had kissed hello and talked for a few minutes, but the whole thing had been basically weird. He felt like he was listening to her from a long way off—like she was talking to him from above water—and everything she said made him a mix of sad and annoyed. Now, he stood in front of a shelf full of bottles, staring at Possible Happiness Syrup.

That name—did it mean that the syrup possibly gave you happiness? Or that it did give you happiness, but not some amazing kind—just whatever was even possible for you? Which in Jacob's case, what would that be?

"Are you going to buy anything?" the guy said.

"Does this work?"

Without even looking to see which one Jacob was talking about, the guy said, "Possibly."

Jacob bought it.

He bought it, but he didn't try it—not yet. The idea was scary, honestly, opening this bottle and drinking whatever was inside just on faith and hope. Instead, he put it on the window-sill next to his bed that night. *In case of emergency, break glass*, he thought.

But Tuesday and Wednesday were, of course, no better. On both days he got a late start—he was having a little trouble getting out of bed—and, after getting dressed with Nine Inch Nails playing on his old boom box and swallowing some cereal, he went off to Baltimore Avenue to the subway-surface car and found nobody there that he knew. It was the same on the Broad Street Line. He knew some people by sight—some folks even waved hello—but nobody he knew *well*. Of course, did you ever know anybody *well*? He remembered what it had been like when everybody was mad at him because of Willow and how Eric had stopped riding with him to and from school. Ridiculous.

He saw Tammy between classes once and he said, "Let's get together this weekend to exchange gifts." And she said, "Okay," and he didn't know if she felt weird about it—probably—but he had this necklace and he was going to give it to her, because maybe that was part of a solution.

Otherwise those two days were more drowned than flailing.

Wednesday afternoon he was on his own again going home—his schedule and Eric's were off somehow, or maybe Eric was with Char. For all Jacob knew, *all* of them were somewhere else, together, without him.

He spotted Leron and the guys on the same subway car, and Leron saw him too. Jacob looked away. What was the point? His eyes landed on an ad for SEPTA—the public transportation company that ran the subway and all the buses and everything. Jacob and his friends had joked about these ads before; the words on the poster said, *We're Getting There*. They actually said that.

At home, after telling Deanna he didn't feel like talking, he decided this was an emergency, and he opened the bottle from Mystic Market. It smelled like cut grass, sort of, and a little bitter, and it tasted pretty much the same, except more extreme, and worse.

There was some throwing up that evening.

In a way, Jacob's mood did shift. While he was vomiting and his mother and sister were standing over him asking questions that he left unanswered, he decided that he was really, really tired of this whole thing. And that it was on him to do something about it.

Once his stomach had calmed down, Jacob made some calls. He told Eric and Tammy and Char and Brian the deal, and told them to spread the word. The deal was that everyone in the Pack—everyone—was going to meet after school the next day. Jacob had something to say.

20

Shortest day of the year," Jacob's mother commented, mostly to herself, the next morning. She was sitting at the breakfast table with her coffee. "We just have to get through today. After that, more and more light."

Okay, Jacob thought to himself. *Just today.*

"Dude, what's this going to be about, this afternoon?" Eric said to Jacob during history.

"Wait and see," Jacob said.

Jacob didn't really know himself what was going to happen. He just knew everybody had to be together.

He also knew that today he was only flailing inside, not drowning at all. It was an improvement. Deanna was right that the key was *him*, *him* being different, *him* not just waiting for things to happen but making them happen. He was different than he used to be—better—and he had to remember that.

After school, everybody did show up. They weren't sitting when Jacob got there—they were standing, some with arms folded, coats and bags ready at their feet—but they were *there*, all of them. Around them was the traffic of kids preparing to go home.

"Great," Jacob said, clapping his hands together.

"So…what's up?" Tammy said.

She didn't come up next to him. They were all standing there like an audience. Couples weren't in couples formation, maybe because of Brian and Alice, one of whom was on one side of the group, and the other on the other. Still—everyone was together. It was *energizing*.

Jacob started with the first thing on his mind. "We need to go ahead and have the White Elephant party. All eight of us."

Char shook her head. "Can't we just let that go? It's not that important."

"No," Jacob said. "We can't."

"It's not a good time to try put everyone in the same room together," Char said.

"We're together in this hallway," Jacob said, gesturing around them.

"You guys should do it," Brian said. *You* guys.

"Right," Alice said, together with Brian in being separate.

Jacob's mind was moving fast, as it had been all day. "No. No. Wait. Listen—okay—never mind the party for now. I've got it. I've got it. Everybody come with me."

"Come with you?" Finn said. "Like in *Terminator*?"

But Jacob only said, "Come on," and he walked down the hall with everyone trailing behind him. He took them down the stairs and along the main hall to the exit.

Tammy caught up with him. "Seriously. Where are we going?"

He wanted to put his arm around her—having a sense of purpose was making him feel a lot better, like he was streaking for the surface—but he held back because he knew Alice and Brian were behind him. "Wait and see," he said. "A magician and his secrets, you know."

Tammy fell back with the rest.

Outside the school, he kept going, right down to the intersection. Eric tugged on his arm. "What are you doing?" he said. It was very cold outside.

Jacob told him, and himself, "I know what I'm doing."

He led them up Olney Avenue, mixed in with other kids going home, the air sharp, his head clear except for a single image. Or a set of images, really, one flashing into the next—but all of the same place.

At the entrance to the subway at Ogontz and Olney, the group surrounded him. Other kids from Central went past them into the entrance, while some other kids he didn't recognize, maybe from the neighborhood, were hanging out nearby.

"Listen," Char said. Her breath came out in clouds. "That's enough. What are we doing here?"

"Field trip," Jacob said.

"Fern Rock," Alice said. "He wants to take us to Fern Rock."

That took Jacob by surprise—how did she even remember?—but he recovered enough to say, "It'll only take a few minutes. It's the next stop north."

Some of them looked confused—Brian, Willow, and Char clearly didn't know what this was about—and the confusion kept everybody anchored in place, until Char said, "Are we talking about, what, a *subway stop?*" She looked down at her new denim trench coat with the white furry lining as if to say, *I'm not bringing this on a subway.*

"I kinda want to check it out," Finn said with a shrug, and Willow moved in close to him, her eyes wide.

Then Brian said, "I really—I really have to go. I'm sorry, Jake. Maybe I'll go with you when school starts up again. Everyone else can go ahead now."

"What's the point, Jake?" Eric said, standing behind Char now.

Jacob looked a little desperately at Tammy. "Jake," she said. It sounded like *please.*

The whole thing was pulling apart—with a little wave, Brian was already on his way down the street, and Char turned to follow him. Eric started to walk, backward, in the same direction, shrugging an apology at Jacob.

Alice stepped up. She said, with her precise little mouth in her very serious face, "I'm going to get on the subway to go home. You should come and do the same thing. It's just North Philadelphia up there, I'm sure. It's just more city." She held his gaze for a few seconds. When he didn't say anything back, she sighed and stepped past him.

Which left Jacob, Tammy, Willow, and Finn on the street corner in the midst of a North Philly desert and a winter wind.

Something burst in Jacob. He began to shout—at Alice, who was gone, at Eric and Char and Brian on their way down the block. "Go!" he yelled, his breath steaming. "*Go!* Just *go!*"

From nearby, one of the hanging-out kids laughed harshly, probably at Jacob.

Jacob stared at the kid and his friends. They were maybe a little younger than Jacob, but there were four of them. Another group, intact and fine.

The kid said something else to his friends, and they all laughed.

Jacob was over there and in the kid's face before his brain had time to work through the situation. "Something funny?"

The kid, who had been leaning against the wall in his puffy blue jacket, was now upright, and right back in Jacob's face. All of them were fully upright, and really close. Jacob could feel that he'd crossed a line. It felt fantastic. "You better step back," the kid said. His breath smelled like watermelon Now & Laters.

"Whoa," came Finn's voice from nearby and far away at the same time.

And Tammy's: "*Jake!*" she said, loud.

"Make me," Jacob said, to the kid, to Tammy, to everyone on earth. His head was clear of the water. And then he shoved the kid, hard, sending him back against the wall. Jacob could hear the knock of his head against the bricks.

"*Jake!*" Tammy screamed. Willow screamed, too, but just a sound.

The kid pulled up off the wall, touching the back of his head once and then coming at Jacob. Who threw one of the punches he'd been rehearsing at Revival. Made contact, and knocked the kid aside. But then the kid's friends got into it and the fight got away from Jacob. A fist to his face, another one, one to his stomach, strobe of light and darkness and back again. Fast, Jacob was down on one knee. People everywhere around him, shoving. And now he could hear Finn right in there among all the bodies, saying, "Whoa, whoa, take it easy, man—he's just having—*whoa*—he's just having a shitty day, okay? Come *on*!"

Jacob didn't feel the pain of it yet. He was staring at a gum spot on the concrete. You couldn't tell what flavor it had been—it was gray now.

After Finn had calmed things—his punk look seemed to throw the kids—and hustled the remnants of the Pack all down into the subway, Tammy tore into Jacob. There was "Are you crazy?" and "What's wrong with you?" and "Jesus, Jake!" and so on like that, and eventually she said, "Just go home," and she sort of shoved him away from her. Jacob stood where she'd shoved him, almost inert now, as she said to Willow, "Let's go see if we can catch Char for a ride." Willow glanced at Jacob, her eyes extra-wide with alarm. And Finn gave him an *I'm sorry* face and told the girls, "I'll walk you, just in case," because they were going to have to go past the hanging-out kids again. Willow nodded and they went to the stairs.

Tammy didn't even look back.

21

At home, Deanna's mouth dropped open. She jumped off her bed, where she had been reading. "Jacob!" Her hand went toward his face automatically but stopped short. "What happened to you?"

"Fight," Jacob said. His face really hurt now—it was worst under his left eye and his jaw, especially on the right side.

"*Fight*? Who are you *fighting*? Oh, when Mom sees this—"

"It was a group of guys," Jacob said, touching his own cheek. Very tender.

"A *group*? Are you *insane*?"

"That seems to be the question," he said. Outside Deanna's window he could see the sun was very low.

His mother, when she got home, did have a big reaction. Her whole face went over to horror at his black eye and bruised jaw. She dropped her purse on the living room floor, more or less wailing, "My baby! Who did this to you? Who did this to you?" She crushed him in her arms. Jacob looked at the purse on the floor. It hadn't spilled, because they lived in West Philly and his mother knew better than to leave her purse unzipped. Instead it just sat there waiting to be picked up.

Jacob, with his mother's permission, skipped the next day of school. It was the last one before break anyway; it didn't seem like there was any point. And he had told her more or less what had happened, so she thought a personal day was a good idea.

By the time Jacob woke up, she had left for work, and there was a note on the floor outside his door. It said *Tonight is Hanukkah*. Which he knew, though he didn't really have any feelings about it.

In the bathroom mirror Jacob surveyed the damage. There was a red half-circle of angry flesh under his left eye, and his jawline was a little discolored too. It all hurt, along with a stiffness in his abdomen. These things were like souvenirs from a trip Jacob didn't understand.

Eric had called the night before, but Jacob told his mother to take a message. The message had been *Call me*. Which Jacob didn't.

Deanna came to the bathroom door. "How are you feeling?" she said.

Jacob laughed a cynical breath-laugh.

"Well, it doesn't look *too* bad," she said, wincing a little.

The two of them spent the day in the living room, watching TV, whatever came on, and not talking about anything significant. Every once in a while, a person on a game show or a character on a soap opera would do something ridiculous, and they'd comment on that, but otherwise they just watched. He wasn't exactly drowning, and he wasn't exactly not.

That night they lit the menorah in the living room window. "Your uncle reminded me that we start with one candle and put them in right to left, but light them left to right," she said. Then she looked up and moved her hands like she was counting or moving objects around. "Yes. That's right," she said.

"I forget every year," Deanna said.

They were both trying very hard to make this cheerful.

"Oh—and we say the blessing *after* we light the helper candle"—their mother pointed—"but *before* we light the other ones."

"What do the blessings mean?" Jacob asked dully. He sort of remembered, but mostly didn't.

"Basically thanking God, or whatever," their mother said, waving her hand vaguely in the air. "Something bigger than ourselves."

Something bigger than ourselves, Jacob repeated to himself in his head. *Something bigger than ourselves*.

"Okay—hair back," she said, and she and Deanna tied their hair back to keep it from any flames. Jacob was a little shaggy himself—no haircut since the beginning of the fall—but no-where near a ponytail yet.

So they lit the helper candle and said the blessings—their mother basically did that—and then lit the one candle for the first night. "It gets nice when there are more of them," their mother said, and then got teary. "I wish you were going to *be* here." Jacob and Deanna hugged her.

"We're here now," Deanna said.

"Well, I'm just a simulation," Jacob said. It was always easy to go into joking mode when his mother was upset.

She smiled, and touched his face, but then her face crumpled again. "My baby," she said.

When emotions had leveled out, in the light of the two candles they exchanged gifts. Deanna liked the cassette and Jacob liked the 10,000 Maniacs tape she gave him. He'd heard some of it somewhere. Their mother cried a little, happily, about the bathrobe from both of them and the slippers from Jacob and the bath salts from Deanna. "You are so thoughtful," she said.

She, meanwhile, had gone all out. "Well, since we aren't go-ing to have all eight nights, I got big things for tonight instead of little things." She held a warning finger up. "It won't be like this every year." What this meant for Deanna was a very fancy sweater—cashmere, maybe?—that made her gape. And for Jacob it meant, unbelievably, a new boom box with dual cas-sette decks. They put the 10,000 Maniacs tape in and listened to Natalie Merchant singing about eating for two, and how it was okay to trouble her, and other things. "I like this," their mother said. "Not like those Really Long *Nails* you usually listen to." Jacob laughed sincerely; she liked to tease him about Nine Inch Nails, and it was funny.

They sat there for a while in their living room chairs, chat-ting off and on, watching the candles burn down, admiring the gifts they'd received, telling each other where they'd found the ones they'd given and if there had been something funny about the store or the shopkeeper. It was nice, basically, though Jacob found himself thinking about that ridiculous store with the rainbow with a hard-on and everything, and then he thought about what happened afterward in Market East, and feelings of all kinds went through him.

"I should just make a call," he said.

"You don't have plans tonight, do you?" his mother said, her face falling.

"No, no." Of course, he *used* to have plans, but there was no need to bring those up. "I've just gotta make a call."

But Tammy didn't pick up. Nobody at her house did. It rang and rang.

Was she avoiding him? He didn't know if she had caller ID or not.

Jacob went back to the living room and tried very, very hard not to think at all about why nobody had answered.

Nobody answered the next three times he tried her that night, either.

Tammy called him the next morning; his mother woke Jacob up at eleven with the phone in her hand.

"Sorry for waking you," Tammy said, subdued.

"It's okay." He was sitting up in bed, touching his still-tender face.

"How are you doing? Physically?"

"Not too bad. Just kind of bruised."

"Yeah. I bet. Listen—do you want to get together? Exchange gifts or something?"

"You sound mad."

"I am," she said. "But I'm trying to get past it."

Which was possibly nice, but then he thought of something. "Wait—where were you last night?"

"What?"

"I called you last night, and nobody answered."

"Oh," she said. "I dunno. So what do you wanna do? Get together today or tomorrow? You leave on Monday, right?"

"You *dunno*? Were you out or something?" Jacob was squeezing the phone handset.

Tammy let out a big sigh. "Well, we figured you wouldn't be into it, anyway."

Jacob went hot, or cold, or both.

"It was Char's birthday yesterday, remember? So she asked the girls to come over."

"The girls?"

"Yeah—me and Willow and Alice. And, well, you know, fuck it—of course Eric was there. And Willow brought Finn."

Fuck it. "So—everybody but me?"

Tammy's voice was a mix of exhaustion and agitation. "*And* Brian. And it wasn't like that. It was supposed to only be the girls, but it came out like that. And plus with the Christmas thing, I just figured—"

"You did the White Elephant?" Jacob said, rubbing his forehead.

"Sort of."

They sat there in silence for a few moments, as Jacob took it all in. His friendship group was fine, actually. It just didn't include him.

"Jake, I knew you were going to react like this. And you were just so crazy on Thursday I couldn't—"

Jacob cut her off. "I get it," he said, pretty loud. "Fuck all of you." And, before she could say anything, he hung up with enough force that the phone made a *ding* sound. There was no need to remind himself to be angry rather than sad; he was fully angry already.

Deanna knocked at his door. "Who were you just yelling 'fuck you' at?" she said, a worried look on her face.

"Tammy," he said through his teeth.

"Tammy? Oh no."

He ran Deanna through what Tammy had just told him.

"Wow," she said, sitting on his bed with him.

"Yeah," he said.

"Well, you were right. Fuck 'em." A nervous charge passed through him as she said that, but she was right. She continued.

"Who needs those assholes? You have too many eggs in that basket, anyway. You can't have friends from only one group."

Jacob nodded. He did. He did have too many eggs in that basket. And the part of him that sensed a well of sadness ready under the anger groped around for another basket. And then he remembered something.

He remembered that the Tribe was having a party at Jessica's house that night. And that there would be adult beverages there.

"Goddamn right," he said. "Just fuck 'em all right to hell."

22

It took some work to get to Jessica's house. Somehow he remembered the address—that wasn't the issue. The issue was finding it on the map and then getting there, *there* turning out to be Chestnut Hill, a different part from where Char lived, which meant getting to Thirtieth Street Station and taking the R8 train out to the end of the line, and then some walking on top of that. He wrote down all of the instructions.

"*Where* are you going?" his mother asked.

"A party in Chestnut Hill."

"But *not* at Charlotte's?"

"That's right," he said. In his head, he added *goddamn right.*

His mother got lost in looking at his bruised face. And then she said, "Okay. But be careful out there. And be home by curfew," she said, "which is—repeat after me—*midnight.*"

Jacob said, "Which is—repeat after me—midnight." That was actually going to be tight, given the R8 schedule. He'd have to leave the party after an hour. But maybe he could be a little approximate with his curfew.

Then they lit the Hanukkah candles. The living room was slightly brighter—there was a helper candle plus two regular ones now. Jacob thought about how you had to have a good helper candle to really get going. Not a crappy one.

On this night gifts were smaller. "Last night was the big night," their mother said. She had gotten the kids books—the one for Jacob was by an author named P.G. Wodehouse—and Deanna had gotten everybody chocolate, and Jacob, who hadn't planned for more gifts, gave out the ones he'd gotten for the White Elephant party. He gave the werewolf back-scratcher to his mother, which she thought was hilarious, and the rainbow box to his sister. *Hard-on* apparently didn't occur to her, and so she liked it fine.

The chocolate was good. Eating was only a little uncomfortable with Jacob's bruised jaw. And chocolate you could let dissolve in your mouth without a lot of chewing. His eye still hurt a fair amount, but even that was already getting better. He felt fully defiant, ready for anything.

Before he left, he thanked his sister for cheering him up that morning. She was getting ready, too—a couple of her friends were going to scoop her up to take her to, of all places, South Street.

Turning from the bathroom mirror where she was checking her eye shadow—blue—she said, "Sure thing, bro. Fuck 'em."

"Fuck 'em," Jacob said. It was becoming like a motto.

Painful face and destroyed social life or not, he was feeling not bad. Active. Angry. Ready. And the party—that right there *would* be a social life thing.

Possibly he was imagining it, but it seemed to Jacob like people were staring at him and his bruises as he walked through West Philly down to Thirtieth Street Station, and then even more when he was in the train station—the light was better in there—and most of all when he was on the R8, which had people in nice clothes on it. And these weren't even the *real* Chestnut Hill people, in the sense of hard-core wealthy; these ones were on a *train*. He didn't see anyone he recognized from school, which meant that he was possibly the only person taking the train to this party. *Whatever*, he thought. *Fuck Chestnut Hill.* He held his wounded face up with a belligerent pride. "West Philly crashes the country club," he murmured to himself.

Once he was off the train, standing in the pretty brutal cold, he pulled out the directions and checked his watch. It was just about nine, so he wasn't fashionably late enough yet, but he still had some walking to do to get there. He got started, turning off Germantown Avenue into more residential streets. So residential, in fact, that after a little while there weren't even any sidewalks to walk on. He had to step onto the grass whenever a car passed by.

Eventually he found Towanda Street, and then he could

hear the party. Some kind of beat that clarified as Young MC's "Bust a Move" as he got closer and saw all the cars parked and spotted the right address on a mailbox.

It was like Char's house. Well, different in its specifics—this one was white, whereas Char's was brown, for example, but both with the big driveways and all the space between them and their neighbors, and just how massive the places were. This one was bigger, in fact, than Char's. It was surrounded by trees that looked like they'd been there since before the land was colonized by white people.

Jacob was jarred out of his trance when headlights hit him and another car pulled up and parked. Kids from his school poured out and ambled past him, laughing, up the driveway to the house. They hadn't paid any attention to Jacob. Somehow that fact sapped some of his *fuck 'em* energy, almost made him turn back—what did he really think was going to happen at this party?—but he was very cold so he decided to follow them at least just to get inside for a minute. He could always leave.

Up ahead the front door opened—the music got louder—and the group of kids disappeared inside. But the door stayed open. A girl with straight brown hair was waiting there.

"Who's that?" she called, louder than necessary, her hand over her eyes as if she were shading them from something. It was Jessica Roth. Her hair was usually curly, but now it was straight. She was in a bright pink dress. Kind of fancy.

Jacob looked down at his own clothes, which were jeans and a Depeche Mode T-shirt under a military jacket. "Jacob Wassermann," he said, by which point he had reached the circle of light in front of the door.

"Jake Wassermann," she said. "Cool. Is the Pack with you?" She looked over his shoulder.

"Nope," he said. "Fuck 'em."

Her mouth dropped open and she covered it with the hand that wasn't holding a cup. She was clearly already a little drunk. "Ohhhhh, shit. Wait—that fight you had—"

"You heard about that?"

"Sort of, yeah," she said. "Was it you and Finn Nolan fighting?"

"You heard about the fight?"

She shrugged. "Everybody did. Ooh, your face. But was it with Finn? That guy is kind of a wastoid, right?"

Jacob thought about Finn breaking up the fight, but then also how he was at Char's the night before. "Basically," he said.

She rolled her eyes. "It's like, whatever, right? Come in."

Inside, Jacob saw that there were already a bunch of people there. So he had gotten the timing right. They were all dressed a lot more preppy than he was. Skirts and dresses on the girls and rugby shirts and button-downs on the boys. Which he should have expected. But also fuck it.

"Let me get you a beer," Jessica said. But then, instead of getting it, she said, "It's in the kitchen," and she pointed.

So he went off to find the beer—getting to this particular kitchen was more of a journey from the front door than he was used to—and said some hellos along the way, mostly in response to other people's hellos. He really did know a lot more people than he used to, and a lot more people knew him, too, at least enough to say hello. The interesting thing was that these folks were mostly of the more popular kind. They definitely stared at his face. He held it up for everyone to see.

The music followed him for the whole journey—there were speakers mounted on the walls of the rooms and hallways. Like the music—now "It Takes Two" by Rob Base and DJ E-Z Rock—was part of the house.

In the kitchen, finally, there was a big keg in a bigger bucket of ice and water. More like a tub of ice and water. Jacob recognized that the silver barrel with the thing sticking out of the top was a keg, but it was the only time he'd ever been in the room with one, so he stopped short.

"Hey," came a voice from next to him—Oscar Kelsey, hanging out with a few other people. "Wass up, Wasserman? You need a beer? Or you just browsing?"

The truth was that at sixteen years of age Jacob had never had one. Well, he had tasted his mother's beer a couple of times and didn't like it. But this was what he was here for, really. "Hm," he said, making like he was in a shop browsing, looking around at this kitchen that was bigger than his living room at home. Cabinets everywhere, including cabinets you'd need a ladder to get to. "You have a nice selection here," he continued, "but what was that you recommended just now? *Beer*, you say? Sounds interesting."

Oscar laughed and then abruptly threw a couple of fake punches. Jacob flinched a little, but less than he would have expected. "Look out for this dude," Oscar said, and then he worked the keg to pour him a beer. Jacob watched him closely so he could reproduce it later.

He took a drink. Beer was just not a good-tasting thing, apparently. "Nice," he said.

"So, you are *fucked* up," Oscar said, looking at Jacob's face. "But how does the other guy look?"

"*Guys*," Jacob said, emphasizing the plurality.

"Whoa," Oscar's crowd said.

"Yeah, I heard something about that," Oscar said. He raised his cup in a kind of toast. "Look out for this dude."

It turned out that Jacob was a minor celebrity at the party. First, he had the Pack thing that gave him basic standing in the first place, but then the fight—there were a few different versions going around, including him taking on a street gang and, on the other hand, him brawling with his friends—that added some spice. It didn't even seem to count against him that he was so banged up himself; that was just evidence of how badass he was. One thing all the versions shared was that he had thrown the first punch. Which was actually true, Jacob reflected.

When he came across Leah Shaffer she actually touched his face. "Can I?" she said, her fingers already on his cheek. Cool fingertips. He very deliberately kept himself from wincing. "Harsh," she said, studying the bruises.

He, meanwhile, studied her. Leah's eyes were green and her hair was still halo-like around her head—curly, but short enough that it surrounded her head and face. She was wearing a shiny black dress that was pretty tight. Jacob took another drink from his almost-empty cup. Leah took her hand back. The nails, still silver, flared in the low light.

"You have…robot nails," he said. The beer was possibly already having an effect.

"How come I never talked to you?" she said.

He shrugged. "Bad judgment?"

She laughed a laugh that was partway a giggle, and then someone swept her away.

The party seemed to swirl through the rooms, and that wasn't just the beer talking—people moved from one place to another, and there were so many places to be that there was always somewhere else to go. Jacob couldn't even tell what all the rooms were for. But they were busy with people now; this party was bigger than anything the Pack had done. Which, fuck 'em again.

He refilled his cup when it was empty.

Everywhere he went people had questions for him. He answered, even though everything already felt mentally slippery. He just answered vaguely.

His path crossed Mike Berman's in a room that was a living room or something. "Here's Rocky," Mike said. Like Oscar, Mike pretended to throw some punches—"*Adriaaaaan*," he moaned in a Sylvester Stallone voice—but Jacob didn't flinch at all this time. Stepped closer to Mike in fact, somewhere between happy and belligerent. Or, of course, maybe those were the same thing.

"Who does that make you?" he said. "Ivan Drago?"

Blurry as he was starting to feel, he could see some wariness in Mike's eyes, even though Mike was four inches taller than he was. But Mike just slapped Jacob on the back, not too hard, and said, "Go get 'em, Rock."

Jacob wandered off, and, on the way, checked his watch. The numbers seemed slightly jumpy. But he saw that it was past the time when he should have left to make the train he would ideally be on for making curfew, and it was getting close to when he would have to go to get the last train of the night.

He found Jessica again. She was dancing in another living room to some 2 Live Crew, her pink dress the brightest thing in the room. "I gotta go soon," he said.

Very unexpectedly, she threw her arms around him. "Noooo," she said, very loud, into his ear.

"I have to get a train." She smelled like a bunch of grown-up perfume.

Jessica pulled away, a bit wobbly. "A *traaain*? No way. Someone will give you…will give you a ride. Where do you live? Germantown? Center City? Why do they *call* it that? It's not even the center, because it's all the way *east*. Well, except the Northeast is further east." She scratched her forehead.

"West Philly," he said. "And Germantown doesn't even have Germans in it."

Jessica laughed almost hysterically, spilling some of her beer. "Oh no," she said, hand on her mouth. She took a pink shoe off and dabbed at the spill with her toe. "Ew, gross," she said. "Now my stocking is wet." Then, suddenly, she looked back up at Jacob. "You're from West Philly? For sure. They fight there."

Jacob thought about that, or tried to.

"*I'm* going to get you a *cab*," Jessica said, "because *that's* a responsible hostess." Saying that, she thrust a hand in the air, but it was her beer hand, so there was more spilling. They both laughed.

"For real? A cab?" he said. He sort of wanted her to put her arms around him again. But she shoved him playfully.

"For sure," she said. "Go back to the party. Come get me when you want a cab, okay? The *hostess*."

Jacob raised his own cup to toast her. These Tribe guys weren't that bad, really. Or at least the girls weren't.

Thinking of the Tribe made him think about how they were mostly Jewish and he was Jewish, whatever that meant, and so he went around the house, weaving through and around everyone, looking for Jewish stuff. Like on one windowsill there were three menorahs—Jessica's parents were away during Hanukkah! Poor Jessica!—and there were some framed Hebrew words for some reason on a couple of walls, and in one place a big picture, a photograph, of a city where all the buildings looked like they were made of packed sand, except this one gold dome. Maybe that was Israel.

He was so immersed in all of this stuff that when someone came up next to him, he said, "Shalom."

She laughed. It was Leah. "What?" she asked.

He was so happy to see her all of a sudden that he hugged her, which made her giggle. "I'm on a Jewish tour," he said. "See this? It's probably Israel."

Now Leah really laughed, bending down over her knees and stumbling a little. When she straightened up, still laughing, she said, "It's—it's Jerusalem. It says *right there*." She was pointing at the bottom of the picture, where it did say *Jerusalem*. In big letters. And then Jacob was in hysterics too. The whole thing had him so unsteady that he sat down on the spot, on the floor, cross-legged.

She sat down, too, which was more work in her shiny black dress. She took off her shoes and curled her legs up under her.

There they were, facing each other, grinning, and Jacob was pretty aware of Leah's body, which was a nice body, and she had very white teeth and dark lips and her hair was a halo around her head.

It was the same kind of thing as the fight two days earlier; Jacob was saying something before he had time to think about it. He was saying, "I want to kiss you a little."

And she said, "Okay."

And then they were kissing, and Leah's lips were very soft, which was different from—Jacob just kissed her harder. Their mouths both tasted like beer.

Things went along from there.

23

Afterward everything was terrible.

"If you throw up in my cab, you're cleaning it up yourself," the driver said without turning around. The car rolled out of the driveway toward the dark street. Behind them—Jacob could feel it even though he didn't turn to look, either—were Jessica and Leah at the front door of the enormous house with the picture of Jerusalem inside. The music was still loud from out here. "You kids shouldn't be partying like that." The cabbie shook his head.

Jacob was already feeling more sober. He had had only a couple of beers, after all. And now he was able to think ahead to his mother, because he was probably going to be late, plus smelling like alcohol. And more than that, he could replay in his head what had happened with Leah. He put his hand on his arm, where, under his jacket, her phone number was written in marker.

They had kissed for a while in the room with the Jerusalem picture, and then, when people started hooting at them, they had gotten up and kind of scampered off to the stairs. "I'm authorized," Leah said, taking his hand with her silver-nailed one, and they went upstairs and found a bedroom—a glance gave Jacob the sense that there were fifty more—and closed the door behind them.

It was amazing how far away Jacob's brain was the whole time. There was nothing in him offering words of caution or support. Even that defiant *fuck 'em* was gone. There was just him doing the things he was doing, and wanting to do them. The kissing even hurt his bruised face a little, and still that didn't bring his brain back.

Pretty soon their clothes were off. Entirely off. He and Tammy had still barely done that. But he didn't think of her then, or only in a flash of comparison—Leah was shorter and softer, curvier. Her breasts were definitely bigger, and Jacob sort of buried himself in them, which made her giggle. But he didn't think about Tammy directly—just how Leah was different. At one point he pulled back to look at her face—there was a night-light plugged into an outlet, so he could see her—and took in her warm green eyes and her dark lips and her round face and he said, "You're beautiful," because she really was. And she grinned and said, "You are so sweet. Kiss me more," and he did.

At some point, because the situation was headed that way, Leah said, "I can't have sex with you right now."

"Really?" Jacob said, closer to a whine than he would have wanted.

"I barely know you." She touched his nose with the tip of her finger.

"Oh."

"But how about this?" she said, and she moved down the bed. When she put her mouth on him, things accelerated fast. Things were over fast too.

"See?" she said, back up face-to-face with him again.

Jacob could barely speak.

After that, they lay together in the bed, warm body to warm body, and Jacob must have dozed, because then there was an experience of abruptly waking up. Leah was there, woken up, too, by his sudden intake of breath, eyes wide at him.

Unfortunately, his brain was there too.

"Oh," he said. "Oh. Oh, wow." He sat up. *Is this the world? This is the world.*

"Do you need to go?" she said, sitting up too.

He looked around, his mind going fast, and saw a digital clock. He *did* need to go, for all kinds of reasons. "I'm sorry," he said, jumping out of bed. "Yeah. I need to go. I'm sorry." He found the light switch—the room looked like a guest room, he saw idiotically, nothing too personal around—and started to put his clothes on, fast, inept.

He heard a sigh from the bed. Leah was there, still naked,

sitting, watching him. "That wasn't some kind of wham-bam thing, was it?" she said, her face a little sad.

"Wham-bam?" Jacob was struggling with his pants in a way that he'd never struggled with pants before.

"I don't do wham-bam," she said. "I just thought, you're funny and smart and you seem nicer than the other guys I know."

Jacob stopped struggling with his pants. "I'm not sure how nice I am," he said. Actually, he was sure that he *wasn't*. Tammy was definitely on his mind now.

"You aren't still with that Tammy, are you?" Leah said, like a mind reader.

"I really don't know," he said, which was true.

"That means yes. I shouldn't have done that," she said, looking down at the palms of her hands.

As frantic as he was, the feelings in Leah's voice, her down-turned face—they made a little howl inside him. Jacob finished pulling his pants on so that he could sit, still shirtless, on the bed next to her. His heart shook in his chest for multiple reasons as he reached out and took her hand.

She looked him in the eyes abruptly, like a challenge. "Tell me something."

"What?" he said.

"Tell me something true about yourself that you usually don't tell people."

It was out before he knew what he was going to say. "I'm mostly sad inside," he said.

She smiled softly. "Yeah," she said. "I can tell."

He stared at her for a few seconds with his mouth partly open. He had an erection again, unexpectedly. Then he remembered Tammy and got up. "I really have to go, for real," he said. "I'm sorry." His heart was all over the place.

"Just tell me one other thing," she said, and he looked her in the eyes. "Do you like me?"

Again it tumbled out of him: the truth. "You seem…like, awesome," he said. "Yeah. I do."

She nodded. "Okay." Then, while he put his shirt on, she said, "Are you in town for winter break?"

He shook his head. The feeling of the moment was now panic. "Mostly not. Well, like half. Listen—my life right now—"

She cut him off. "Call me when you're back," she said, like it wasn't even a controversial thing.

Neither one of them said anything in the bedroom after that. Jacob, in all kinds of agitation, watched her get dressed, still wobbly. He felt like he couldn't just leave her there to get her clothes on alone.

And then they went down the stairs and Jessica called a cab company and the three of them stood waiting for it near the front door, Jessica and Leah laughing about something, Leah standing closer to him than he could exactly handle, and he tried to breathe as calmly as possible. When the cab got there, Jessica gave the driver some money, which added unexpectedly to the feeling of embarrassment that Jacob now understood he had carried down the stairs, and Leah, to his surprise, produced a marker and grabbed his arm to write her phone number on it. It took a very uncomfortable few seconds. When he had his arm back, he got into the cab. He didn't kiss her goodbye. He waved. She frowned a little at him and pursed her lips in thought, but waved back. And then he went down the driveway.

"I mean it," the driver said now. "You're going to have to clean it up."

Jacob's mother was awake when he got there, again sitting in the living room, just waiting for him. "It's almost one o'clock," she said, her mouth tight.

"I'm sorry," he said, keeping his distance because of the possible smell of alcohol. Though maybe she wouldn't be able to smell it because she had a glass of her own stuff next to her.

"When you get back from your father's," she said, grim, collecting her glass and getting up from the chair, "we're going to have to change some things."

And then the tension inside him blew up unexpectedly and

he was yelling. "*God*, Mom! Don't you think I have enough shitty stuff going on right now?" After which he stomped past her and up the stairs, feeling basically the same as when he had shoved that kid at Ogontz and Olney.

This time the person didn't push back.

The next morning Jacob's brain—hungover not from alcohol but from regret and embarrassment and anger and self-loathing and even the terrifying curiosity he was feeling about Leah— was fully with him. He saw it all clearly: the fact that, even if he and Tammy were fighting, and maybe done, they were not *officially* done, and he was crazy about her, right, and yet he was with Leah last night, who he'd never even thought about in that way before. Though he was, now. Her phone number was there on his arm, loud. And then on the other side were his shitty, shitty friends, and that included Tammy, and it took Jacob a while to get out of bed, he was so caught up between all the things he was thinking and feeling.

Over breakfast—it was more like lunchtime, but he ate breakfast—he tried to decide what to do. He and Deanna were leaving for Chicago the next day, which gave him one day at home to reach out to Tammy or anyone else from the Pack, if that was what he was going to do—Eric, maybe, or would Brian or Finn understand? Finn had said, "Girls suck," hadn't he?

It was hard to decide what to do. In terms of getting advice, his mother was already at work, doing a Christmas Eve double shift for the time-and-a-half, and anyway maybe she would be mad about last night. But Deanna was home; he could hear her listening to INXS upstairs. But he couldn't decide whether he should bother her or not. In fact, he ended up sitting at the table for quite a while in total indecision. He heard "Devil Inside" from upstairs, and then "Need You Tonight," and then "Mediate," and "The Loved One." And then a pause for Deanna to flip the cassette over, followed by "Wild Life." That was when Jacob finally got up.

Eric answered the phone after a few rings. "Hey," Jacob said.

"Hey, Jake. 'Sup?" Eric's voice was even and bland.

"Are you in the neighborhood? Can you hang out right now?"

"Now?"

"Yeah—if you could."

After a couple of beats, Eric said, "Sure—okay. You can meet me here. But give me a half hour."

When Jacob got to Eric's house, Eric came outside and closed the door behind him. "Feel like walking?"

Jacob didn't—it was twenty degrees outside—but Eric was already down the porch steps, so Jacob followed.

"I can only be a little while. Christmas Eve and everything. My folks are getting everything ready in there."

"Right," Jacob said. He had forgotten about that.

They started off down the street. Jacob couldn't decide what to say first—something about how furious he was about the White Elephant party, or something really guilty about what he'd done at the party last night. He was going to have to talk about that eventually; he and Leah had been kissing out in the open, so word was going to get around.

"So you heard about Char's house," Eric said, deciding the matter. "The soiree or whatever it was called."

"Yeah," Jacob said. The anger surged up inside him, ready.

"You know, that was really kind of an accident," Eric said. "Char didn't *want* to leave anyone out, so she made it just the girls, but it was her birthday, so obviously I came. And Finn came because Willow told him about it and she didn't realize."

"Which left me out," Jacob said. "*And* Brian."

They turned onto Spruce Street and headed east. It was viciously cold.

"We didn't mean to," Eric said. "We talked about inviting both of you, once everybody was there—"

"But then you didn't."

"Well, it's not like we could have invited Brian with Alice there. And so then if we called *you*, he would have been even more left out."

"This is such bullshit," Jacob said, shivering. His hands were in his pockets and they were still cold.

"Well, dude, you've been acting *crazy*."

Jacob stopped in his tracks. "Don't fucking call me that," he said. "Tammy calls me that and I'm done with people calling me that."

"Jake, you hit a kid for no reason. And then you told Tammy, 'Fuck all of you'?"

Jacob just stared into Eric's eyes for a few seconds. Then: "So what you're saying is you *didn't want me there*."

"You're not listening," Eric said.

"Did you guys ever even like me?"

"See?" Eric threw his mittened hands up. His face was as red as his hair. "Jake, this is what I mean."

"You only ever liked my jokes," Jacob said, partly to Eric and partly to himself.

"Come on, Jake."

"I was right the first time. Fuck you," he said, and then he turned and walked toward home.

Despite the cold, he kept going when he got to his house, east and south toward Clark Park, which was a real park, unlike Spark Park. His head was boiling. Anger, for sure, and also other stuff. Even though he hadn't brought up Leah—by that point it seemed to Jacob that he didn't owe it to Eric, who by the way was the same guy who'd abandoned him because of stupid Willow back when everything got started—it was definitely on his mind. Mainly as a thing of guilt, because he hadn't officially been broken up with Tammy. He hadn't even decided for sure that he *wanted* to break up with Tammy; *fuck you* wasn't the same thing as a decision. Or was it? And had *Tammy* decided anything? Maybe not. Probably yes. How would he know? He knew he needed to call her.

When he got to Clark Park, which was pretty barren for a park, actually, he sat down on a very cold bench and looked at the leafless trees and thought about crying.

And had he done wrong in terms of Leah herself? She said she didn't do *wham-bams*. Is that what he just did?

He remembered freshly that when he told her he was mostly sad inside, she said, "I can tell."

He pictured her face, put his hand on his markered arm, felt guilt and also like he wanted to talk to her. But he stayed on the bench. He also pictured Tammy's face. Jacob hated himself and a lot of other people, let himself spill back and forth between anxiety, fury, grief, and total bafflement.

The next day, he and his sister left for Chicago.

24

The first thing their father did when he met them at the airport gate was hug them both in big bear hugs—Deanna first and then Jacob. The second thing was that he held Jacob at arm's length and said, "Ouch," wincing at Jacob's shiner. It was getting better, but it was still there. And then, third, Jacob still at arm's length, his father shook his head and added, "And an *earring*?"

"Yeah?" Jacob had meant to make it sound like a statement, firm, but it had come out more like a question, like something he was putting out there in hopes of confirmation.

Instead his father shook his head again, smiling wryly, one eyebrow raised over his sharp brown eyes, and said, "Well, who's hungry?"

That was a regular question from his father; there was always a lot of eating with him. And yet he was not a particularly heavy guy. Big, maybe, in the shoulders, but not heavy. Not even a paunch lately.

Jacob and Deanna were both hungry. Why not?

Sitting in the back seat of the car while Deanna talked about college up front with their father, Jacob still felt hungover with regret and agitation. He hadn't made contact with anyone else after that bad walk with Eric. Well, he had tried to reach Tammy once, but her father had picked up and said, "It's not a good time," and it was in a gruff voice, so maybe he knew about some of what was going on, but of course that was the voice he always had, so maybe he didn't know anything. And it was Christmastime, so there were other reasons why it wouldn't be a good time.

"Could you ask Tammy to call me?" Jacob said.

Her father grunted and that was that. Jacob had left Philadelphia without getting to tell Tammy what had happened.

And maybe she was going to find out from someone else now. Probably he should ask his father if he could make a call when they got to the condo. Though it would be long distance. And it was Christmas itself.

Meanwhile Leah's number, though a little faded, was still legible on his arm.

Jacob sighed and watched gray Chicago go by.

The first time they had visited their father in Chicago he had driven them all around, right from the airport, to give them a tour of the city. And it was almost like he was an official tour guide, because he knew a lot about Chicago. It was actually pretty impressive. Throughout the week that first time, he had so many tidbits: this is the river that they turned green every St. Patrick's Day; that's where the Blues Brothers knocked all those Nazis off the bridge; that's the haunted theater; that's the base-ball stadium named after chewing gum; that's where Al Capone got his shoes shined. Just about everywhere they went—and they went a lot of places—he had some fact about it.

The tour-guide thing had calmed down some since then, but still he kept them busy when they visited. After the airport this time he drove them into town—sometimes his father turned his head to ask Jacob something, to work him into the conversation, but it was awkward and Jacob was distracted, so eventually his father gave up, and Jacob just watched the backs of their heads as they talked, his neat brown hair above the neck of his turtleneck sweater and her big brown curls pouring down even over the seat. They got lunch at The Berghoff in the loop, and then they went to the Art Institute afterward. It was a good museum. Jacob had favorites among the paintings there, including Vincent Van Gogh's sad little bedroom, Edward Hopper's sad little diner, and Claude Monet's sad little water lilies.

"They're not sad," Deanna said. "They're just plants, in the water."

"It's the colors, maybe," Jacob said, looking close up at the painting until it decomposed into splotches of paint.

"They're just colors," Deanna said.

After that they went back to their father's condo in the suburbs. "We'll go back into the city tomorrow," he said as he drove them out. "Tonight you can settle in a little." *Settle in* made Jacob wince. "And we'll maybe get some Chinese food or something. Do Hanukkah."

They spent the evening in the condo, which was open and bright even in the winter and a lot like the other ones on either side. It shocked Jacob each time, how much better off their father was than their mother. He sent child support, of course, and probably some kind of alimony, but still she always seemed to be just scraping by. And he went out to eat whenever he wanted. There, in front of them, all kinds of Chinese food, more than they could eat, spread out on the big living room table, and *Spies Like Us* going in the VCR, playing on the living room TV. There were also TVs in each bedroom. Their father had all the latest everything.

Jacob looked over at his father. He had had a beard when Jacob was a kid, and his hair had been a little shaggy, but that was the 70s, and now he was trim and clean-shaven. He had gone from glasses to contact lenses a few years earlier too. Still there was something bear-like about him—as if he might suddenly rear up and start roaring. It made Jacob wonder how he, Jacob, could have turned out like this, when his father was so *strong*.

On the windowsill the Hanukkah candles burned their way down. They had exchanged gifts already—his father thanked Jacob for the tie, which now Jacob was worried was maybe a cheap thing, and Deanna for a book by James Michener, and then he had brought out the presents for the kids. For Jacob, there was, awkwardly, a new boom box, this one with a cassette deck *and* a CD player. Jacob's mom was not going to be happy about this.

He hadn't asked his father yet about making a long-distance call. It was their first night together, after all, and Tammy would probably be busy since it was Christmas, and besides Jacob didn't really want to. Why would he want to call his official *girl-*

friend to tell her he had taken his clothes off with another girl? Well, and more than that.

Maybe he should call Leah instead.

"Are you watching?" his father asked, shaking Jacob from his thoughts.

"What?"

"Are you here with us?" his father said. He had an eyebrow raised. Was he watching Jacob in order to make sure Jacob was watching the movie? His father was smiling, but still the whole thing was strangely intense. Then both of them turned back to *Spies Like Us*.

Jacob was still partly lost in his thoughts, though now they involved his father too. It was like a second wake-up when Deanna and his father laughed at the same time, a very similar moderate laugh. Dan Aykroyd had done something funny in the movie.

Jacob resolved to pay attention.

For some reason he still had the boom box in his lap.

The next morning, he did ask about the phone call. He and his father were fighting, which is what always happened after a short time of being together. This time it was about a recurring thing, which his father called Jacob's *attitude*. At eleven o'clock his father had had to come wake him up, and Jacob's sluggishness getting out of bed and his draggy mood at the breakfast table—the condo had a breakfast nook—were all too much for his father.

"Do you not want to be here? Is that the issue?" His father, who had already eaten, was sitting opposite him with his big arms crossed.

"I'm just tired," Jacob said from behind a bowl of cereal. "I just woke up." He also had not slept well the night before. Tammy. Leah. The Pack. Tammy. Leah. The Pack. He had been close to crying a bunch of times.

His father said, "That doesn't explain why you were off in outer space yesterday. You were completely elsewhere."

"I don't know," Jacob said. "I guess I'm just tired in general."

"Well," his father started, "we don't get to see each other very often—"

I'm not the one who moved to Chicago, Jacob thought.

"—so I'd appreciate it if you could work on your attitude—"

There's the word.

"—so we can all have a good time."

Jacob snapped. "Could you give me a break, Dad? Jesus. Just because I'm a *little* tired and distracted doesn't mean I have an *attitude problem.*"

"Your attitude *is* a problem if it messes up this visit. You and your black clothes—" he gestured at the Bauhaus T-shirt Jacob was still wearing from yesterday—"and your moping around. I need it to stop."

"Why are you making such a big deal out of this? It's not bothering Deanna."

His sister, who had also apparently eaten, called back from the living room, "Please don't bring me into this."

"You know, this whole gloom-and-doom thing isn't going to do you any favors in the long run," their father said.

"Oh God," Jacob said, looking down at his cereal, which was on its way to falling apart in the milk.

That *Oh God* set his father off, and the attitude question got more attention for a while, until Jacob finally said, "Okay—I'll try, okay, Dad? I'll try. I'm just a little distracted because, because I need to get in touch with someone back in Philly to tell them something important. If I could just make a phone call." And Jacob could see that this was landing reasonably well with his father, who glanced at Jacob's arm and the phone number in feminine handwriting on it—the number had been covered up the day before by a flannel shirt—and so it was pretty stupid that Jacob reacted to the glance by saying, "They even give you a phone call in *jail.*"

The fight went on from there. It lasted through breakfast, and then the whole thing continued in a Cold War feeling afterward as the three of them went out to get lunch—right after Jacob's breakfast—and then it followed them into the mall movie theater, where their father bought them all tickets to *Tango & Cash*. Deanna was trying to keep things cheerful with more college talk, and their father was back into the mode of telling stories and dropping tidbits, but it felt forced, and there was palpable tension between Jacob and his father as they settled in to watch. When the lights went dark and the movie began, they all went silent. It was a relief to Jacob. Still, aware that his father was probably watching him watch again, Jacob focused his eyes on the screen.

As it turned out, it was a pretty entertaining movie—buddy cop stuff—though seeing Sylvester Stallone did remind Jacob about Mike Berman calling him Rocky at the party, the party where so much happened after so much had already happened.

By the end of the movie, helped maybe by Tango and Cash's victory over the bad guy in the hall of mirrors, the Cold War had thawed some.

"Enjoy the movie?" his father said.

"Yeah," Jacob said, and they nodded with adequate satisfaction at each other.

But then, instead of taking them back out into the winter and the car, his father walked them deeper into the mall.

"What are we doing?" Deanna said.

Their father indicated the department store ahead of them. "Happy Hanukkah."

"Wait—what do you mean?" Jacob said.

"Is this one of those deals where we have fifteen minutes to grab whatever we want and it's ours?" Deanna asked.

"I'm heading for Electronics," Jacob said. They were both joking, but Deanna's question didn't seem completely crazy.

Their father laughed. "Not quite," he said. "I want to get particular *kinds* of things for you, but I wanted to do it *with* you, so you could pick out styles and sizes."

"Ooh," Deanna said, hopping a little hop mid-step. "What kinds of things?"

Their father looked them over and said, "Well, I think you could both use new coats."

"Ooh," Deanna said again, with a clap.

But Jacob looked down at his military jacket, feeling an irritation rise up inside him again. Sure, the jacket wasn't warm enough sometimes, but he had trouble imagining that this mall department store, with all the glittery Christmas decorations hanging everywhere and the Muzak playing overhead, was going to have anything like the *styles* he liked. Still—he held his tongue this time.

Inside, Deanna said, hopping again, "Can I just...?" She pointed at the women's section.

"Go ahead," their father said. "Pick out something you like."

"Price limit?"

Their father shrugged. "Don't worry about it too much. Everything's on sale anyway."

"Wooo!" Deanna hooted, skipping off.

Don't worry about it too much. Their mother had never said anything like that about money, ever.

"Find us in Men's," their father called after her. He turned to Jacob, clapped him on the back. "Let's pick something out for you."

Let's. "I'm not going to get anything preppy," he said.

His father didn't engage that. "Let's just look," he said, and they found the escalator.

There were plenty of preppy coats, of course—expensive-looking brown wool coats and beige suede things and multicolored ski jackets as bright as confetti—but Jacob found a couple of decent things in there too.

"How about this?" he said, holding up a black leather jacket. It wasn't exactly the Skinz look—a little long and slick, and no chrome studs or zippers anywhere—but it was still a leather jacket.

"Does that work for vegetarians?" his father joked pointedly.

He was right. Jacob put the jacket back.

Eventually they were able to compromise on a long, dark gray wool coat. It was too fancy for Jacob, but it was gray and he could wear it in. Hit the lapels with some *Meat is Murder* pins or something. And at least he and his father weren't fighting.

"Okay," he said. "Should we find Deanna?"

His father waved a dismissive hand. "She'll be a while. And now we've got to get you a shirt and pants."

"What are you talking about?"

"We're going somewhere nice tonight. The kind of place that doesn't go for jeans and a T-shirt about burning down the establishment."

"Why are we going someplace like that?" Jacob said, an urge to fight picking up in him.

"I *like* places like that," his father said, "and you would, too, if you could open your mind. They've even got meatless options. You know," he said, waving his hand in the air, "pasta. Besides, we're meeting Bill."

That last comment was meant to put an end to the debate. Bill was Jacob's father's boyfriend and had been for several years now. They didn't live together, but it was a serious thing. And Jacob's father knew that it was awkward for his kids, him having a boyfriend—other than Deanna asking once how Bill was doing, his name hadn't come up at all during the visit so far—and he also knew that his kids *liked* Bill. All of which meant that Jacob was stumped for what to say in response. His father had obviously known that was going to happen.

"Come on. One nice shirt, one nice pair of pants," his father said. "It won't kill you."

But ten minutes later, standing in front of the changing room mirror, blue button-down shirt and khakis on, Jacob suddenly felt his heart slumping in his chest. His clothes looked like more expensive versions of what he used to think was cool, before the Pack. And here he was wearing them now. Who was this guy in the mirror? What was he even doing here? This was like some strange other planet, far from where his real life was.

But of course the first planet, the one where his real life was, was a wasteland now. And so maybe this *was* his world. Gravity seemed to intensify as he stood there, until he actually sank to the ground, the four walls of the changing room close around him.

After a while, there was a knock on the door. "Jacob?" his father said. He paused and then knocked again. "Jacob?" This time he sounded annoyed.

Which annoyed Jacob, which was a crack in the thing that was weighing him down. "Yeah, okay," he said.

When he came out a minute or two later, wearing those clothes, Deanna was there, too, a long white coat over her arm. Her eyes went wide at the look he was sporting, but she read Jacob's face and kept her mouth shut. Their father, on the other hand, said, "See? You clean up nice."

Jacob didn't have the energy to make a retort. He just looked down at himself. Collar, buttons, crease in the pants, neat, spiffy. "Okay," he said, turning to go back to the changing room.

Things were calmer for the rest of the afternoon, partly because Jacob was tired. His father was happy because of the successful shopping—Deanna had even gotten a scarf and gloves—and he didn't mind Jacob going off to take a nap, a nap that was actually Jacob lying on the bed, gravity back in force.

An hour later, Deanna came into the guest room and sat down on the bed next to him. He didn't bother to pretend he was sleeping. "What's going on?" she said.

He shrugged.

"Is this about you and Dad?"

Shrug.

"Jacob, what happened at that party you went to?"

Shrug. He could have told Deanna, maybe, but what he had done—what would she think about what he had done? And besides he couldn't seem to get his mouth to work.

Deanna sighed. "Well, Dad sent me in here to tell you we're leaving in a half hour and you should probably get ready."

Jacob nodded.

"He's going to be really excited about you coming out with these new clothes all wrinkled from lying on the bed in them."

Shrug. Though actually that cheered him up a little.

"We're going to see Bill," she said. "You like Bill."

Jacob nodded.

And then Deanna leaned over and got her arms under Jacob and actually hauled him up into a sitting position. It was kind of shocking. He sat there blinking at her.

"It's an Italian restaurant," she said. "There are going to be good vegetarian options. Pasta and stuff. Okay?"

It took a few seconds, but finally something shifted and Jacob said, "Okay."

The restaurant they ate at that night was dim and sleek and very modern. Jacob saw how he would have stuck out in his regular clothes, though that made him wonder what he was doing here, rather than questioning his regular clothes. He was doing better than he had been during his non-nap nap. Still he felt sort of slow inside.

Bill was already at the table. He stood to greet them; Bill was very tall, and a balding blond. He and Jacob's father didn't kiss hello—they didn't do that in public—but they clasped hands meaningfully, for just a second. Then Bill turned to the kids with an eager smile on his face. "Now here's who I was *really* waiting for," he said in his deep, rumbly voice. He winced a little at Jacob's fading bruises, and then hugged him and his sister in turn. Jacob hugged back, maybe a little more than he'd meant to. But it was nice having someone excited, and only excited, to see him.

As they sat down Jacob saw his father and Bill squeeze hands again. They had met through their jobs somehow; they didn't work for the same company but they worked for companies that interacted with each other, both of them doing business things that Jacob couldn't really picture, and the two men had interacted enough times that things had gotten started between them. And then, on a visit maybe six months later, Bill had been officially introduced to Deanna and Jacob. During that lunch, Bill and their father were so nervous—and their father was never nervous—that both of them knocked over water glasses. Jacob remembered his food—a Reuben sandwich—sort of floating in the ice water that had pooled in his plate. Still, it had been nice.

He didn't have a problem with his father being gay, or he didn't think he did. Well, maybe it was unusual to have a gay father, but anyway apparently that wasn't what had broken up the marriage to Jacob and Deanna's mother—their father had discovered he was gay later, and he told everyone before he ever met Bill. Though probably it was always there, under the surface, making trouble in the marriage. Jacob knew what it was like to have something under the surface, causing issues. But his father had brought his stuff out and now everything was fine, whereas Jacob's thing—whenever it bubbled up, the problems got worse.

Jacob snapped back into focus at the dinner. His father and Bill were telling a funny story together about this crazy camping trip they had taken—hard to imagine his father camping, but there it was—where they were constantly worried about bears. "I actually put bells on the front flap of the tent," Bill rumbled.

"As if that was going to help if a bear showed up," Jacob's father said, laughing.

"I thought we needed a warning."

"Bill," his father said, putting a hand on his arm, "it's not like there was a back door to escape through." His eyes were almost twinkling.

That was the most surprising thing about his father being gay. It didn't seem to Jacob that his father was easygoing enough or wide-open enough to be gay, or even straight, really—anything that involved being vulnerable with another human being. And yet when he was with Bill he was both lighthearted and open.

Maybe you just needed the right person.

So they ate their really good food—Jacob had eggplant parmesan—and the mood was bouncy, and they all told funny stories. Even Jacob finally did, when Bill asked him about school; he told the one about Mrs. Hudson, who was normally really strict, but who one day came in completely stoned on cold medicine. She kept laughing and couldn't pronounce "Odysseus."

Late in the meal Bill asked about Jacob's bruises. Jacob was almost too embarrassed to answer; this wasn't the crowd that would be impressed with him taking on multiple kids. He looked at his father's interested expression; they hadn't talked about it directly yet. "I got in a stupid fight," he said.

When it became clear that Jacob wasn't going to elaborate, Bill nodded. "I remember stupid fights," he said.

Jacob smiled tentatively, gratefully.

"Just think," Bill said. "In a few decades you'll be in some other nice restaurant"—he gestured around—"remembering *your* stupid fight. And you'll think, 'Boy, that was a long time ago.'"

Jacob's grateful smile widened.

The dinner lasted a long time, in a good way. And even though they were all completely full after their main courses, they got dessert too.

When the three Wassermans stepped back into the condo, his father told Jacob it was okay to make his phone call. "Not *too* long, okay?" he said.

And so Jacob went upstairs to his father's office and sat in his office chair and made the call he needed to make.

"Hi." Leah's voice was sort of bright and sort of bored at the same time.

"Hi," Jacob said. He felt like he was thundering inside. "It's Jacob." He started playing with the pens on his father's desk.

"Oh, hey!" she said. "That's cool."

He felt the way he had with Bill—a warmth inside to find someone excited about him.

"Are you back in town?" she asked.

"No," he said. "I'm still in Chicago. I just—I just wanted to say hi."

"Ohhhh," she said. "That's nice."

"Yeah. I—"

But then she broke away to yell something off to the side. "I *got* it, Dad! It's for *me*! Jesus Christ! It's not even your line!"

"Wow," Jacob said, when there was a pause. "I—"

But she wasn't done. "Jesus, Dad! I don't have to tell you who it is! Can I have some fucking privacy?" He heard a slam, like a door slamming.

"Okay," she said, her voice sweet again. "I'm back."

"Wow," Jacob said again. "That was really something."

"I know. 'Rents are heinous. How's Chicago? They have crazy hot dogs there."

"That's true." Jacob was scrambling a little to keep up. But it was true that in Chicago they liked to put a thousand different things on their hot dogs, some of which were terrible ideas. "I haven't had any, though. I'm a vegetarian."

"I should be a vegetarian too," Leah said. "When has a cow ever tried to eat *me*?"

Jacob laughed. It was like English class. Leah didn't say much in that class, but when she did it was usually pretty interesting. Like when they were in a poetry unit and she raised her hand in the middle of something and said, "I think rhyming is boring. Book, took, schnook. Who can't do that? Look, crook, shook, cook, hook. When are we going to read some *blank* verse?" Or when they were studying *Macbeth* and she said that the play should have been all witches, all the time. Even though actually the witches were bigtime rhymers.

"So what *have* you been eating?" Leah said.

Jacob smiled and told her about the eggplant parmesan, and then that led into talking about being out with Deanna and his father and Bill.

"That sounds cool," she said.

He picked up a glass paperweight that had a bunch of paperclips trapped decoratively inside it. "What have *you* been eating?"

"Uch," she said. "Nothing. Garbage."

"Huh," Jacob said. "Like, out of restaurant dumpsters, or the garbage cans at home?"

Leah laughed for a little while about that—maybe even thirty seconds. And then she was done and she said, "That was nice, the other night."

Jacob was caught off-guard by the turn in the conversation. The thunder inside him returned, strong. But after only a little hiccup of time he said, "Yeah. It was," because it was, as long as he could block out the rest of his life that was surrounding it.

"I especially liked the talking afterward. Which is a very girl kind of thing."

He chewed on his lower lip a second and then said, "I'm sorry I was so weird."

"Are you still with Tammy, or what?"

Talking to Leah was like being in a pinball machine. But again he just said the truth. "No," he said. Because, really—if it hadn't been decided before, it was now.

"Good," she said, and there was a pause.

"What have you been doing over break?" he asked, just to ask something.

"Nothing," she said. "Extreme nothing. When are you coming back?"

"Saturday. December thirtieth."

"Ooh," she said. "Jessica's having a New Year's Eve party. Well, sort of her parents are. But there's going to be an old people section and a young people section. Separate, different rooms. Anyway, you've gotta come."

"Cool," he said. "I got some new clothes." And he told her about his new shirt and pants, because they were more Tribe-style than what he usually wore.

She said, "I don't know. Maybe your black T-shirts are more you."

Jacob smiled. "Maybe."

His father, who was apparently just on the other side of the office door, suddenly called in to him. "Are you almost off?"

Jacob jumped, and said, "Yeah, Dad," while scrabbling instinctively at the pens on the desk to get them back into order.

"Okay," his father said.

"I gotta go, I guess," Jacob told Leah.

"Sure," she said. "You should get your own line."

"I don't even live here."

"That's a pretty good point, Jacob. A-plus. You should call me again. I think you're nice."

"Okay," he said, pinballing. "But I'm not always nice, I don't think."

"Well, duh," she said.

And then they said goodbye and Jacob hung up. For a minute after that, he sat in place, staring at the phone. He felt good.

The next day there was another family outing. Well, first Jacob had to get out of bed, and *then* there was a family outing. He'd had another night of not-great sleep, though this time only partly because of bad things on his mind. A lot of what was keeping him awake was *up* energy. Energy named Leah. Anyway, his sister had to wake him up at eleven again.

"Just come downstairs cheerful," she said. Nobody wanted another day of fighting.

"I can do that."

The warning turned out to be unnecessary, though—their father was closed up in his office doing some work. Whatever he did for his job, there was a lot of it to do. It seemed like he was probably important, as a person. Maybe that was what confidence got you. Anyway, Jacob whisked up a couple of eggs and made a piece of toast and sat down to eat his breakfast with Deanna, who had again already eaten.

"We're going to have lunch soon," she said.

"I figured."

After a moment of quiet, Deanna asked, "Hey—now that you're not a zombie, can you tell me what's going on?"

Jacob thought about that. There was *so much* going on. Where could he even begin? "Well, I think I met someone," he said.

Deanna blinked. "What do you mean? Like, in Chicago?"

"No—in Philly."

"Like a girl somebody?"

He bit a corner of his toast off and nodded.

"Wow," she said. "That was fast."

"It was at that party I went to the night before we left." As he said that, though, some agitation picked up in his chest. He didn't want to get into everything with Deanna.

"*Really* fast," she said.

Deanna's talk about fastness was turning the agitation into a buzzing. "Well, I didn't really *meet* her then. I already knew her a little."

"Still fast."

Jacob didn't know what to say. He dug into his eggs to give himself time to think.

Deanna bent her head down to catch his eye. "You sure you don't want to take a break, just spend some time with yourself?"

Jacob put his fork down, hard, and some egg scattered. "Nobody would want that," he said.

They were staring each other down, him angry and her surprised, when their father came in.

"Lunch, anybody?" he said, an eyebrow raised at Jacob's breakfast.

They ate lunch out again—their father liked to do meals out. Tex-Mex this time. When Jacob asked what they were going to be doing that afternoon, his father looked him over and said, "I'm thinking the barber," which set off a brief argument. His father had been kidding, but still.

Actually their father had bowling planned, and Bill met them at the bowling alley, where they traded in their regular shoes for ridiculous ones.

Jacob couldn't remember the last time he'd been bowling, but it was long enough ago that on this day he bowled like it was his first time ever. He released the ball too soon so that it smashed into the lane and bounced, or too late so that it made an arc and then bounced, and at bad angles so that the ball hit the gutters again and again. Everybody else was a lot better, and they all had advice. Jacob rolled his eyes at all of it, except when Bill was giving the tips; then Jacob nodded politely and rolled his eyes only in his mind. He didn't really mind being bad at bowling; it seemed like it might even be a good thing to be bad at bowling.

He found himself imagining telling Leah about it later. In fact, he realized he was keeping a kind of running narrative in his head, as if he was preparing it for her. *I suck at bowling*, he'd say. *I think I broke their floor.* And she'd laugh and say, *What even is bowling, really?*

His father gave him the most advice. "Just lay it down," he said. "They're going to kick us out of here if you keep attacking the lane like that."

But Bill gave him a boyfriend smack in the arm. "Control freak," he said. And Jacob's father laughed, which is not what he would have done if Jacob had said it.

What was the deal between Jacob and his father? He thought about that, along with everything else—well, the good parts of everything else—throughout the rest of the afternoon. It just seemed like something about him was a problem for his father. His sleep habits, a problem; his hair and clothes, problems; his attitude—his personality—a big problem. Through the bowling, the ride back to the condo, the take-out deep-dish pizza dinner, the Hanukkah they *didn't* do that night, maybe because Bill wasn't Jewish, the inevitable movie on the VCR—Jacob couldn't figure it out, why a son would be such a big problem for a father. It wasn't like his father gave Deanna a hard time. Maybe Jacob was just a problem in general.

Fuck 'im, he ultimately decided.

When his father pulled out a second film—this one was called *Bird*, and it was about a jazz musician—Jacob said he was going to do some reading. He got a questioning eyebrow from his father, but that was about it.

Upstairs, Jacob went past the guest room and into his father's office. He hadn't asked about making another call because he knew what the answer would have been and he was going to make the call regardless.

He closed the door quietly behind him and picked up the phone without even turning the light on, his heart going fast as he dialed.

"Hi," Leah said.

"Hi," he said.

"I had a feeling. But I was off by forty-five minutes. Wait. Forty-eight."

"Which direction were you off?" he said, smiling.

"Why are you talking so quiet?" she said.

Jacob explained that he probably wasn't supposed to be calling her at all, which made her say, "Awww. Okay, well, I'll be quiet too, in sympathy." And then, in a voice that was quiet at first, she told him about what she'd done that day, which was ice skating, and how it had been in West Philadelphia at the University of Pennsylvania rink, because her father had graduated from Penn's business school and sometimes he was *Nostalgia Man.*

Jacob, in a voice that stayed quiet, told her about bowling and how bad he was at it, and she said, "Seriously, they should give out trophies for the *worst* bowler. Because why are we bowling?"

"Seriously," Jacob said.

"Fathers are so cheesy. Are you going to take me to that club when you get back?"

"That club?" Jacob scrambled to catch up with another swerve.

"That one you go to with your friends," she said.

"Revival? Would you want to go to that?" He tried to picture Leah in her kind of high-end, fashionable clothes dancing in the middle of all the punkness and gothness. But then again, Char had gone there—and at that point he tried to shove all those people out of his head again.

"I have some black clothes," Leah was saying. "I think.

Somewhere. Wait—are you coming to Jessica's New Year's Eve party or not?"

"Yeah," he said. "Definitely."

"Cool."

They talked for only a few more minutes, until Jacob decided that he was pushing his luck, and then Jacob said he would call her again, and that he *would* take her to Revival, though it made him feel anxious and very strange to say it—"Cool," she said—and after they had both hung up, he sat in the desk chair feeling dizzy for a minute—was he getting a chance to start over?—and then remembered he was pushing his luck and sprang up and slipped out of the room. Forgetting that he was supposed to be reading, he went back downstairs in time to see the jazz musician get arrested for something to do with drugs.

Jacob didn't get the chance to call Leah the next day or night. His father kept him and Deanna busy with the aquarium and a movie—*National Lampoon's Christmas Vacation*—and with a running argument about *the future*, Jacob's, which Bill wasn't around to defuse. If it hadn't been for having Leah to think about, Jacob was pretty sure he would have exploded. But he pictured himself and Leah floating peacefully, although not like the fish he'd seen in big tanks that day—he and Leah were floating on top of the water—and it kept the tension from igniting. Wouldn't it be cool to just float like that?

He was getting better, along the way, at not thinking about anybody in the Pack. He had decided that *Fuck you* was, in fact, a breakup, with Tammy and then with everyone else, and he had decided to leave it tied up neatly in his head like that. Whenever he did think of any of them—an image of Tammy's face up close might flash into his head, like light flashing off her glasses, and he'd feel guilt complicated by anger—he just repeated the *Fuck 'em* mantra and forced his thoughts in a new direction. It mostly worked.

Be the person who's not depressed, he told himself.

Friday was their last full day in Chicago, and their father had more plans for them. He did some work in the morning—Jacob mainly slept, though not *quite* as late, because he had fallen asleep more easily the night before—and then they did lunch out again, and then the planetarium, which they'd been to before and which was very cool. Well, the "Revolution in Measurement" exhibit wasn't too amazing—a bunch of astrolabes and sextons and inclinometers and some placards explaining how the French Revolution had produced the metric system—but the sky show was amazing. They sat back, Jacob, Deanna, their father, and Bill, and the room went dark and the dome ceiling became the night sky. It was kind of miraculous, how real it felt. Even when they launched off into the universe it felt real, aside from a few goofy laser-light animations. And there was this comforting voice talking about space, which made the room feel like it was floating. As the universe swirled and changed overhead, Jacob pictured himself floating in it with Leah. It was even better than the floating-on-water image.

That night—it was the final night of Hanukkah—their father dropped the surprise gift of tickets to a Chicago Bulls game.

Jacob wasn't really a sports fan, but even he knew about Michael Jordan. Michael Jordan had a Wheaties commercial, and was famous enough that sometimes he was an expression. The same way you'd say *Brilliant, Einstein* when a person did something stupid, or *Okay, Shakespeare*, when a person said something pretentious, you would say, *Ladies and gentlemen, Michael Jordan*, when a person did something clumsy. So the thought of seeing him play sounded good even to Jacob.

The seats were close enough that they really *could* see him. They saw him hit jump shots and free throws and three-point shots and score fifteen points in just the third quarter, and thirty-four total. At one point he grabbed the ball away from the star of the Spurs—that guy's name was Robinson—and took it up for a dunk with his tongue sticking out. They could see his tongue from where they were sitting. And then he knocked the ball to a teammate when the Spurs tried to inbound it and the teammate dunked. Michael Jordan was everywhere, doing everything. Watching Michael Jordan play basketball made it seem to Jacob that anything was possible. When he came to the sideline for a break, he smiled like he was playing for fun. Like some of the kids Jacob would see, but never join, playing back in West Philly. Back when he hung out with Leron and those guys, sometimes they'd set aside the video games and go play basketball in the real world, and that's when Jacob would go home.

But maybe that had been a mistake. Who knew what Jacob was capable of? Maybe there had been a lot of mistakes? Maybe anything was possible. He pictured himself flying up off the court to dunk the ball, his own tongue out, Leah cheering in the stands.

It was pretty late by the time the four of them got back to the condo, and so everybody just went to bed. Bill even stayed, which was not something that frequently happened when Jacob and Deanna were there. But probably they weren't doing anything sexual, Jacob reflected from his guest bed, not with everybody in the condo. Anyway, Jacob was distracted, buzzing, to the point where he would have believed it if Deanna had told him his body was making an actual buzzing sound. But she didn't; she'd fallen asleep quickly, the way she usually did.

Jacob waited as long as he could before getting up and sneaking downstairs the best he could through the dark, to use the phone that was on the kitchen wall. That was one thing that was the same between his father's house and his mother's house—a phone on the kitchen wall. He sat down on the floor, his back against some low cabinets, tapping the number into the handset in the dark.

"Hello?" Leah said.

"Hey. It's Jacob." He was speaking even more quietly than the other night.

"I thought so," she said, and then she yawned. "You know, it's pretty late."

POSSIBLE HAPPINESS   191

"Oh, I'm sorry," Jacob said. "Did I wake you up?"

"I don't know," Leah said.

"I'm sorry," Jacob repeated. "I wasn't even sure you'd be home. I thought you might be out."

"Nah," she said, sighing. "Last night of Hanukkah and everything."

"Happy Hanukkah," he said.

"Happy Hanukkah," she said.

"But I guess it's over."

"Nope. Jewish days go till the next sundown. Did you go to Hebrew school?"

"No," he said. And then, "So, is being Jewish…is that a big part of your life?"

She thought about that for a minute. "I don't know. It just *is* part of it, I guess. But I'm not, like, an Orthodox rabbi or something."

Jacob laughed, maybe a little too loudly, but then got it under control.

"But it's not a big thing for you, being Jewish?" she said.

"Not so far. Not yet."

"Okay."

"Okay."

"Well, happy Hanukkah," she said again.

"I didn't get you anything."

She giggled at that. "You can get me something later. Hey—do you want to go out before Jessica's party? Maybe, have dinner?"

"Yes," he said.

"We can eat plants," she said, and that threw him until he realized that was a reference to him being vegetarian. Then he laughed. "I don't like all plants, though," she said. "I'm not a fan of cauliflower or broccoli, which are the same thing as far as I'm concerned. Or celery. Or big chunks of onion."

"Okay," he said. "We can—"

Which is when the lights came on.

"Are you making a long-distance call?" his father said from the door. He was in a very soft-looking bathrobe, but his face— Jacob was blinking in the light and trying to recover—his face was hard. "Are you?" he asked again.

Jacob didn't answer—in his ear, Leah was saying, "What's happening?"—but the answer must have been obvious, because his father said, "Say goodbye and hang up the phone."

"Leah," Jacob said, "I gotta go."

"Totally. It's late anyway. Call me when you get home, 'kay?"

"I will," he said. "Bye." And he stood up and put the handset back in place gently, as though it was still important to be quiet.

"Do you think it's okay to make a long-distance call without even asking me?" his father asked, crossing his arms and standing like a bouncer. His father was big on questions like that, where there was only one right answer, and it wasn't the one that matched what you'd actually done.

"I did ask you," Jacob said.

"Don't be deliberately obtuse. You asked me *once*, for *one* call," his father said, one finger up in the air like a blade. "And now—"

"Jesus, Dad! It's not like you're running out of money." Jacob threw his arms wide to indicate the condo at large.

"That's my business. It's not your money to just spend however you like."

"Are you kidding? I *know* it's not my money. Do you know how we live back in Philadelphia? I'm a hundred percent clear it's not my—"

"I send plenty of support to your mother. It's not my fault if she—"

"Don't," Jacob said. His father was going to say something about his mother spending the money on alcohol, and she did spend some money on alcohol, but it wasn't like that was going to make the difference between his father's lifestyle and his mother's.

His father was visibly fuming from being shut down

mid-sentence. "I don't know who the hell you think you are," he said, "but if you were growing up in this house—"

"This house? This house in Chicago, that you bought after you *left Philadelphia?*"

"Goddammit, Jacob."

"Well, I'm not living here. And thank God. Because you can keep your money—"

"The money you were just spending? That goddamn money?"

"I'm *sorry!*" Jacob yelled. "I'm sorry my existence cost you a few—"

His father took a looming step closer. "Don't give me that bullshit."

"What do you *want* from me?" Jacob said, taking his own step closer. "I'm leaving tomorrow, so don't worry—you won't have to play Dad anymore."

His father's face was clenched with anger. "You sarcastic son of a bitch," he said, sounding like his teeth were almost gritted. "I ought to smack you right in the mouth."

Later, Jacob would wonder why he didn't back down. His father had never been physically violent with him, or with anyone, as far as Jacob knew—he'd never even said anything like that before, as far as Jacob could remember—but he was an intimidating man all the same, and the possibility of violence seemed real right then. Regardless, Jacob didn't back down. Instead, he said, in a low, even voice, "I would punch you right back."

Everything stopped.

Neither of them said anything for a long moment.

Then, finally, his father: "You would, wouldn't you?"

"You're goddamn right I would," Jacob said.

They both went silent again. His father didn't seem worried—just shocked. They stared at each other, breathing almost audibly.

After a while, his father said, "Let's sit down," raising his hand to indicate the breakfast nook.

Jacob followed his father out in silence and sat across from him. He took hold of the salt and pepper shakers—little white and black cubes—and spun them with not much force on the table. Neither one made a full rotation. He spun them again, with more energy, and they went all the way around. He said, "You've been on my case since I got here."

"No, I haven't."

Jacob looked him in the eyes. "My earring, my clothes, my hair, my attitude. You're trying to change everything about me."

"I'm your *father*. It's my job to guide you."

Jacob pushed the shakers aside. "Dad, you don't even *know* me. How are you supposed to guide me when you don't know me? Don't you think you should find out who I am before you try to change me?"

That caught his father short. He didn't say anything at first, his big hands together and still on the table, his lips pressed together. Jacob remembered what he had looked like with a beard. Warmer.

The condo was completely silent, and the only light was in the kitchen and the breakfast nook.

"You wouldn't let me get to know you if I tried," his father said.

Which caught Jacob short, in exactly the same way.

"Who are you, Jacob?" his father asked.

Jacob searched for an answer. He searched for a while. Then he said, "I'm trying to figure that out."

His father nodded in the light of the breakfast nook.

They stayed up for another couple of hours, talking. Once they had both calmed down, they talked about mainly minor things, like school and work, when they went to sleep and when they woke up, the things they usually ate, winter, Philadelphia and Chicago. They talked about the basketball game they'd just seen, the planetarium, bowling, the restaurants. And they talked about the past, what it had been like when Jacob was a kid and the Wassermans were a nuclear family. Family trips, favorite board games, even a couple of funny stories, like the time Jacob had gotten a marble stuck up his nose. And they got into less minor things, too, for both of them, like the fight Jacob had been in, and about his father and Bill and how there was a possibility of them moving in together. They talked about the salt and pepper shakers, which his father had picked up in some home goods store that he couldn't really remember, and pretty much the whole time they were talking about how to get life right.

The next morning Jacob's father took him and Deanna to the airport and hugged them both goodbye, bear-like, forcefully. And then Jacob and his sister got on the airplane and flew back to Philadelphia.

25

When they got home, things were kind of a mess—things being the house, which was physically a mess with newspapers and coffee mugs and drinking glasses and plates scattered around, trash overflowing in the kitchen trash can; and things being also their mother, who was emotionally messy. On the one hand she was overwhelmingly happy to see them—hugging and re-hugging and saying, "Oh, this is *so* nice"—and on the other hand she was always on the verge of tearing up. Jacob got the sense that she had been doing some of the drinking that his father had almost mentioned the night before.

But Deanna took the reins right away, and they all spent the afternoon cleaning up together—"It's so nice to have you both here," their mother said—and catching up too. Or sort of catching up; there were unspoken rules about debriefing after a visit with their father. Their mother was allowed to tell them everything she'd been up to, which was working a lot of shifts, but she mostly saw her work as a downer and didn't want to dwell on it. As for Deanna and Jacob, they were sharply limited in what they could say about Chicago. If they talked about things that pointed to their father's financial success, that would upset their mother; if they talked about Bill, that would upset their mother because their father had found someone and she hadn't; if they made it sound like they'd had a lot of fun, that would really upset their mother. So, without needing to plan it, Jacob and Deanna both participated in offering an edited version. They talked about bowling, but Jacob emphasized how ridiculous he thought bowling was; they talked about seeing movies, but Deanna added a feminist critique of those movies; they talked about the dullness of the suburbs and the astrolabes at the planetarium, and also how their father had to take time to work for some of the visit. "You'd think he could take one week off," their mother said, a pleased kind of irritated. They didn't mention the basketball game at all; their mother had already commented on the new coat and scarf and gloves Deanna had been wearing. "It's good *he* can afford things like these," she'd said. Jacob's new boom box was still tucked away in his suitcase.

It was weird, Jacob reflected, how when you were with one parent sometimes you could see the good in the other. At one point late in the night before, when they were talking about some of the small things, his father had abruptly said, "I'm not trying to change you, Jacob. I'm trying to make sure you're going to be okay."

His mother suggested Chinese food for dinner, and neither Deanna nor Jacob mentioned that they'd had Chinese food twice during their trip to Chicago. Plus the place on Baltimore Avenue was pretty good. You couldn't eat there, really—there were just a couple of small tables where you waited for your food to get ready, and then you carried it out, waving to the couple who'd prepared the food back behind the bulletproof glass—but Jacob's mother called ahead and then they went to pick it up as a family and bring it home as a family.

For the first few minutes of dinner, all the talk was about *try this, pass that*, and then their mother asked, "So, what are we thinking about for New Year's Eve?" Jacob and Deanna both stopped chewing mid-chew. "They asked me if I'd take a late shift but I thought we could spend the time together instead."

Deanna spoke first. She cleared her throat and said, "There's this party. Some of my high school friends."

Their mother's face fell. "But you just got back."

"It's only one night," Deanna said. "We're here now. What about the three of us go to the Mummers parade on New Year's Day?"

Their mother turned heated eyes on Jacob. "Well, I know you're not even *thinking* about going out to a party after you broke curfew for the umpteenth time before you left. You and I still have to talk about that."

"Wait," Jacob said, "are you saying I *can't* go out?" His heart was beating hard; he needed to go. "I kind of have a date."

"You have a *date*?" Deanna said, putting down her chopsticks altogether.

Jacob ignored her. "We haven't worked out the details yet, but we were going to go out first and then to a party."

"Well," his mother started, "I know you really like this Tammy, but you see her all the time, and we need to talk about—"

"It's not Tammy," Jacob said quietly, using a fork to stir the little mound of rice on his plate.

"It's not Tammy?" his mother said.

"It's not Tammy," Deanna confirmed.

"I can't keep up with you," his mother said, and it could have been an affectionate line, but instead it was flatter. Almost bitter.

"Are you saying I can't go?" Jacob said. He felt his heart going.

His mother considered. They sat waiting in a room filled with the smell of Chinese food. "I think there have to be consequences for you breaking curfew," she finally said.

"Mom!" he protested, suddenly standing, suddenly caught up in an angry energy. He wanted to throw his plate at the wall.

The two women looked at him in surprise. He was surprised, too, but that didn't eliminate the anger.

Then, "Don't ruin the dinner," Jacob's mother said. "There have to be some consequences."

"Jacob," Deanna said, tugging on his shirt.

He sat down, but he didn't say anything else for the rest of the meal. According to his mother, who gave her analysis at the end, he did ruin the dinner after all.

While his mother cleaned up and put the food away with a lot of slamming and banging downstairs, and Deanna closed herself up in her room for safety, Jacob dialed Leah. He didn't quite realize that he'd brought his dark mood with him until he heard himself responding to Leah's normal "hello" with a very sullen "hello" of his own.

"Whoa," Leah said. "Do you want to try that again?"

"I'm sorry," he said. "I just found out I'm grounded and can't—we can't go out tomorrow. I can't go to the party, either."

"Wait—why?"

"Because I was late for curfew after Jessica's party."

"Because you were late for curfew after Jessica's party?"

"And a couple of other times," Jacob said.

"Hm," Leah said. He could picture her pursing her lips, making her features a little rounder. "I kind of have to go in a minute, out with my girls—"

"Yeah, it's okay," Jacob said, back in the sullen voice.

"Jesus—lemme finish, Jacob," Leah said. "What I was saying was, can you put me on with your mom first?"

He blinked. "On the *phone?*"

"Yeah," Leah said. "Just for a minute."

Jacob, not knowing what else to do, set the phone on his bed, went downstairs, and pointed to the phone on the kitchen wall. "Hey, Mom," he said to her aggravated face, "could you pick up for a minute?"

His mother exhaled sharply. "Pick up the phone?"

"Just for a minute. I actually don't know why," he admitted.

But she did it anyway, and Jacob sat down on the floor and listened, warily, to his mother's side of the conversation.

"Hello?... Well, hello, Leah. I don't think we've met.... Well, I hope we will too. Can I ask—.... Yes. That's right. And it's really a family matter.... Yes.... Is that—.... You don't need to apologize.... Well, that is helpful, but this is about his previous actions.... Hm?.... Yes." She glanced at Jacob, something softer in her face. "I know he has.... Yes. That's true.... Yes. You've made your point, Leah.... Yes. You're right about that.... He is...." Jacob's mouth hung open now. "Is there going to be alcohol?... I mean, among the kids?... Well, you see, that kind of thing—... Sure, I appreciate your honesty. I just don't know if—... Sure... That's reassuring... Sure." She sighed. "Do you know that he has a curfew of midnight?... Well, sure, 12:30 or 12:45 to catch the New Year.... Well, thank you, but I'm not going to hold *you* responsible; I'm going to hold my *son* responsible.... Sure, honey. I appreciate that.... Sure.... Sure. Okay. Well, I'm going to hang up now and let you talk to Jacob again.... Yes.... You too. Goodbye."

His mother put the handset back, and turned to Jacob, a hand on one hip. "That is some young woman right there," she said, wonder and admiration plain on her face. "*Twelve-forty-five*, youngster. No later or you're toast."

Jacob blinked and then got up and bolted up the stairs and grabbed the phone off his bed. "What did you *say* to her?"

"I really gotta go," she said. "Can I pick you up at your house tomorrow at six-thirty? My father says there's a good Ethiopian restaurant in West Philly that I bet is near you."

He said sure, gave her his address in a kind of amazement, and hung up. He noticed that he had a full-on erection.

Leah showed up at his door the next night right at six-thirty, very pretty in a dark blue dress. Jacob was underdressed again, his khakis upstairs in a drawer, but at least he had put a sweater—black—over his black T-shirt. And he was wearing his new dark gray coat.

For a moment they just smiled at each other, and then Leah waved over his shoulder. "Hi, Mrs. Wasserman," she said in her bright voice, her silver nails twinkling in the light.

Jacob turned to see his mother in her nurse's clothes leaning, bemused, against the wall. "Hi, Leah," she said.

He got them out of there before his mother could change her mind.

The Ethiopian restaurant Leah had in mind was just a few blocks over, at Forty-Fifth and Locust—Jacob had actually been there before a couple of times—and they zipped over in Leah's Jetta. "Mostly mine," she said. "I think it'll be all mine when I go to college." Feeling shy about Leah because they hadn't kissed hello or even touched each other yet, Jacob peered around. It was a pretty nice car, and it looked almost new. She drove it fast from stop sign to stop sign.

Ethiopian food seemed like it could possibly be intense for a first date, having your hands in the same dish, the same *food*, and then eating directly with those hands, but of course they had already been a lot more intimate than that. Besides, this restaurant was a very slow one, so after ordering food—vegetarian platter for two—they had plenty of time, sitting at a low circular table that was woven out of something, before eating intimacy kicked in.

"By the way, I've never had Ethiopian food before," Leah said.

"Oh—I hope you like it," Jacob said.

"We'll find out," she said.

Then they both debriefed about their breaks, the things they hadn't told each other on the phone. Leah had been on a short ski trip with her family and another family over Christmas and otherwise she'd been at home, bored and sometimes seeing friends. And Jacob went over the funny parts of his Chicago time. He talked more about the bowling, and mentioned *National Lampoon*, which it turned out she'd seen too, and liked it better than he did. He told her about the way his father teased Bill at the game about how he was on his way to getting as bald as Michael Jordan.

Then, "What was the story with your dad when you had to get off the phone?" she asked. "What was he so mad about?"

"I wasn't supposed to be making long-distance calls," he said.

"Bummer," she said, playing with a curl of her hair. Otherwise she was sitting on her low wooden stool in a very ladylike way, upright with legs crossed.

"Yeah." And then, instead of trying to make a joke about it, he added, "But we had kind of a good talk afterward. It was okay."

"That's good," she said.

Then there was a pause, during which Jacob panicked, because what if there was nothing else to talk about? "What kind of music do you like?"

"Really?" she asked, like she couldn't believe the question. "What do you want me to say, Bobby Brown, Paula Abdul, Roxette?"

"I don't know," he said. He had the sense that he'd bored her by asking that. He shifted on his stool. It would have been good to be in a chair with a back. "I think my favorite is Nine Inch Nails."

"I bet," she said.

Then, even though it was still a little obvious, they went into other favorites—TV, movies, things to do. Jacob noticed that there were a lot of interests where they didn't match, and also that the whole thing seemed to keep Leah bored.

"You never asked me what I asked you," Leah said out of nowhere.

"What do you mean?"

"To tell you something I don't usually tell people."

"Oh," he said, and she waited for him to ask, her green eyes blasé on him. "So tell me something."

"I worry," she said. "I worry about *everything*. I saw this one guy for a while who said that the reason I can't stay on a topic is because bouncing around stops me from getting worried."

"Oh," Jacob said. "A guy from our high school?"

"Huh?" She paused with a curl of hair around her finger. "Oh, not seeing like *dating*—seeing like *counseling*. This was a grown man. A doctor, or like a doctor."

"Oh," Jacob said. He didn't know anyone else who had seen a doctor for the things they thought or felt.

Just then the food arrived, a big platter of lots of food dolloped around on some spongy injera, and a small plate of extra folded injera to eat with.

"Vegetarian platter for two," said the waitress, an older woman, maybe about the age of his mother. But she didn't seem particularly tired.

When she'd left Jacob said, "Thanks for telling me that."

Leah smiled at him softly. "Sure," she said. "I like talking about real stuff. Now, so, we're supposed to use the bread to eat this or something?"

Jacob showed her what he understood about how to eat Ethiopian food, and they dug in. It *was* intense, having their hands in the same dish, the same food, and eating with those hands, licking their fingers sometimes. Intense in a different way from what they'd already done. But the food was good—Leah liked all of it, especially the red-brown stuff, and they talked about ordinary things, like classes and the looming idea of college and their parents, and they talked about random things, too, swerving with Leah's swerves in conversation. Things they didn't like to look at, the farthest they'd ever traveled, how they felt about books as physical things that you could hold. It was a mix—sometimes they bounced off each other, like when Leah said her farthest place was Greece, and Jacob said his was Chicago, but sometimes they connected too. Like how they both thought that maybe New England would be a nice place to go to college. Not that Jacob had ever seen New England in person, obviously. But it sounded nice.

By the end, Jacob was unbelievably full, and there was food still left over, a lot of which was on her side of the platter. "Are you full?" he asked.

She patted her stomach. "Uch. Totally."

They paid—Leah said they should split it—and then went out to the cold car. Despite that cold Jacob found himself saying, "I'd like to kiss you," and Leah said, "It's nice how you always ask first," and so they kissed for a while. He again noticed how different it was from kissing Tammy—softer, mostly—and realized it was the first time he'd thought about Tammy for the whole date. He also realized that it would not be a good idea to think about her anymore, so he pushed the thought roughly away and reached out for one of Leah's breasts. His hand met winter coat.

"Um, in a car in the middle of a neighborhood?" she said.

"Right. Sorry."

She smiled and started the car and they drove off to the party. Leah again drove very quickly. Even at times, frighteningly. They raced out of West Philly—"This neighborhood is *rough* in some ways," she said—and then she built more speed on West River Drive, and when she reached Lincoln Drive, threw the car hard into the curves. Jacob was pretty sure they got airborne a couple of times. He even had the thought that it wouldn't be such a terrible way to go, in a car on a date with Leah Shaffer. He reached out and held her right hand.

"Don't worry," she said.

"You either," he said, remembering what she'd told him at dinner.

That made her smile for a long time.

They got to Jessica's house in one piece, kissed some more in the parked and cooling car, and Jacob felt keenly that he really was being given a chance to start everything over. That maybe his mother was wrong; what if there *didn't* have to be consequences? After a while, the two of them got out of the car—Jacob wished they could stay there but didn't say it—and walked up the driveway to the front door. The person who opened it wasn't Jessica this time but a man in a sports coat and slacks, whose face told Jacob he was Jessica's father. In a voice that was all gravel, he said, "Kids party in the basement."

As Leah led him back to the stairs, he said, "The basement?" His own basement was a dark and spidery place where you did laundry and then got out of there as fast as possible. When they moved in they found an old baby food jar on the dirty shelves that ran alongside the basement stairs. It was filled with clear liquid and was labeled *HOLY WATER*. Jacob figured it was for the vampires that very likely lived down there somewhere.

"It's a finished basement," Leah said.

Jacob gathered what that meant when they made their way down the stairs. Wall-to-wall carpeting, lamps, couches, TVs, a refrigerator, a ping-pong table, a pool table, and a separate sound system from upstairs. Tone Loc playing. The space was huge—probably the size of the upstairs—like a whole other house that Jacob hadn't even seen the last time he was here. "Wow," he said.

The room, if you could call it that—it was open, just with pillars instead of walls, but it seemed too big to be called a room—was already populated. Not as many kids as at Jessica's last party, but a couple dozen scattered around. Jacob put his coat down in the pile by the entrance.

"Leah!" came Jessica's voice, and then Jessica herself was there, arms thrown around both Leah and Jacob. He felt something spill on his neck. "Oh!" she said, pulling herself and her red cup back. Jacob could smell beer.

As if she'd read his mind, Jessica said, "My parents are cool with drinking as long as it's a special occasion and as long as it doesn't get out of hand."

Leah said, "I told your mom there'd be some alcohol. But I promised her I'd drive you home sober."

"Okay," he said.

"So we'll just have a little," she said. "Well, I will. You can do your thing, either way."

"Yay!" Jessica said, and just like that she grabbed Leah to bounce her away. "I need her for a minute!"

"I'll be back," Leah called to Jacob. Jessica pulled her up the stairs, and she was gone.

Jacob was suddenly alone at the party, which made his heart go fast. He recognized some of the people there, but not as many as last time—some of them looked like private-school kids, maybe from Germantown Friends or one of the other good ones. For a minute he just stood at the edges of the group of people closest to him, like he was part of it, them with their sharp polo shirts and him all in black. They were talking about skiing, which to Jacob was an imaginary thing, basically fictional, but now he'd been with people talking about it twice in one night. After a couple of awkward glances from the group, he decided he really needed a beer.

Getting to that beer required going past the ping-pong

table, where it turned out Mike Berman and Noah Lieber were playing some kind of game against a couple of very, very blond kids that Jacob didn't know. They had set up a bunch of cups on both ends of the table and were bouncing the ball back and forth toward each other's cups.

"Balboa!" Mike called over the music, launching a punch that caught Jacob on the shoulder. The kind of thing that was supposed to be friendly.

"Hey," Jacob said.

"You got next?" Mike pointed at the table. He already looked a little unsteady, and Jacob realized that there was beer in the cups, and that they were trying to get the ball to land in the beer.

"I bet he'd be killer at this," Noah said, cracking himself up.

"Nah," Jacob said. "Just going to have a beer."

Mike repeated, "Just going to have a beer," but for some reason in a kind of stuffy British accent. "Cheerio," he said, turning back to the game.

Jacob shook his head.

The beer was in a keg again—how were Jessica's parents okay with this? In any case, Jacob remembered from last time how to work it, and soon he had a cup of beer. Mostly beer, plus thick foam. Surveying the room, the people he sort of knew and the people he didn't know at all, all the rich white kids partying to rap music, he remembered what his life had been like before he'd been discovered that fall. And he realized that when he went back to school in a week he might not have anybody. Well, Leah, hopefully. Plus maybe her friends? The Tribe? Oh boy. With that in his head, he tipped his cup up and drank the whole thing down, right through the foam that tasted even worse than the beer, and then he filled up again and drank some more. Where was Leah?

"Dude, can I get in there, or are you the bouncer or something?" said a preppy kid in penny loafers, snickering.

"Jessica's family *would* totally hire a bouncer," another kid said.

Jacob took another big swig and walked away. He spotted

someone he knew a little bit from math. Or maybe he would go talk to Stacy Adams or one of the other girls from the Tribe. They were huddled up on the far side of the room. On the way, though, he passed the ping-pong table again. "Yo, Wasserman," Noah said.

"Stand right there for a second," Mike said, and for some reason Jacob did, long enough for Noah to pitch a ping-pong ball into his beer. Right in.

Jacob had thrown his cup before he knew he was going to, before he knew he was angry. There wasn't much left in the cup, but what there was spattered on Noah's and Mike's shirts. Mike grabbed Jacob's sweater. There was some beer spattered on that too. "Dude, what the fuck are you doing?" Mike said, Noah close behind him.

Jacob felt all the anger now. He didn't know what was going to happen next—all he knew was he was starting to lose the ability to back down—but just then Jessica and Leah and Stacy were in there, and Leah was saying, "Take a *chill pill*. Mike, there was already beer on your shirt, you slob."

Oscar, who had come over too, said, "Dude, that's true."

Mike looked down for a long moment. And then he started laughing out of nowhere, and Noah was laughing, too, and Oscar. More than made sense. "Totally," he said. "Okay—just get Rocky out of here so we can play."

Leah took Jacob's arm and separated him from the situation. As they walked off a few steps, he asked her why she hung out with those guys. His heart was pounding.

"Yeah, they're kind of dickheads sometimes," she said, shrugging. "Sometimes they're fun too, though."

Jacob realized that the only thing he wanted was to be alone with Leah. Not at a party, not even out at a restaurant, not with anybody but her. And not even because it would be great to see her naked again, but because just about everybody and everything else was a problem for Jacob. So many problems. If he could just be alone with Leah, maybe he could hold things in place and keep things fine. His heart was still pounding.

He put his hand on her cheek and said, "Do you actually want to get out of here instead?"

And she opened her mouth to answer, but then seemed to see something over his shoulder. "Oh," she said.

Jacob turned, his hand still on Leah's face. There weren't enough people in the room to block his line of sight, and so even twenty feet away he could see the people coming in from the stairs. He could see Char, and Eric, and Tammy.

And as he stood there, touching Leah Shaffer and staring back at them, they could see him too.

26

Even before Tammy did or said anything, Jacob felt like everything inside him was crashing together. It was like a wall had broken inside him. He took a step backward and his hand dropped from Leah's face.

"Great," Tammy said now, her glasses flaring with light. "Are you serious?" She had her hand up, indicating Leah.

"Tammy," Jacob said, but he didn't have anything to follow it.

Tammy crossed the space to him. "That was fast. I'm glad you're doing so much better."

From somewhere in all the inner chaos, anger stepped forward. "Hey," he said. "After what you did, I was pretty sure we were—"

She waved his words away. "Oh, we were done. We were done when you told me, *Fuck you.* We should have been done a while before that, if I'd had any brains." As Jacob's anger abandoned him, Tammy turned to Leah. "Good luck, girl," she said. "You know, he's not what you think he is."

Jacob looked back in panic at Leah's blank face, and then at Tammy's angry one, and at Eric and Char, wary behind her. He was aware that other kids at the party were starting to watch this too.

Tammy kept going, ranting at Leah. "You know, on the outside Jacob's all laughs, but *inside*—" Jacob felt his heart banging around again, but this time like it was trying to get away— "inside he's just a train wreck. A total fucking mess. He pretends, but the truth is that he's—" she turned her eyes back on him and jabbed his chest with a finger, and it was rougher than any punches he'd ever taken—"he's broken."

With that, she turned and stomped to the stairs and up them.

Char gave Jacob a sad look and followed. Eric stood there just a moment longer, his face a mix of things, and then he went too.

For Jacob, it seemed like everything was suddenly in slow motion. The crashing inside him, the heart trying to get out of him, the party on all sides, like it was all happening at a quarter speed. The air was thickening around him, into water. The beat of the music thumped like tired, reluctant feet.

"Hey," Leah said, touching his arm.

Jacob looked at her. She was so pretty, with her halo of hair and her green eyes that were trying to read his face. "She's right," he said. "She's right." His voice sounded slurred to him, like it was being dragged out of his mouth.

"Hey," Leah said again.

"I just need to be alone for a minute," he said. A little still-functioning part of him could see that he was sinking toward something big and awful, and that maybe if he could just get away from everything, just for a minute, maybe he could stop himself from going into it. Without looking back he went heavily up the stairs, until the sounds of the downstairs party blended into and then got replaced by the sounds of the first-floor party. He looked around for a bathroom but didn't see one right away, so instead he went for the front door, passing a little roughly by some well-dressed grown-ups. "Oh," one said. He kept going, walking right along the edge. He just needed some air, maybe.

But when he got outside, even though it felt like fifteen minutes or more had gone by, Tammy was still there, with Char and Eric. They were arguing. "No," Tammy was saying. "That's not—" And then she saw him. "Great. Are you following me now? Do you have something you want to say to me?"

Jacob's mouth was open, but it took a few seconds to say "No. No—I'm sorry." And then he said it again, because he so was. "I'm sorry."

Tammy breathed in and out through her nose, steam in the cold. It was very cold out. Jacob had left his coat downstairs.

His first serious girlfriend stared at him with an unreadable face while people who used to be his friends looked on.

Tammy stepped close to him again. For just a flash, Jacob thought it was possible that she was going to say something that would make it all okay. She cleared her throat before speaking. "You know," she said, and their eyes were locked through the bulletproof surface of her glasses, "the whole thing is more sad than anything." And she did sound sad instead of angry. "Because you know she can't save you either. I couldn't save you, and she can't save you either." She tapped him on the chest. "Because this is who you are."

When she turned away and walked off, Jacob dropped his eyes to his feet, feeling things slow further, thicken further. The air, as cold and biting as it was, was now heavy water pressing on him. Soon he would be at the bottom of the pool.

"Hey—do you need a ride?" Eric said.

"We can't give him a ride," Char said. "We have Tammy."

"I know—I just thought—"

"It's okay," Jacob said, still looking at his shoes. "Thanks."

"Okay."

Char gave him a pat on his arm, and then she and Eric left too.

Jacob stood there for he didn't know how long. Long enough to hear a car engine start up and fade into the distance, for sure, but beyond that he didn't know. It was only when he realized that Leah might come looking for him that he got moving.

Jacob walked down the driveway and turned right at the street. He remembered the way to the train station.

Walking through the dark and bitter cold streets—he had left his coat behind—getting to the station, waiting for the train, getting on and getting off, walking through West Philly—he was only remotely aware of any of it. Like his body was moving him without any connection to the rest of him, down so deep inside that it was almost gone.

His house was empty. Deanna was at her party and his

mother was doing a late shift for extra money. He saw that he was home before curfew. His mother wasn't there to see. It didn't matter.

Jacob went upstairs to his room. The phone rang, but he didn't pick it up. He just got into bed, clothes and all, and let himself go away.

27

Jacob stayed in bed for four days.

Sleeping and not sleeping.

His mother tried to get him up, and Deanna tried to get him up, but after a while they just resigned themselves to bringing him food and sitting with him, and trying to talk to him here and there—he didn't know about what—and leaving him alone again.

When he was alone, Jacob slept and he didn't sleep. He ate a little of the food. He stared at the radiator next to his bed, which clanged sometimes. He felt how much every part of him weighed. How much the air weighed on him. Time was slow and endless. His shades were drawn, but strips of hard light got in around the edges and moved unstoppable across the wall. The room turned all the way dark eventually. Like the bottom of the ocean.

For the most part he didn't even think. When he slept he didn't dream, and when he didn't sleep his mind was almost blank. It couldn't make its own thoughts; it could only receive things, dumbly. Radiator. Wall. Light. Dark. Be the person who isn't depressed. *Clang*. You've been acting crazy. A tray of partly eaten food. Tell me something you usually don't tell people. The heavy, heavy blanket. She can't save you. The sound of his sister's or his mother's voice, their hands on his arm. Jacob wrestling the angel. This is who you are.

Sleeping was better than not sleeping.

There were a few phone calls while he was in bed. He ignored them. Then, on the second day, his mother brought him the phone and said, "It's Leah."

He kept his head on the pillow in the pillow and shook it slightly, slowly. But she put the phone on the bed with him and left.

After a minute he picked it up.

"Hello?" she said.

"Hello," he said, buried in the pillow.

"You're sad," she said. He nodded, but of course she couldn't hear that. "Yeah," she said. "Is there anything I can do right now?"

Jacob tried to think about that. Leah was—he liked her. But there wasn't anything she could do. Tammy was right. "No," he said.

"Okay," she said. There was a long period of silence with them both on the phone, and finally she added, in a voice that he hadn't heard from her before, a voice that sounded worried, "Listen—just call me when you're on the other side, okay?"

The other side? The words were strange to Jacob.

As though reading his mind, Leah said, "That's what my counselor called it. When I was having anxiety. He said you just have to make it to the other side."

"Oh," Jacob said.

"Okay," came Leah's voice. "Call me then. I have your coat too."

And then Jacob went back into his sleeping and his not sleeping. Mixed in with everything else were those new words, *the other side.*

His mother collected the phone while he was sleeping. A lot later she came back and told him she'd called his regular doctor and his doctor had suggested bringing him in to see someone. He worked with someone who would be good to talk to. By then it was the third day, and the idea was for him to go in on Friday, two days from then. It seemed impossible that he would be able to move by then.

Other calls came in but he turned them away, and didn't even pick up when his mother left the phone on the bed. Eventually the person would hang up and the phone would go over to that angry repeating sound that was supposed to get you to hang up your end. But Jacob just listened to it. He wondered if the sound would go on forever if he let it. But after a while his mother would come to take the phone away again.

Thursday Tammy called and he did talk to her. Not the first time she called, but the second.

"Hello," Jacob said. The handset was on one side of his face, and the other side was deep in the pillow. He knew from his bathroom trips that the pillowcase was pressing its wrinkles into his cheeks.

"Hi," Tammy said. "Listen—I called to say I'm sorry."

That surprised Jacob, in the dim place in him where he could feel surprise, but he said, "You were just telling the truth." His voice was like syrup, thick and sticky.

He could hear Tammy breathing. "I was angry. I'm still angry. But it was only part of the truth. Like, one way of looking at it."

Jacob didn't say anything. He didn't know what to say.

"I'm just saying I'm sorry."

"I'm sorry too."

They stayed on the line in silence for another minute, and then she said goodbye, and she hung up. Jacob waited until that angry repeating sound came, and then he hung up too.

He lifted himself partway off the pillow—a thousand pounds—and looked over at the dresser, where the box was with the necklace in it. He should maybe get that back to Mr. Bocek somehow. Mr. Bocek could give it to Tammy as a father gift, maybe.

School would be starting again on Monday. What would Jacob find there, if he went? What would be left? Some of the calls he'd turned away had been from friends. Char, Eric, even Alice. His father had called too.

Jacob put his head back down on the pillow for a long time.

Later he sat partway up and pulled the window shade aside. The light was painful. But during the day Spark Park was there, visible. What used to be a building, now wood chips. Somebody had called it a park.

Jacob let the shade drop closed and let himself drop back into sleep.

The next morning his mother managed to get him out of bed. Out of bed and dressed and into a car she'd borrowed from a neighbor so that they could go to the doctor. "I met him yesterday," she said. Jacob hadn't even noticed her leave the house. "He's nice," she said.

He watched West Philadelphia go by, watched the buildings of the University of Pennsylvania crop up. That's where his mother had wanted Deanna to go, so that she would be close by, but Deanna hadn't applied to any schools within a hundred miles. Probably his mother now expected him to apply to Penn. He saw that likelihood the way he saw the neighborhood— through glass. Through water. They crossed the South Street bridge and wound their way down past buildings and houses until they got to Graduate Hospital. For a moment, staring at the hospital, Jacob wondered if his mother was going to put him in there and leave him.

Inside they took an elevator and a hallway and found an office where inside the colors were warmer than the rest of the building and where a receptionist told them they would have to wait for only a few minutes. They took seats in the kind of chairs you could have in your house. There were pictures on the walls, a potted plant. It didn't seem like the kind of place where a person could have you committed.

His mother tried to make conversation, but he couldn't give her more than noises of acknowledgment. Jacob was some- where between receiving thoughts—plant, chairs, this is who you are—and forming thoughts of his own. His own thoughts were hovering near him, and they were not great.

After some time the receptionist called his mother, who went into the next room—"I'll be back soon," she said—and after some more time she came back out again. "He wants to talk to you by yourself. If that's okay," she said.

Jacob got up and went into the next room. It was like a

miniature living room—more plants, a coffee table with a love seat on one side of it and an armchair on the other. A man was standing in front of the armchair. He was wearing a gray sportscoat. He was younger than Jacob had expected, maybe almost ten years younger than his mother. The man stuck out his hand. "Hi, Jacob," he said in a soft voice. "I'm Dr. Daniel Barol." He was smiling in a way that was a little bit sad. Like he was already feeling what Jacob was feeling, *because* Jacob was feeling it. "Have a seat."

Jacob sat on the love seat.

There was silence for a minute. He could feel the doctor watching him, knew the doctor was waiting for him to do or say whatever he was supposed to do or say. But under an ocean of water he didn't know what that was. "I'm sorry," he said.

"Jacob." He looked up, saw Dr. Barol's eyes. "Please don't feel you ever have to apologize in here. No matter what you're feeling or thinking. I know you're in pain. But I want you to also know that *whoever* you need to be, while you're here, is absolutely okay. Is fine. Is *welcome*."

And that was it. Before Jacob knew what was happening, he was crying. But not crying actually—sobbing. Sobbing harder than he could remember ever doing before. It almost felt like throwing up, this heaving violence in his body. He was down on one knee in the carpet, his face in his hands, when Dr. Barol came to him and put a hand on Jacob's shoulder. It turned out that it was somehow possible for Jacob to cry harder. Dr. Barol sat on the coffee table, that hand still on Jacob's shoulder.

Then, when the heaves started to slow, Dr. Barol moved them to the love seat, where Jacob sank back into the sobbing. He was trying to get ahold of himself, but it was like trying to hold a storm. "It's okay," Dr. Barol said. "You don't have to stop." And Jacob let go altogether, let himself fall tumbling into the storm, let his body get tossed around in it, this feeling between misery and rage, this pummeling inside. Jacob sobbed and pressed his hands into his face, sobbed and pounded his fists on his thighs, sobbed and gasped and even roared. There were no thoughts behind all this—just him pouring himself out, just him feeling all of it, all the way. Dr. Barol sat with him.

It lasted a very long time.

What finally broke through the crying were hiccups. They started up at some point, and got stronger until it became hard to cry and breathe at the same time. Slowly, his body made the choice to breathe. Then he was sitting there in smacked-face astonishment, only hiccuping. He looked at Dr. Barol's calm face and actually laughed a wet laugh, like a cough, in surprise.

"I have the hiccups," he said.

"Yes," Dr. Barol said. They both laughed.

Then the doctor started breathing audibly—slow in, slow out—like an example. His hand was still on Jacob's shoulder. Jacob tried to breathe with him, broken up repeatedly by hiccups. He kept trying. And over time he got closer to the doctor's breathing, until finally his own was ragged but regular, and the hiccups were gone.

Jacob finally said, "How long have I been here?"

Dr. Barol glanced off to the side. "Just about…fifty minutes."

"Oh God," Jacob started. "I'm so—"

Dr. Barol's hand got firm on Jacob's shoulder. "No," he said. Jacob's apology dissipated in the air.

The doctor sat back, let Jacob's shoulder go, and looked thoughtfully at him.

Jacob shook his head wearily. He laughed a small laugh. "Wow."

Dr. Barol nodded at something he saw in Jacob's face, and smiled. "I'd like you to come back and see me again," he said.

Jacob breathed out. "Okay."

"Maybe we'll even talk next time," the doctor said. And his eyes were so warm as he said it that Jacob laughed, and the doctor laughed, and it was so, so nice.

Afterward, he and his mother made another appointment

with the receptionist and then his mother took him out to lunch at a place that served veggie cheesesteaks. She said she'd been wanting to try it.

"How was that?" she asked him about the appointment.

Jacob nodded. He felt bone-tired, but not like he wanted to go to bed.

"You're—you're okay with seeing him again?" she asked.

He nodded, picking up his veggie cheesesteak. It was pretty good. He could tell that his mother was tearing up a little, which was okay. "Yeah," he said. "I think that would be helpful."

When they got home, Deanna said that Eric had called and left a message. "He said he'll see you next week," she said.

"Okay," Jacob said.

For the rest of Friday he sat with her and watched game shows and soap operas on television. It wasn't like drowning, exactly.

On Saturday, in the middle of more TV, he got a very unexpected call—Mr. Bocek. "Are you ever coming back to work, or what?" he wanted to know.

"Oh," Jacob said. "I thought because of me and Tammy—"

"I like you better if you're not dating my daughter," he said. "And you believe in work."

"Okay," Jacob said. "But—"

"Tammy said it's okay," Mr. Bocek said.

And that was that. They arranged for next Tuesday and hung up. There were tears in Jacob's eyes, but the good kind. Or were they maybe *all* good?

On Sunday he called Leah. She wasn't there when he first tried her, but he called her back and got her later.

"Are you on the other side?" she said.

Jacob looked around his sparsely decorated room. The shades were open and it was bright in there. "Well," he said, "I'm out of bed."

"That's good," she said, a smile in her voice. "Hi, Jacob."

28

On Monday morning school was back in session. Jacob got out of bed, showered, got dressed, had breakfast, and went to Baltimore Avenue, where he caught the subway-surface line. Eric wasn't on there, but Jacob's timing had been basically random, so he wasn't really expecting to see Eric there. Sitting next to a woman who seemed to be on her way to work, Jacob watched West Philadelphia and then, after they went underground, the tunnel walls.

At city hall he went through the dark tunnels to the Broad Street Line platform and stood among the other scattered kids there. Across the two sets of tracks he saw one of those *We're Getting There* signs and he laughed softly to himself.

"Hey," came a voice.

Jacob turned. Leron was there, by himself. He'd gotten a haircut and was now sporting a not-very-high-yet hi-top fade. "Hey, Leron," Jacob said.

"Hey—what you been up to?" Leron said. "Besides throwing down on the corner."

Jacob laughed. Leron was talking about that fight from before break. It seemed like a long time ago. Jacob had checked himself out in the mirror that morning and saw that his face was pretty much back to normal. "I went to Chicago," he said. "How 'bout you?"

"We went down to DC, saw my grandmoms and grandpops."

They both nodded at each other and then the subway came. They found seats together inside.

"Where's everybody else?" Jacob said. "All your crew?"

Leron smiled. "I could ask you the same thing."

"I dunno," Jacob said. "Guess we'll find out at school."

School, where the Pack would or wouldn't be meeting, where

things would be awkward or okay or somewhere in between, where word would be getting around about all kinds of things—the fight, maybe, him and Tammy, him and Leah, him and either one of the Tribe parties. Plus the countless unknown rumors that would be going around about anybody and everybody else. It was a big school, and it wasn't like Jacob was at the center of it.

Still—he wondered what he would find when he got there. The subway walls rushed by.

"Guess it's just you and me, then," Leron said.

Jacob smiled. "Yeah."

"Yo, what'd you get for Hanukkah this year?"

So Jacob told him about the two boom boxes—he still hadn't told his mother about the second one, which he'd put in the back of his closet—and the crazy new clothes, and the basketball game he'd gone to with his father. That last news floored Leron, who had the *Jordan vs. Bird* game for Commodore 64 at home. They had played it together before, though it was awkward because Leron always made him be Larry Bird so that the races would match. *The great white hope!* he'd yell when he was scoring on Jacob's Larry Bird. Anyway, they talked for a while about the real basketball Jacob had seen in Chicago, and then Leron talked about the stuff he'd gotten, which was mostly more video games—*License to Kill, Stunt Car Racer, Batman.* Leron said he'd been playing them all day, every day since his family got back from DC. He had a lot to say about the games. He finished with "I'm ready to kick *anyone's* ass. If you want, you can come over sometime and I'll kick *your* ass."

Jacob laughed. "Sounds great," he said.

Then they talked about their jobs, which they both apparently still had, and Leron asked Jacob about his "love life," and Jacob basically held his tongue about that. Not because it was bad—he thought maybe things were pretty good—but because he wanted to keep it close to him. Leron, meanwhile, was still with Latia.

By the time they got to the Wyoming stop, two stops before Olney, conversation wound down. It was only a few minutes, but they felt like significant minutes to Jacob. There was a limit to how much they had to talk about. Maybe it was like that with everyone, ultimately.

When the train pulled into the Olney station, Leron stood up, and Jacob didn't.

"Not getting up?" Leron said.

"Not yet."

"What, you live on the train now?"

"Nah," Jacob said. "Just something I want to see."

Leron gave him a sideways look.

"I'll catch you at school," Jacob said. This wouldn't take long.

Leron shrugged and nodded goodbye with a smile, and joined everybody else getting off.

The doors closed and they moved on toward Fern Rock. Hardly anybody was on—two other guys, older, alone in two places in the car. Jacob watched the dark walls outside the windows.

After a minute or two, those walls started to get lighter, and Jacob realized that was sunlight. The subway was going to go aboveground for the last stop. He hadn't expected that.

Without planning it Jacob snapped his eyes shut—and kept them that way.

He could tell when they were outside, the light cranked all the way up against his eyelids, but he didn't look. He left his eyes closed as the train rolled along, left them closed as it pulled into the station, and kept them closed as the doors opened, staying open longer than usual.

There was the sound of footsteps. And then, "You getting off here?" came a voice that Jacob figured must be the conductor's.

Jacob knew that Alice was right. There was no way that there was an oasis three or four minutes away from Ogontz and Olney. There could only be a concrete platform and some low houses, maybe, another neighborhood struggling to get by. It was never going to be what he'd pictured. But—and this was the thing that he was really getting now—it didn't matter what was out there. It wasn't going to be anything out there that made the difference for him.

"Kid?" the conductor said. "You awake?"

"Yeah," Jacob said, his eyes still closed. "I'm not getting off here. I'm going back to Olney."

"Okay," the man said. "It'll be a minute."

"Okay," Jacob said.

After a while the train got moving again. Jacob kept his eyes closed. The train made that rhythmic metal sound of rolling along, and Jacob kept his eyes closed, listening to the sound. He didn't open them again until the light changed around him and he knew for sure that he was inside.

ACKNOWLEDGMENTS

It's amazing to see your own work in print, neat and tidy between two covers. Finished, published, it starts to look like something that was always meant to be here—inevitable. But this novel was never inevitable; it was the result of eight years of work, and lots and lots and lots of help along the way.

First of all, in the early stages of getting my thoughts together, I leaned heavily on the music of the late '80s, and I owe big thanks to the members of the Posse for reminding me what we used to listen to, as well as some other details from back in the day—not to mention for changing my life in high school! I'm so grateful for you. If this was a yearbook page, it would have to read 2GETHER + 4EVER = 6CESS. A special shoutout goes to Becca Ewing for her friendship and support as I thought about what it would mean to bring this book into the world.

Thank you to the retreat center known as The Porches, where this idea started to take form. And I owe a lot to the wonderful Virginia Center for the Creative Arts, where residencies enabled me to work on the manuscript in a concentrated way. This work was also supported by Fellowships from the DC Commission on the Arts and the Humanities—thank you, DCCAH.

Drafts of this book benefited enormously from feedback from the brilliant writers in my writing group: Melanie McCabe, Emily Mitchell, and David Taylor—and Angie Chuang gave me timely feedback toward the very end too. N. West Moss was crucially helpful with her insights on an early draft. These are excellent writers, folks—check out their work.

The publishing process, meanwhile, has been great. I'm very grateful to Jaynie Royal and Pam Van Dyk for their steady stewardship of Regal House, and especially Jaynie for the care she put into *Possible Happiness*.

Above all, I want to thank my family. My mother, father, and stepmother have been there for me again and again and again over the decades—and I don't know who I'd be without my sister, Karla. Whether she wanted to be or not, she was a kind of second mother to me in my tween years, and has always been one of my favorite people on the planet. I love you all. And Rachel and Reuben? The people around whom I can most be myself? Who I love and treasure so much that I can barely begin to express it? THANK YOU.

And thank you, reader. Thanks for being here. I hope you find something significant for yourself in these pages.

Book Group Questions

1. Would you recommend this book to others? Who in your life would get the most out of it, and why?

2. What character did you most identify with in the story? Why? Which character did you identify with least? Why?

3. This book takes place in 1989. In what ways would Jacob's experience probably be different today, particularly concerning his depression, but also his relationships to others? In what ways would it be the same?

4. What contribution does humor make to the experience of reading this novel? And in what ways is the book also serious?

5. What contribution does music make to the story?

6. Do you think Jacob has changed significantly by the end of the book? If so, how?